Cassie Connor loves caps weekending in Nice and wherever she goes. She's never finished *War and Pe* motto is CBA – Can't Be A and inventing her own always so much better. Hudson in her debut novel, *Love Under Contract*, proves the point perfectly.

Also by Cassie Connor

THE BIG GAME

CASSIE CONNOR

One More Chapter
a division of HarperCollins*Publishers* Ltd
1 London Bridge Street
London SE1 9GF
www.harpercollins.co.uk
HarperCollins*Publishers*
Macken House, 39/40 Mayor Street Upper,
Dublin 1, D01 C9W8
This paperback edition 2025

1

First published in Great Britain in ebook format
by HarperCollins*Publishers* 2025
Copyright © Cassie Connor 2025
Cassie Connor asserts the moral right to be identified
as the author of this work

A catalogue record of this book is available from the British Library
ISBN: 978-0-00-866291-2

Printed and bound in the UK using 100% Renewable Electricity
by CPI Group (UK) Ltd

For my dearest friend and agent, Broo Doherty, for her stalwart support and so much more.

Prologue

LILY

'It's Donaghue taking it all the way to the touchdown!' roars the announcer.

Oh my God, I don't believe it. Tate has just scored in like the fifty-ninth minute. On the sidelines, the whole cheerleading squad is going crazy. I'm jumping up and down, screaming my head off. The noise is so wild I only just hear the final whistle.

The Radley Rangers have just won the college football championship for the first time in the college's history. It's a huge moment for the whole team: the players, coaches, everyone behind the scenes – and, of course, for the girlfriends and cheerleaders. It's been a long, hard-fought season, but all that is forgotten in the golden glory of victory.

On the field, the players peel off their helmets, grinning like lunatics. Tate catches my eye and blows me a kiss. My heart flips at the sight of his ever-boyish grin and those sparkling blue eyes. All I can do is grin back at him – all gorgeous six-foot-four inches of him – happiness fizzing in every vein, drinking in the sight of all that toned muscle, the tousled hair and the sheer joy on his beautiful, chiselled face. He heads my way, where I'm celebrating with the other cheerleaders, being slapped on the back by his nearest team-mates. But he's like a heat-seeking missile locked on me. I meet him halfway and jump into his arms. Hot, sweaty and still breathing hard, he scoops me up and kisses me, hot mouth and hungry tongue and I kiss him right back. It's the sort of kiss that should come with a health warning. Christ, I'm horny as hell.

'Fuck, Lily,' he murmurs into my mouth. 'I could do you right now.' His hands clasp my bottom, his fingers straying just a little close to the edge of my tiny shorts. 'Tell me you're wet for me.'

I nip his ear and squeeze my thighs harder around his waist. 'What do you think?'

'I think if I get a hard on out here, the scouts are gonna notice.'

I laugh. 'I'm sure they've noticed you, period. You're bound to get picked for the draft now.'

He kisses me again. 'Nothing's certain yet.'

He's so modest. He's one of the best ball players on the team and, hell yeah, I'm biased but everyone knows he's a real talent and that fame and fortune are going to come knocking in the next few months. He's worked hard to achieve everything he's been dreaming of for the last nine years. I'm so happy for him. This might just be the happiest day of my life, even though, when he is drafted, we won't get to spend as much time together.

Fuck off, negative-thought weasels. Nothing is going to spoil today's party, especially not tonight.

Tate and I have been holding off having sex. It sounds crazy, as we've done everything but. It's just we both wanted to wait. Plus, it was super-hot, enjoying the build-up. He's made me come in plenty of inventive ways and I know exactly how taking him down my throat makes him moan – but tonight we agreed would be *the night*.

'Congratulations, babe.' I nip his lip as I slide down his body. 'Tonight, you get a hero's welcome, with all the trimmings.'

Coming up behind him, Coach Silverman puts an arm on his shoulder, prying us apart with a crooked smile. 'I need to borrow the big guy, Lily. You can have him back later.'

'Congratulations, Coach.' I smile at him. He's tough, fair and nothing like the grizzled old coaches you always see on TV and in films. Mark Silverman, with his dark hair greying at the temples and his shark-lawyer, three-piece suits, lives up to his name. A silver fox, he could easily model sweaters for one of those hot older-men catalogues.

'Thanks, Lily. We've got press interviews, and there's a scout from the Giants who wants to talk to you, Tate.'

My eyes go to Tate's. The Giants. That's his dream team. Although the way the draft works it's not always a given he'll get picked, this season they've got pick number six, so there's a very good chance.

Tate leans down and kisses me again. 'See you later, babe.'

I'm mesmerised by his very fine ass in those tight

football pants, which show off every sculpted muscle. He looks over his shoulder at me and shoots me a smile that sends a torpedo of heat right between my thighs. I swear there's suddenly an extra swagger in his stride. I let out a breath, trying to ease the flush heating my body. It's always been like this, since the day I first laid eyes on Tate. I can't wait to get up close and very naked with him later. It's been a long time coming.

For the next few hours, it's a circus. Every time I get near Tate, he's whisked off to speak to someone new, but it's fine because I'm with my friends from the cheerleading squad, Becky and Angel. They're both a bit glassy-eyed, as much with alcohol as with happiness.

'We did it,' says Becky, toasting the air with her plastic cup. We're all still in our cheerleading kits, which, despite it being January, are only marginally bigger than bikinis. 'We really did it.'

She looks around, catches the eye of one of the team and puffs out her chest. She's lucky. Despite all the training and being dead skinny, she still sports a 32DD.

'Put it away,' says Angel, rolling her eyes.

'You're just jealous,' challenges Becky, laughing.

'No, that's li'l 32A cup, here,' says Angel with a laugh, nodding at me.

I pat my flattish chest complacently. 'At least they don't get in the way.' I'm the tallest on the team, but also the skinniest.

'Do you think anyone noticed I was a beat out?' Becky is a worrier.

'No one noticed,' Angel reassures her. 'And your toe touch jumps were spot on. You know they're gonna give you a place on the team next year. Quit worrying. You've got this.'

'I've gotta get through the audition first.'

'You will,' I say, placing a reassuring hand on her shoulder. All three of us are here on cheerleading scholarships but there's no guarantee we'll get a place on the team next year. Personally, I don't care that much. Cheerleading was a means to an end to get here, but it's not something I'll be continuing with when I finish college next year. Both Angel and Becky want to work their way up and join one of the big football teams' cheerleading squads. They have a clear plan. Me … I have no clue now. I've been living in the States for the last six years. I came out to school here while my dad worked for the UN and I stayed on. Dad is expecting me back next year, but things change. I'd like to stay. With Tate. We haven't talked about the future but sometimes you just know that you're meant to be together. That's us. I've never felt like this before. Like I couldn't breathe if he wasn't with me. Like a light is turned on inside me every time I see him. And I see that same emotion in his eyes, too. That moment of wonder, where neither of us can quite believe we found each other.

My cell phone rings and I expect it's someone wanting me to congratulate the team on their behalf. It's not. It's Alice, my dad's housekeeper. I frown and move to the edge of the room where it is a bit quieter.

'Hey Alice.' Is she ringing to remind me it's Dad's birthday next week? Or just for a catch-up? I haven't spoken to her for a few weeks.

'Lily… Oh, Lily…' Her breath catches on a sob.

Something cold grips my heart, squeezing it with icy, spiteful fingers. I gasp at the chilly sensation, focusing on the sudden pain.

'Dad? Is it Dad?' It can't be. For his age he is almost superhuman. You've never seen a fifty-year-old in better shape. Unless there's been an accident. He's all I have. Mum died when I was a baby.

'Lily, sweetheart. I'm sorry. He's had a heart attack. He's in the hospital. You need to come home.'

It's amazing how quickly you can organise yourself in an emergency. Within minutes, I've booked a flight to London Heathrow out of Boston Logan and arranged a cab to take me to the city. All I need now is to go back to my hotel room, grab my passport and some clothes and speak to Tate. I hate to spoil his evening, not that it really will. He's going to be on a high for days. Besides, he'll get it. He understands my dad is all I've got in the way of family, just like his dad is for him. We share that in common. Both our mothers left us, mine dying when I was a toddler and Tate's leaving when he was a teenager. The lack of a maternal relationship in our lives doesn't bother either of us, though, not when we've got our dads.

I've got everything packed in a small holdall. Now I just

have to find Tate and explain what's going on. I'll be back in a couple of weeks if not before. My dad's the last person you'd expect to have a heart attack. I mean he's not just super fit, he's literally bombproof. He was in the SAS – Special Forces – when he was younger, and I'm pretty sure he's done plenty of secret-squirrel stuff covered by the Official Secrets Act, although he's never breathed a word. But as they say, sometimes actions are louder than words. Since the age of five, he's been teaching me self-defence and survival skills to prepare myself for any eventuality. Honestly, my childhood was far from ordinary. I can stitch up a gash, shoot a can out of a tree at fifty paces, hold intelligent conversation with royalty, handle a bow and arrow and grace a catwalk. To date, these skills have not served me particularly well in college, but then my dad comes from a very long line of eccentric Englishmen, thirteen of them to be precise, as he's the fourteenth Duke of Landsfforde, not that I tell people about that here in the States. I get enough attention because of my British accent.

I return to the celebrations, anxiety pulling tight at my shoulders as I scan the bar. I don't want to leave but I need to get home to my dad. Tate might even insist on coming to the airport with me, but I won't let him. This is his party. His triumph. I'll share it with him as soon as I get back.

I can't see him anywhere, which is unusual because my Donaghue antennae are always primed to his wavelength, and vice versa. It's a joke between us that we can always find each other in a crowded room.

'Hey, Andy. Have you seen Tate recently?'

Andy, one of his teammates, pauses mid-swig of his

beer. 'Yeah, two minutes ago with his dad. I think they were headed down to the locker room. Frank probably wants to get a selfie with him down there.'

'That's cute,' I say. I bet Tate's dad is thrilled with the win. He's so proud of his son. I've only met him a couple of times, but it's obvious he thinks Tate is a champion and is going to go all the way.

I hurry along the corridor, which, after the crowded football field, is virtually silent, and the further I travel down into the bowels of the building, the more muted the celebrations become. My dance shoes barely make a sound on the concrete floor and I occasionally glance back, a little creeped out by the dim light and the feeling of being alone.

I breathe a sigh of relief and smile at myself for being so silly when I hear Tate's familiar voice.

'I know, Dad. But the draft—'

I pause for a second, wondering if I should interrupt.

'You,' Frank's tone is sharp and uncompromising, 'have gotta be showing them you're serious about your career.' He spits out his words like machine-gun bullets. Fast and furious. 'Training hard. Committing yourself one hundred per cent to the game. This is where it gets real.'

I've heard him say similar things before, although perhaps not quite so vehemently. Frank is nothing if not committed to Tate's career, which is great, but sometimes I think he's a little bit too invested – not that I'd dream of ever saying so to Tate. He adores his dad, who has apparently made a lot of sacrifices over the years, including giving up a lucrative executive job so that he could make sure Tate got to all his training sessions, selling their house and downsizing to ensure that Tate went to the best school.

'Sorry, son, but you have to give her up.'

I frown. Who does Tate have to give up? His car that he endearingly calls, Hermione, because it needs magic to keep it on the road? His favourite massage therapist?

'I know.' Tate's sigh is so heavy, I can almost picture his despondent face. 'You've been telling me for a while. But we won today. I don't need to make any decisions until the draft in April.'

'Tate, you're just dragging things out. And what happens when you get picked in the draft? You two could be at opposite ends of the country. Sure, Lily's a real nice girl, but she's going back to England one day.'

I freeze. Me? They're talking about me. That's not possible. Tate and I love each other. We're a team. I don't hold him back. I lift him up. He's told me so.

'But not yet,' says Tate and he sounds a little desperate.

Tears prick my eyes and I smile. He loves me and I love him.

'Just give me until the draft. It's only a few months. Then I'll finish things. Surely, I'm allowed to have a little fun between now and then. It's not like it's serious or anything.'

His nonchalant words hit me like hailstones: sharp, hard and icy. My stomach feels as if it's been hollowed out with a spoon. I want to bend double and wrap my arms around my waist to hold the pain in. Tate's going to finish with me. I never saw this coming. It never even occurred to me. We love each other. I was so sure he felt the same about me…

A little fun. That's what I am. A stopgap until his real life begins.

Now I'm standing here feeling like the world's biggest idiot.

The pain in my stomach starts to grow, pushing out and out and out. I can barely contain it. Tears are running down my cheeks.

Frank speaks again. 'I don't know, son. Now's the time to show them you're still putting the hard yards in. You're young, you've got your whole life ahead of you. Don't throw it away on some girl. Women don't get it. They want to settle down, have kids. They want all of you. A ball player, especially at the beginning of his career, needs to keep his edge.'

'I know, Dad...' Tate carries on talking but his words are now muffled as if he's moved to a different part of the room.

I've heard enough. My hand is over my mouth as I try to decide what to do. Do I slink away and pretend I haven't heard? Do I march in and confront them both? That's my preferred option. My dad taught me to stand up for myself. He taught me that I can rely on no one but myself. He taught me independence.

Dad.

Fuck Tate. I'm not going in there. Not now. I need to get away. Regroup. I can't do this now. I back away down the corridor, fearful that they might come out of the locker room at any moment.

I have a plane to catch.

Chapter One

LILY

Eight Years Later

London Heathrow had been grey and drizzly, but arriving at JFK, it was bright and crisp, and my hotel, the Waldorf Astoria, is every bit as fancy and wonderful as its reputation.

I'm not due downstairs in the ballroom on the main floor – where I'm joining the charity gala dinner – for another forty-five minutes, but I want to get the lie of the land before I meet Winston Radstock III in the bar. Thank fuck for double espresso, which I've been mainlining since I woke up. My body clock is wrecked, despite the comfort of the million-thread-count Egyptian cotton sheets on the sleep-a-family-of-five bed. The Astoria is the full five stars, which I'm certainly not complaining about.

The lift opens into a large foyer, which I'd had a preview of earlier when I sneaked in to make an unscheduled delivery. The walls are lined with white leather benches, and urns of blousy flower arrangements are everywhere, the scent of lilies puffing additional pungency into the heavily fragranced area. I eye a couple of people queuing to walk through security a few metres away.

Following the crowd, I approach the brunette holding a clipboard. She's petite and absolutely dwarfed by the man-mountain security guard standing next to her. Both are wearing earpieces. I smile to myself knowing full well the devices are window dressing – an accessory to make them look the part.

The brunette gives me a welcoming smile, which tells me I'm right on the money when it comes to my appearance. I'm not vain, but I know that with my blonde hair (thank you, Viking ancestors) styled into long loose waves, very pre-Raphaelite, the sexy dress and the smoky eyeshadow and sultry red lipstick I'm wearing, I've nailed the 'armed and drop-dead gorgeous' part of my assignment.

I tug at the halter neck of my show-stopping scarlet-silk dress, which does great things for my small boobs but leaves nothing to the imagination. At least its thigh-length slit means I can move quickly, if I have to. And though my matching red heels aren't exactly conducive to setting any world records, close protection means close protection.

'Hi, your name?'

I smile back and lean over her clipboard. 'There.' I point.

Her eyes go a little wide but then she regroups quickly. I'm used to my name drawing attention, today it's a deliberate part of the strategy.

'Oh, you're Mr Radstock's guest.' She gives me a speculative look. 'Go right in.'

She ushers me in through the double doors to the art-deco ballroom, which is pure glitz, with an enormous ice sculpture at its centre and misty-white balloons strung up in long elaborate helix strings around the walls. In the adjacent room, I glimpse dozens of round tables adorned with crisp tablecloths, gleaming silverware and expensive crystal glasses – with guests in formal evening gowns and smart tuxes. This is definitely a thousand-dollars-a-table affair.

There's still half an hour before I meet Winston – who owns an American football team, the Austin Armadillos – in the bar area. According to my boss, Winston's been having some issues with death threats to someone in his team, posing significant danger. I've been hired to provide close protection, though I'm not yet sure for whom, as Winston insists it's on a need-to-know basis. I would argue that I need to know, but as he's a close friend of my boss, I've been overruled.

I snag a glass of Veuve Clicquot and weave my way through the rapidly filling room. I don't know a soul but it doesn't bother me. I'm too busy getting the measure of everyone. Shifty-eyed man with his wife – he's clearly worried that his mistress, who's standing with her back to him, is going to come over and cause some trouble. Then there's the bored wife trying to stem her fury while her husband is scrolling through his phone, ignoring her, despite her frequent nudges. Handsome young guy is trying to work out who he can approach to score some 'recreational uplift'. Young couple, newlyish weds are simply enjoying being part of the scene. I'm betting from the width of his shoulders and both of their naïve, wide-eyed stares, that he's a recent draft to the team. They're cute and so sweetly in love, it's a novelty. In my line of work, you don't always see the best in people but I can't help smiling at their obvious delight and pride at being here.

And that, right there, is exactly why being sentimental is a mistake.

I'm hit, and hit hard as a man barrels into me. Worse still, to add to my humiliation, flashbulbs illuminate in quick succession capturing the spill on camera.

While I'm trying to gather my well and truly scattered wits lying in a crumpled heap on the floor, a large hand appears in my peripheral vision, offering to help me up. Lordy, he is big ... muscular thighs barely contained by his very expensive suit. My eyes track up past a determined, chiselled jaw. His mouth is sexy-sulky, and the crooked nose adds a certain something, but it's the eyes: blue and blazing, first with apology, then anger—

'I'm so sorr— Lily?'

What the—? Fuck. Fuck. Fuck and fuck some more. Of all the people in all the world to bump into, it just had to be him.

Tate Donaghue. Of course.

'Tate,' I squeak, like an overgrown guinea pig looking up at him. Oh my. My mouth dries, the transformation from boy to man is... Holy hell ... he's even more gorgeous. But there's also something harder and more dangerous about him. He exudes testosterone through every pore.

My eyes widen and it takes every bit of my willpower

not to smooth my hand up his chest, cup his neck and pull him in for a kiss.

A slow, not very friendly, smile crosses Tate's face. I feel like I've just come face to face with a hungry tiger, and with my hormones misbehaving so badly, I'm not sure I've got it in me to run.

'Lily. What the fuck are you doing here?'

Chapter Two

TATE

I'm trying to hang onto the ends of my totally justifiable, white-hot anger. Fucking Winston has hired me a fucking bodyguard … without even asking me. I'm fuming as I change direction, suddenly deciding to head for the bar, and bowl over a woman in my path like a ten pin. My apology implodes when I realise exactly who this woman, wearing a smoking-hot red dress, is. It's been almost a decade since I last saw her.

Lily fucking Heath.

The sight of my college girlfriend, her blue eyes wide and shocked, sprawled at my feet in firecracker scarlet silk, like she's spread out on a satin sheet, pushes my blood pressure into the might-have-a-stroke-at-any-minute zone.

Lily Heath.

I haul her to her feet without any finesse; I really don't want to be touching her. A spark of electricity shoots up my arm. I ignore it. Just static. Basic physics. But the unfamiliar sensation pulls me up short and I lose power. Lily canons into me, her hand hitting my chest, and there it is, that instant burst of fireworks, attraction to the power of ten. My brain short-circuits and the throwaway, 'Do I know you?' that I've been practising for the last eight years doesn't even get out of the starting blocks.

I'd always planned to be casually cool, in a didn't-we-once-date, I-think-I remember-you, dismissive kind of way. Instead, my furious emotions burst out. The words 'What the fuck are you doing here?' tumbling out like I give a shit.

My notorious self-control is shot. Me, the guy famous for calming down his teammates, who's ice cool on the field, now wants to punch something. I want to put my fist into the wall.

It's her. Lily Heath. Lily fucking Heath. The woman I hate with every fibre of my being, and then some.

I pull myself together and this time I say with icy ease, 'Again. What the fuck are you doing here?' My teeth are gritted so hard I could grind walnuts to dust as I stare down at her. She's tall for a woman. Five-eleven. But I've still got a good five inches on her.

'Working,' she says, brushing down the fabric of her dress that billows around her legs, bringing a flashback of her thighs either side of my face as she sat on my shoulders at an outdoor stadium Killers gig. 'An apology wouldn't go amiss, you know.'

That's rich. She walked out on me and she's talking about apologies. Sure, we had an awkward video call where she explained her dad had been sick, but she refused any support I offered and then I never heard from her ever again. She ghosted me. I ram a hand in my pocket, clenching my fist out of sight.

'For what?' I ask.

'Knocking me over.'

'Didn't see you,' I snap. It's rude but I don't care.

'Seriously? That's all you've got?' Her voice is husky even though her eyes flash with a touch of anger.

There's no way sorry is going to pass my lips. Instead, I pull up a bored look. 'Is there anywhere you need to be right now?'

'As a matter of fact, there is,' she snaps.

'Well, I suggest you get there.' I give her an insincere smile and watch as she lifts her chin and looks down her nose at me.

'Nice seeing you again. Not.'

'Childish,' I observe, acting equally dumb. What the fuck is wrong with me? Why did I have to have the last word.

She raises a haughty eyebrow and looks at me as if I'm something she's spotted on the bottom of her shoe after walking through a farmyard.

My heart is performing a tumbling routine worthy of Simone Biles, but I hold her gaze. Fuck, she's even more beautiful than I've been remembering and, standing there with her hip jutted out as if she's ready to take me on, she's cute, feisty and brave. Exactly as she was back in college.

Her lips have tightened, twisted and pursed in the last few seconds – as facial gymnastics go, it's understated, but it's there all the same. I'm convinced she's trying to work up a comeback. Funny, the Lily Heath I knew was never lost for words. Sharp, even spiky, but always honest and forthright, loyal and spirited. She had this super British confidence that yanked me in the first time we spoke. It had been one of her many attractions. As a ball player in college, you get a lot of attention. A lot of action. Lily was never impressed by that and made it quite clear that I was nothing special the first time she met me. I had to pull out all the stops to get her to go on a first date. She said it was because I wasn't used to being turned down.

Lily turns and stalks off. Sad loser that I am, I watch her every step of the way. I'm mildly puzzled by the fact that she's made a beeline for the dining room, and out of sheer nosiness, I follow at a discreet distance, wondering if she's meeting someone in there. Why is she here, of all places? How did she get on the guest list?

The room is empty, everyone is gathered around the bar and the area overlooking the roof terrace. I'm intrigued when Lily walks right to the back of the room, disappearing behind the plants for a few seconds. She comes out of the other side of the planters, pushing something into her purse, and I have to turn away quickly and move back into the crowd before she spots me. I am not the least bit interested in Lily Heath. I couldn't care less about her. But I am intrigued – and that's all it is – as to what she's collected and put in her purse.

One beer later, the only one I've allowed myself, and I'm with the guys. Most of the team is here tonight before we fly out to New Orleans in the next couple of days.

'You okay, Tate?' asks Blake, my closest friend and one of the team's linebackers. 'You seem a little edgy.'

I look at him. I can trust him with my life, and I'm so shaken, I say. 'Remember when I first met you.'

'Yeah,' he grins at me but lowers his voice. 'How could I forget?'

He's not kidding, I was a mess. Nearly dropped out of college. Was benched from the team for not showing up to practice. Skipped gym sessions. I nearly lost everything.

'I just saw her.'

Blake's face mirrors the shock I'm feeling. 'Shit, man. Here? Now?' This time the question is quiet and urgent.

I just stare at him.

'You're not going to freak out on me?' he asks worriedly.

'No,' I say with a bucket-load of indignation, as if that's the last thing that would ever happen to me.

He cocks an eyebrow. 'First time I met you?'

'That was the one and only time,' I fire back at him, even now a little embarrassed by the way I'd fallen apart that day in the locker room. 'And you've been a good friend ever since. Thank you.'

He claps me on the shoulder. 'Way to cement a friendship, huh? Tell someone to take deep breaths into a paper bag.' He's studying me now. 'How do you feel? Seeing her again.'

'Fine,' I say, stiffening my spine. I am not going to let history derail me. This is my time. The best season of my life and I'm playing the best ball of my life. Nothing is going to get in my way, least of all Lily Heath. I dredge up a curt smile. 'It was just unexpected, that's all. I didn't have time to prepare – and I was already pissed.'

'Pissed? You?' Blake's surprised. I've got a reputation for

being driven on the field but with iron control. I never lose it. The team rely on me to keep tempers cooled.

I change the subject.

'Winston has hired a fucking bodyguard?' I jab my thumb towards my chest. 'For me. Fuck's sake.'

'You're kidding.'

'If only I was. He got another letter today. I mean who even mails letters these days?'

'You said they weren't serious.'

'They aren't,' I say, exasperated. 'Just some crackpot, yanking his chain. But Win is rattled with the game coming up, plus the d-i-v-o-r-c-e, which must not be mentioned, so these crazy threats are sending him over the edge.'

'He's just looking out for you.'

I give Blake a look. He has a tendency to think the best of everyone.

Before I can answer, a white ball of fur comes careering towards me and starts dancing and yapping around my ankles, jumping up and down for attention.

'Hey, dog, stop.' I lean down and scoop up the little Pomeranian into my arms. He's quivering with over-excitement and nerviness. 'Now just cut it out, little man,' I tell the fluffball. 'How does something your size have so much attitude?' The dog quietens and there's the usual grin on his foxy little face. 'Don't even—' Before I can finish the sentence the dog has lunged at my face, lavishing it with friendly licks, which are so not welcome.

'Maybe you can borrow the dog to protect you,' teases Blake.

'Ew, dog,' I hold the dog at arm's length and pointedly

ignore Blake's comment. 'Not in the face. I don't know where the tongue's been. You disgusting creature.' With a long-suffering sigh I hold onto the wriggling mass that is Teddington Bear the First just as his owner, Pammie Radstock, comes rushing over. Long legs on elegant heels, her luxuriant blonde hair arranged in a mass of sexy-just-out-of-bed curls, Pammie is poured into a dress made to emphasise every one of her considerable assets. She is one gorgeous woman, and she's aged gracefully and elegantly. She's also the boss's wife.

'Teddy, you naughty boy.' She waves a chiding finger at the little dog. 'Naughty, naughty, running away from Mommy.' Then she bats her eyelids at me. 'He just adores you.'

'Mmm,' I reply, grimacing and still holding the dog as far from my face as possible.

'Can I get a picture of my little baby with you?' I roll my eyes, but Pammie's already turned to Blake. 'They just make the most adorable couple, don't they. Just so sweet together. Him so big and muscly, and Teddy so little,' she croons in a baby-doll voice.

'Yeah, Mrs Rad … er…' Blake tugs at his collar. 'Very cute.'

Her face falls and her eyes fill with sadness. 'I'm still Mrs Radstock. Winston might have moved on to a younger model, but I'm still married to him.'

'Yes, ma'am,' sputters Blake.

None of us know what went wrong between the two of them. They've been married for twenty-five years and always appeared to have a solid marriage. Not that I'd know anything about that. My mom bailed when I was fifteen. She lives in Canada now with a new family, and with my schedule, we rarely touch base. I don't bear her any ill will, though, and my dad has more than made up for her absence.

'Now let me take our picture.' Pammie elbows Blake out of the way and takes out a tablet from one of her regular, outsized purses and muscles in next to me and the dog to take a selfie, after which she smooths down her curls with a self-congratulatory stroke.

'Pammie, you've got to stop doing this,' I say. The woman is causing us all a whole heap of trouble. I mean, I have nothing against her, she's a sweet woman and obviously suffering, but I really don't want to be dragged into her marital break-up.

'Doing what, Tate? I can't help it if my dog loves you.'

'You know what I mean.'

'Sorry, darling, no idea.' With that she grabs one of the dog's paws, waves it at me and sashays off on her sexy high heels, and I mean sashays, a sassy wiggle to her bottom as she is absorbed into the crowd, the dog now tucked under one arm, her huge bag clamped to her side by the other.

I shake my head.

'Let's hope Win doesn't see that picture,' says Blake.

I shrug. What else can I do? Pammie's hurting and she still owns part of the club. Win is mad as hell at her, and no one knows why. It's turned into a game of one-upmanship and her weapon of choice is TikTok. The videos she posts invariably get picked up by the tabloids. And then Winston gets grumpy and bawls the team out.

'You know she's been seen a lot with her Swedish tennis coach, Sven something-or-other, but it's so clichéd. Winston's convinced something is going on. The guy is half her age and Pammie's always had more class than that, don't you think?'

That's one of the things I like about Blake, he's astute when it comes to people.

I vaguely listen as he talks on, my attention caught by a couple of people moving through the crowd.

'For fuck's sake.'

'What?' Blake turns and cranes his neck to see the recipient of my scowl. 'Ooh, who's *that* with Win? She's a looker. Don't tell me she's Pammie's replacement?'

My stomach drops. Please, God, no.

'Don't be ridiculous,' I snap, because in a million years I did not predict this scenario. 'She's half his age.'

'Puh-lease. Are you crazy?' Blake raises an eyebrow. 'Since when did a healthy bank balance affect that equation?'

'Who's the honey?' asks Marvin, this season's rookie, sidling up to us and glancing round. 'If Pammie sees her, shit's really going to hit the fan. Look at those legs and'—he groans—'that is a fuck-me mouth, if ever I saw one— Ouch! What was that for?'

Marvin rubs at his ribs where I've just given him a sharp jab.

'Show some respect,' I snarl.

Around the room, everyone is watching Winston. On one side of him is his usual sidekick, the team manager, Shane Dooley, who, despite his VIP status, is not a total dick; on the other side, gliding along beside him, is the serene beauty that is Lily Heath. The three of them stop to greet John Tierney, Head of Security, and together they stand in a small huddle. Meanwhile, my brain is going into overdrive.

Lily said she was working here. No way. Don't tell me Lily Heath has just walked back into my life on a more permanent basis. Not when I have the biggest game of my life coming up.

Chapter Three

LILY

'Winston Radstock the Third?' I ask, approaching the bar. It feels daft saying 'the Third' out loud, it's not like I knew One and Two. I smile politely at him, and I'm the epitome of smooth professional once more. Inside it's a very different story. My insides feel as if they've been rattled about, rearranged and abandoned in the wrong places after my encounter with Tate bloody Donaghue. Discombobulated doesn't begin to describe it.

Whisky glass in hand, Winston swings round from the bar to face me. More handsome than his pictures suggested, he's a tanned, fit sixty-something, with a wide smile and very white teeth.

'You must be Lily.' He sizes me up with the shrewd assessment of a corporate shark, despite which there's a likeability about him. 'Do I shake your hand?' His mouth curves very slightly into a smile. 'Or will you toss me over your shoulder like some super ninja?'

I like him straight away. I extend a hand and say with a polite smile, 'I assure you, it's perfectly safe.'

'Phew.' He leans in and says in a loud indiscreet whisper, 'I mean, you don't look like your typical close-protection officer, but Pennington tells me you're the best.'

I want to say Pennington, my boss, exaggerates. But, one, he doesn't, and two, this guy is paying a lot for my services. I simply nod.

I'm horribly aware that all eyes are on me, which is really not how I would have orchestrated things but Winston Radstock III is the client and this is how he wants to play it.

'Can I get you a drink, Miss Heath?' asks a short man on the other side of Winston, who is dressed in an extremely sharp suit and bears a passing resemblance to a slightly less rumpled Ed Sheeran. 'I'm Shane Dooley, General Manager of the Austin Armadillos.'

'Nice to meet you. And, please, call me Lily. Soda water, thank you.'

'Excuse my manners,' says Winston, gesturing at a man who's been scowling at me with undisguised scepticism. 'This is John Tierney, Head of Security.'

I'm unfazed. I've met attitudes like Tierney's a dozen times over, but as I turn to greet him, I spot Tate, and my heart does that stupid miss-a-beat thing – just like the very first time he spoke to me back in college. He's among a group of what have to be ball players, they're all huge. Their stares are by turn: admiring, the tall, lanky guy; suspicious, a handsome guy to Tate's right; and downright hostile Tate, of course. As if I've wronged him. I give him a cool stare and turn away. Fuck my traitorous heart. I'm cool, professional and totally in control. That heartsick, lost girl is long behind me.

'Nice to meet you, gentlemen,' I say. 'Shall we find a place to talk? Pennington said you'd fill me in some more once I arrived.' I gesture to one of the empty booths on the other side of the bar area. Winston smirks as he catches Tierney tightening his jaw. Mr Head of Security is clearly one of those men who underestimates women and is allergic to them taking charge.

We sit, and the three men fidget with their drinks, all of them have small tumblers of what I'm guessing is whisky.

'So, Mr Radstock,' I prompt, as no one else seems to want to get to the point.

'Call me Winnie, everyone does.' There's a blank look around the table. 'Almost everyone.' No one interrupts. 'Okay, no one does. I'm Winston. I was gonna try Winnie out for size. I feel like I need to change things up a bit since you know…' Around the table the others give sympathetic smiles. I nod along.

'I understand that one of your players, Don, has been receiving threatening letters,' I say. I've seen them. They're creepy and insistent. Proper old-school cut-out letters stuck on paper type-thing.

'At first I thought they were a joke, but your boss didn't agree.'

'No. We've looked at them. And had one of our profilers study them, too. It's easy for a troll on social media to dish out threats but these … well, someone is going to some trouble to make their point, not once but over and over.

They're quite fanatical,' I add, remembering the profiler report. 'They've fixated on this particular player, for some reason, but it seems as much because he's an intrinsic part of the team. Why don't they want him to play?'

'Because,' explains Shane, the manager, 'Don is pivotal to our success. His talent and work ethic are the glue that holds the team together. None of them ever want to let him down.'

I nod, maybe I should have done a bit more homework, but I couldn't bring myself to open Pandora's Box. It's a point of principle. I avoid anything to do with American football, I have no idea who the stars are. Okay, Tate was first pick for the Patriots in his first season, but I never checked again after that. It was bittersweet knowing that he'd achieved his dream of playing pro-football.

I fold my arms, as much to keep the memories at bay as to maintain my professional image.

'Whoever's sending these letters seems to know the movements of the team between now and the Superbowl. Which events they're attending, when they're flying into New Orleans, where they're staying, which I understand is confidential. Is there any chance of a leak within the organisation?'

Tierney's look of disgust says it all. I hold up my hands. 'I have to ask.'

'There are no leaks. Everyone with access to that level of information has been on the team for years. We're family.'

Winston nods vehemently. 'Family.'

'Can you think of someone who has a grudge against Don?' I ask.

The men exchange glances. 'No one,' says Tierney. 'I mean, he occasionally plays the field. Has a bit of a rep. But I think this is more than a disgruntled bunny boiler. Why insist he's axed from the team?'

'Bunny boiler?' I give him a deadly stare. 'Because women have no right to call men out on bad behaviour.'

He shrugs but goes a little pink. 'He doesn't have time for relationship commitments. Always training. His absolute priority is the team. No one thinks otherwise. I don't think that the threats are coming from that quarter. Plus, why are they coming to Winston?'

That was a good point.

'We don't want news of this getting out,' says Shane, exchanging a nod with Winston. 'We need to focus on the football. And if this got into the media – the hysteria would be even more crazy than it already is.'

From my time in college, I know football dominates the tabloids and social media over the few weeks leading up to the finals.

'Okay. So, when do I meet Don?'

The men look at each other, like a bunch of boy scouts hiding a confiscated magazine. I sense there's something they're not telling me.

'Tonight,' says Tierney, as if he drew the short straw. 'He's here at the dinner. You're sitting next to him.'

'Great. And I assume he knows about our cover story … as to why I'm around.'

There's that covert glance among them again.

Winston looks at Shane as if he might rescue him, but Shane just nods encouragingly.

'The thing is … well…' Again, Winston looks at Shane, who looks at Tierney.

I take pity on Winston. His uber-cool corporate-shark persona seems to have taken an early holiday.

'He's a bit resistant to having a new girlfriend thrust upon him?' I supply for them. 'Especially one who is actually his undercover bodyguard. Thinks it might cramp his style?' I give them a warm reassuring smile. 'Don't worry, I've done this a few times before. I'm very good at keeping it professional. It's all part of the job. After a day or two, he'll be used to me.'

'Of course. You're a professional.' Winston's gratitude is palpable.

I nod. It's true. This isn't new territory. I've done plenty of protection work, looking after people in the public eye. Posing as the party girl in plain sight.

There's a lull in conversation around the room and then the tapping of a spoon on glass. We're being invited through to dinner.

'Why don't you introduce me and then we can go from there?' I suggest.

All three men look down at their drinks.

Interesting. Why so skittish? 'Is there a problem?'

This time they shuffle in their seats. It's Shane who caves first.

'Thing is, Miss Heath.'

'Please call me Lily,' I say.

'Thing is, Lily.' He glances at Winston. This time his wince is more pronounced. 'He's refusing.'

'Refusing?' For some reason I think of a horse baulking at a fence and I'm confused.

'Oh, you mean he's reluctant to have protection?' I ask. Now this is a new one. Most 'details', as they're known in the business, are happy to have the reassurance of someone looking out for them.

'Not so much reluctant,' says Tierney, with a very faint hint of triumph. 'Adamant.'

'But,' says Winston, in that trying terribly hard to be positive way, 'I do have the final say. I hold the winning card. I own the team. He has no choice if he wants to play.'

I frown at that. 'Kind of counter-productive because that's what the person who's threatening wants.'

He nods and sighs. 'Which is exactly what Don says. He's playing hard-ass.'

'He is a hard-ass,' interjects Tierney. 'And hard-headed. The guy's not taking the threats seriously.'

'Thing is, when we told Don we had arranged protection, he was furious. Hung up on me. He's not happy at all.'

'Understatement of the century,' mutters John.

'But he has to have protection,' sighs Winston. 'I'm not dicking around. The boy is like family. If anything happened to him, I'd never forgive myself.'

'Have you tried that line on him?' I ask. Emotional blackmail is one hell of a tool.

There are blank looks all around the table. Men.

'Have you sat down and discussed it with him? I take it this was a phone conversation.'

Again, doubtful looks.

'Does he know you've already hired someone?' I ask.

'Not yet,' says Winston.

'When are you proposing to introduce us?'

'In about five minutes?' says Shane diffidently.

I smile brightly. It's a job. I'm a professional. Just another day at the office.

'Come on, then, let's get on with it.' With my British accent I probably sound just like Mary Poppins.

Here we go.

Chapter Four

LILY

As we enter the packed ballroom, a shiver of foreboding comes over me. If this guy really is in danger from a crazed fan, this is not a great venue. There are too many exits and too many people. It's a crush.

Tierney catches my eye. 'Everyone is scanned when they come in from the elevator. No weapons.'

'Unless they're already staying in the hotel and have access to the service stairs,' I point out, and open my clutch to show him the glint of gunmetal sitting pretty next to my lipstick and perfume. 'I visited earlier. Hid it in one of the plant holders.'

His eyes widen and he glances around actually looking worried.

'But it's quite a public place,' I say reassuringly. 'And invited guests only.'

This is utter bollocks. If anyone is determined enough, they'll find a way in, which Tierney should know as well as

I do if he's any good at his job, which I'm beginning to doubt.

As if we're a royal entourage, the crowds part as we head to the front of the room and I realise that Winston Radstock III is *someone*, and a well-liked someone, judging by the waves and smiles he receives as we pass through.

We come to the table in the middle at the front. There are place cards at each setting ... and I don't believe it – Tate is standing on the other side of the table. He looks up at me and his face goes blank. Great, just what I don't need. Please don't let him be sitting on this table.

'You're over there,' says Shane Dooley and points to the chair right next to where Tate is standing. He ushers me round towards the seat. 'Just here.' I stand behind my chair and eye the name cards on either side of me. Fenwick Easton and Tate Donaghue.

I glance at Shane and wrinkle my brow in confusion. Luckily, Shane gets the message and smoothly takes charge. 'Lily, can I introduce you to Tate Donaghue. Winston calls him Don.'

My heart takes a nosedive in my chest.

'Tate.' I smile mechanically, or is that manically. Bollocking bloody bollocking hell.

'Tate, this is Lily Heath,' says Shane. 'She's sitting next to you.'

Tate doesn't say a word. A small flame, a pilot light of anger, fires up inside me. How dare he try and make me look inconsequential? I might not have meant anything to him, eight years ago, but surely he can at least extend some good manners right now.

'At this table,' says Shane, a little desperately. 'Right here.' He indicates my empty chair. There's a growing silence around the table as people are tuning into the awkward atmosphere, their bodies leaning in as if to hear better.

Tate just glares at me from beneath dark, narrowed eyebrows. He's really perfected the whole brooding-hero thing since I last saw him.

'Mr Donaghue,' I say politely, and hold out my hand.

He raises an eyebrow and although he takes my hand, he doesn't say anything. I'm conscious of the warmth of his palm encased around my fingers, before he drops my hand like I'm contagious.

Are we really going to pretend we don't know each other?

'Nice to meet you,' I say, summoning up my professionalism. I need to get him on side, not antagonise him.

Shane gives me an uncertain smile and backs away to his place on the table next door. There's a stodgy silence that's only broken by the scrape and rustle of chairs at the other tables. At table ten, we all follow suit and sit down. Tate proceeds to completely ignore me, turning to the guest on his other side, and around the table, conversation picks up with low murmurs.

On my left, Fenwick, one of the Armadillos' sponsors, chats away to me with friendly ease, for which I'm very grateful as I'm hyper-aware of the tense mountain of pissed-off man on my right. It's like all my senses are tuned into a Tate Donaghue frequency, and my whole body is quivering with pent-up energy. I focus my attention on Fenwick, who is thankfully a big Anglophile and asks me lots of questions about London and Oxford, after I told him I hailed from Oxfordshire.

Eventually, however, etiquette dictates that Fenwick turns to talk to the woman on his other side, leaving me with little choice.

'Could you pass me the water?' I ask Tate.

He picks up the jug, and for a moment I wonder if he's going to dump the contents into my lap, but to my surprise he pours me a tumblerful, the ice clinking against the glass.

'Thank you,' I say.

'So, you said you were working. Who for?'

'Mr Radstock,' I say. It's going to come out at some point.

'Winston?' Tate wrinkles his nose, a familiar dimple appearing in one cheek. I stare at his smooth-shaven skin, my heart skipping merrily over two beats as I recall the same, much cuter, puzzled expression on his face years ago when I used an English phrase Tate didn't understand. When he'd teased me, his blue eyes had crinkled as he called me his Sexy Brit.

'What are you doing for him?' he asks, oblivious to my inner trip down memory lane. His fingers toy with the tines of the fork in front of him, reminding me that Tate never could sit still.

I take a breath. This is when I should leap in and explain, but we're interrupted by a waitress bringing out the starters.

'Starter for you, Mr Donaghue,' says the very young,

pretty and slightly breathless teenage waitress, her cheeks already pink with hero worship. Her hands are shaking as she places the plate in front of him.

'Thank you, Serena,' he says looking at her name badge and then lowering his voice. 'All a bit fancy, isn't it? When I was your age, I waited tables and I was always terrified I was going to drop the soup in someone's lap.'

She turns even pinker, but her smile is pure gratitude. 'I'm real grateful they're not serving soup tonight, sir.'

As she walks away, I can't help myself.

'That was nice of you,' I say.

'I am nice,' he replies. His blue eyes give me a piercing stare and his mouth twists slightly, those lips almost close enough to kiss. Despite his disdainful expression, he's still gorgeous, and an immediate invisible connection fizzes through me. My heart actually flutters, full-on beating wings, trapped butterfly in my rib cage, the works. Like I'm nineteen again, he's the football heartthrob everyone has warned me about, and I'm trying to be indifferent, except it's not that easy. Tate Donaghue was, then, and still is, gorgeousness and sexiness personified in one glorious package. I honestly thought that distance and dislike would have immunised me to him. Instead, I have a craving to taste his lips one more time. My body wants to know the feel of him again. The heavy weight of his breadth against mine. My mouth has dried with pure longing.

I smile back, a little regretfully.

His smile immediately vanishes and is replaced by a tight, curt expression. A timely reminder, I'm nothing to him.

Thankfully, the delicate plate of smoked salmon and green salad in front of me gives me a new focus for my attention. I'm embarrassed by my body's stupid reaction, and snatch up my knife and fork. I've taken just a couple of hasty mouthfuls before I catch Tate's quick look of disappointment.

'Just once at one of these dos, I wish they'd serve a burger,' he mutters.

Although the comment isn't directed to anyone, I feel I ought to acknowledge it.

'They didn't get the protein memo, I guess,' I say.

He shoots me a glare. Not only does he not want protection, he's even less likely to want it when he realises it's me. And as for the undercover girlfriend – I almost laugh out loud at that one. How am I going to convince anyone that he's into me, when he looks as if he'd rather kill me and chop me up for shark bait? Sexual chemistry, that's all it is, I tell myself. We always had it in spades. I have no emotional feelings for Tate. They're buried six-feet under with fifty floors of skyscraper on top of them – never to be exhumed.

Tate's mouth purses and I'm drawn again to those lush lips, which still look eminently kissable even when he's scowling at me.

'Did you want red or white wine?' he asks.

'Just water, thanks,' I say. I'm officially on duty, even though I could murder a white wine. I continue to tuck into my starter to deter further conversation, and luckily, the girl next to Tate does her best to monopolise his attention, which amuses the hell out of me, because I can tell he can't decide which of us is the lesser of two evils.

I turn to talk to Fenwick again. In contrast to Tate, he's charming and totally devoted to his wife and twin boys, which fills plenty of the conversation for the next fifteen minutes. When the next course arrives – chicken, dauphinoise potatoes and wilted spinach – I notice Tate tuck in with enthusiasm. He makes short work of the meal, and his plate is clean before I'm even halfway through mine, but then making polite conversation with a neighbour does slow you down.

Maybe it's because my body has some muscle memory where Tate is concerned, but something makes the hairs on the back of my neck stand up. Tate has become very still, which is uncharacteristic. He's always been one of those people in constant motion. A hand tapping, a foot jiggling, fiddling with a pen, the label on a beer bottle. I can't quite put my finger on what is wrong, but it's as if he's suddenly being careful with his body. Not making any sudden moves. It's then that I hear his outward breath wheeze just a little. I listen carefully. His breath rasps out of his chest.

'Tate? Are you okay?' I ask in a low voice, my body sliding into on-duty mode. Alert, aware and ready for trouble.

'Yeah,' he says but he deliberately evades my gaze. I watch his Adam's apple dip.

He doesn't look right. There's a very slight sheen to his brow. And am I imagining it, or do his lips have a blue tinge to them?

I listen harder. He coughs and I know I'm not imagining

things, he sounds a little breathless. 'Tate?' I ask again in a firm voice.

He turns and his mouth is fused in a grim line. He pats his chest and says through gritted teeth, 'Don't make a fuss. I'm just going outside a minute.'

He pushes back his chair, and I catch Winston's eye, shaking my head slightly, already on my feet. I want Winston to understand he can rely on me, and I'm not about to let Tate Donaghue out of my sight.

I follow Tate into the lobby area and it's very noticeable that he doesn't protest at my presence when he sits down, patting his inside pocket.

Shit, his lips are swelling before my eyes.

'I don't feel right.' His blue eyes hold mine, candid and direct.

He pulls open his jacket and delves into the inside pocket. His face creases and I see the first stirring of unease in his expression as he checks his outside pockets.

'What are you looking for?' I ask, holding my own breath. I've seen Tate have an allergic reaction once before, not quite like this. Someone had thrown a peanut in the college bar one night and he'd caught it before it hit him in the face. That time the response was swift and mild, but instantaneous – leaving him with a nasty rash on the palm of his hand. That was how I found out he had a severe peanut allergy.

It was also the night he first told me he loved me. After he'd explained about the rash on his hand, I flounced off and he chased after me.

'Lily, what's wrong with you?' He'd tried to hold me, but I wriggled free.

'What's wrong with me?' I demanded. 'What's wrong with you?'

'I'm fine,' he said, holding up his hand, which was absolutely not fine at all. It was a mass of ugly, red hives distorting its shape. 'It'll go down.'

I couldn't speak for a second, pure rage boiled through my veins.

'Shouldn't you have an EpiPen or something? And shouldn't you have told me that you have a severe allergy?'

'I have got an EpiPen. I just haven't got it with me.'

'What do you mean you haven't got it with you,' I'd replied, even more furious at his admission.

'I forgot it. It's not a big deal, Lily.' He'd looked a little sullen, as if he knew damn well it was but didn't want to admit being in the wrong.

I wasn't letting him off the hook.

'Not a big fucking deal,' I yelled at him. 'You could have died!'

And then I'd burst into tears, which was so not like me, but I couldn't bear the thought of him not looking after himself properly.

My tears shocked him, and he pulled me into his arms and kissed their salty tracks. 'Hey, Lily. I'm sorry. I didn't mean to…'

I looked up at him. 'You scared me. What if you'd eaten it? And you didn't have the pen and I didn't know.'

'Hey,' he tried to soothe me, but I shook him off.

'No, Tate. I'm mad at you.'

'Mad at me because I didn't die.' The corner of his mouth lifted.

'Don't joke about this.' I pointed at him. 'It's not funny.'

He took me in his arms, genuine remorse in his beautiful blue eyes. 'I'm sorry. It's not funny and I should take it more seriously but … I hate people thinking I'm weak.'

'You're an idiot.' I told him, although my heart was pounding with the realisation that if anything happened to him, I'm not sure I'd have survived.

'That, too.'

'The thought of anything happening to you frightens me,' I whispered to him. 'Promise me you'll carry it in future.'

I'd always been so careful with my emotions, ever since I was ten years old and came down one morning to find, without any warning, that my dad had gone and I was being driven to boarding school and handed over to the principal by his driver. I learned later that he'd been called away on the first of many secret assignments, and after that he was an unreliable quantity in my life. It pretty effectively prepared me for the fact that loving someone makes you vulnerable. Dad wanted me to be tough and self-sufficient.

Tate had taken both my hands in his and clasped them over his heart. With the other, he cupped my face, meeting my eyes. 'I promise, Lily,' he'd whispered. 'And I'm sorry for frightening you. You know I wouldn't do that for the world. Not when I love you so much.'

'EpiPen?' I ask now as Tate searches his suit jacket again, as if he might have missed something the first time.

His breathing is sharp and hoarse now. Panic darkens

his eyes. My heart clenches and I feel real fear. He could die. This isn't something I have control over. Suddenly, this isn't a job. This is Tate.

'It's not here,' he rasps in a hoarse whisper. 'It's always there. I always carry it.'

'Do you have a spare nearby?' I ask, horrified by the tears that have suddenly appeared from nowhere.

'Not here. Home.'

'Stay calm,' I say and give him a reassuring smile, even though I want to take his face in my hand and place a kiss on his forehead. 'You're going to be fine.'

This is where my advanced first-aid training kicks in.

'Lie down.' I push him down onto the couch, prop cushions up behind him and raise his legs. 'Don't move. I'm going to call an ambulance.'

'No,' protests Tate, shaking his head, a mutinous line to his mouth. He grabs my hand urgently. 'I'm not going to the ER. Team doctor. Get the team doctor. He's here.'

I pull out my phone and call Winston.

'Where are you?'

'Winston, there's been an incident. Tate has had an allergic reaction. You need to get the team doctor out to the lobby with an EpiPen. Right now.'

'Is he okay? What happened? Where is he? What—'

I cut his questions short. 'Doctor, now. Lobby area. And make sure someone keeps his plate of food and whatever he was drinking. Put them in a sealed bag. Tierney will know the drill.'

Seconds later, a young man appears at a sprint run, carrying a black rucksack. Before he reaches us, he's already rummaging in his bag and produces an orange EpiPen.

'Tate?' he asks, assessing Tate's face and prodding his lips. 'How you doing?'

'Been better.'

The doctor hands over the EpiPen. 'This will help.'

'Thanks, Doc,' says Tate and holds the pen to his upper thigh, pressing the lid down hard with his thumb.

There's dead silence as the doctor and I stare at Tate.

'I'm not dying,' he says, glaring at us. 'You can both stand down.'

A few minutes later, Tate's breathing is already starting to ease, and his colour is returning – not to exactly normal, but much less near-deathly than it was. He still looks wiped out and I can tell that he hates it because he's scrunched up his eyes and tilted his head back as if he doesn't want to acknowledge either of us. The team doctor, who was watching him carefully, is now on the phone to Winston.

Reluctantly, Tate's gaze moves to me.

'What did you say you do, Lily?' he asks. 'Like, what exactly are you doing here?'

I take a breath. I might as well tell him.

'I'm your new bodyguard,' I say.

'Fuck.' He closes his eyes and shakes his head. 'No way. Over my dead body.'

'Well, it almost was,' I tell him, grimly. I hadn't expected the threats to turn to reality, or at least not so soon.

But it seems someone has just tried to kill Tate Donaghue.

Chapter Five

TATE

M an, I'm as weak as a kitten. Getting dressed earlier drained what little energy I have. I'm under doctor's orders to rest for the next couple of days, which means I'm supposed to be staying at home. Screw that. I need to speak to Winston and the team.

'Dude, just listen to them,' says Blake, who I've conned into swinging by my hotel room and come with me to Winston's New York apartment for a showdown with management at four-thirty.

Blake's supposed to be on my side, but he's clearly not read that memo.

I should phone my agent and keep him in the loop. He'd soon tell Winston to ditch the idea of a bodyguard, but he'd also tell my dad, who would not keep quiet about this and probably insist on calling the National Guard in.

In the taxi to Winston's, I rest my arm on the edge of the window, grateful for the hotel's underground garage. The paps are out in force today. Word got round pretty quick that I'd 'collapsed', and my phone has been blowing up, not just from press hysteria, but with calls from my worried teammates, too.

Unfortunately, the team doc's press statement about an allergic reaction has not quelled rampant speculation. According to social media, I've got anything and everything from gastric flu, epilepsy, IBS, chicken pox, had a nervous breakdown, right through to terminal cancer.

'I don't need a bodyguard. What's that gonna say to the world? More importantly, what's that gonna say about the team. That we're running scared?'

I clench my hands into fists. I certainly don't want Lily Heath anywhere near me – my close protection detail or not. I might not have seen her for eight years, but my body hasn't forgotten her. Sitting next to her last night was hell on Earth. Every time I breathed in, I could smell her perfume, subtle and sexy and very different from the light, citrussy fragrances she used to wear. A constant reminder that the gorgeous girl of my college years has grown up. She's now a woman. And a super sexy one at that.

Over the years since we dated, my brain has developed an unhealthy curiosity about Lily – wondering how her lithe, toned body might have changed since I'd last touched her. Back then, she was sinewy muscle and long limbs. Tall and lean. She has filled out, just a little since then, but she is still as slim as a blade and though she's always been strong, I had to wonder what sort of protection she could offer as a bodyguard. Sure, she could always look after herself at college… Her crazy dad had taught her how to do that, he was big on self-defence. So I guess I shouldn't be surprised at her line of work now.

'I'm telling them no way,' I announce to Blake now. 'If Winston insists, I'll quit the team.'

'Fuck off, you will,' says Blake. 'We need you, dude, and let's be honest, you need us. Football is your life.'

'Then back me up,' I say, like a sulky toddler.

Blake rolls his eyes. 'Is it really gonna hurt you to have a little back-up. A shadow hanging about now and then, making sure that some obsessed stalker isn't going anywhere near you? Plus, she's pretty easy on the eye.'

'It's the principle,' I growl, ignoring his last sentence. 'It's like, the message is that I can't handle myself.'

Not to mention she's the one woman I don't want to have anything to do with.

'These two weeks are important,' I growl. 'We have to get our head in the game. I don't have time for this shit.'

When we arrive at Winston's fancy apartment block and walk into the huge, brightly lit foyer, I'm greeted by a chorus of excited yips as Teddy the Pomeranian, comes streaking across the floor, his claws skittering on the hard surface before he launches himself at me.

'Little dog, what is your problem?' I say to the wriggling mutt, who, as usual, is desperate to kiss my face. I look around, and sure enough, Pammie is trotting around the corner. Despite the weather, which must be twenty-six degrees Fahrenheit, she's in tennis whites – a tight sport's vest and ass-skimming skirt. She looks fantastic, though closer up, I see a tiredness around her eyes, which tells me more.

'Oh, there you are, Teddy,' she trills. 'He just loves you, Tate. Don't you, baby.' She bends to fuss with the dog and kisses him on his nose.

I don't ask her what she's doing here. I don't want to know. I seem to see more of her now that she and Winston have split up than when they were married.

'What are you doing here, honey?' she asks. I'm so used to her being the boss's wife, I answer without thinking.

'Seeing Winston about something.'

She frowns. 'I've got a meeting with him at five-thirty, so I hope you won't be long. The lawyers I'm having to pay for are very expensive.'

I hand her the dog. 'Just admin stuff,' I say blandly, then smile at Pammie because she looks kinda sad.

Tears well up in her eyes. 'I wish Winston would stop all of this.' She glances over to my right where a tall blond man has appeared. 'Thank God for Sven, he's being such a support. Have you met him?'

'I haven't,' I say.

'Well, let me introduce you.'

But as she hails the man, he turns his face away. Maybe he's a little shy, or nervous. Can't say I blame him. He's on enemy turf here, and apparently Winston is convinced they're having an affair. I'm not so sure.

'We'd better head up,' I say, and Blake and I move towards the lift up to the penthouse, which is Winston's second home. He maintains an office and boardroom up there, as well as at the Stadium in Austin.

'That little mutt sure does love you,' says Blake.

'I've no idea why. I've done nothing to encourage it.'

'Don't you like dogs?' Blake asks me.

'I love dogs, just not ones that want to lick me to death.'

'Don't let Pammie hear you say that,' says Blake with a laugh.

We're buzzed into the penthouse foyer, and straight into the office on the left. Winston's private secretary, Amanda, looks up, her eyes turning misty.

'Tate, darlin' boy. How are you? Shouldn't you be resting up?'

She's the mother hen for the team, sweet as pie until you cross her. She's already up and out of her seat clucking round me.

'I'm fine, Mandy. Just fine.'

'If I'd known you were comin' in, I'd have baked you some cookies.' She puts her hands on her hips and tuts. 'You better go on through. They're waitin' for you. Quite a kerfuffle you're causin'. Now, you behave and do as you're told. The team needs you.'

Blake grins. 'That's what I've been telling him.'

I glare at them both. The whole world is against me today.

As I open the door, the voices in the room quieten. Sitting around Winston's round table are Winston, the head of security, Shane and … of course, Lily.

Lily. My eyes are immediately drawn to her svelte figure in black cargo pants and a well-fitting T-shirt that outlines her contours. My heart slams against my ribs with walk-into-a-wall awareness. It's as if there's no one else in the room. Just her, looking golden. I remember the last time I ever saw her all those years ago. Legs wrapped around my waist, her skin flush with excitement, eyes full of promise. I want to close my eyes and shut her out, but she fills the room with her presence. Today, she's channelling Lara Croft, and fuck me, is it sexy. Her blonde hair is scooped up in a high ponytail which shows off her delicate, patrician features. She looks neat, tidy and professional, but I already have a pretty good idea what she'd look like all mussed up. An image, one of many imprinted into my memories, comes to mind, Lily lying tangled in my bedsheets with the morning sunlight slanting over her body when I came home from an early-morning run. That slow sleepy smile she greeted me with.

The rattle of the cups on a trolley brought in by the housekeeper brings my thoughts back to the present, and I stand aside as she starts unloading plates of sandwiches and cakes. I blink away the memory. I'm a fool. Like my dad said, Lily weakened me. After she left, I almost didn't make the draft. That's what I have to remember. Her being here for the biggest game of my life is pure bad luck, but it's not going to affect me. Not this time.

'Hey Tate, how are you feeling?' asks Winston. To be fair, he does look genuinely concerned, but then he's invested one hell of a lot of faith in me, not to mention money.

'I'm fine,' I growl. Truth is, I want to sleep for another six weeks and every muscle in my body aches with tiredness. My brain is mush. And I'm feeling anxious.

Despite knowing these are well-documented post-anaphylactic symptoms, it doesn't quell the doom-laden, gnawing sensation of anxiety gripping me with sharp teeth. I don't want anyone to see this, especially not Winston and the team, who are relying on me.

'Man, it's good to see you on your feet,' says Shane. 'You looked a bit grim yesterday.'

'Thanks,' I deadpan. 'Needed to hear that.'

'Sorry,' he says. 'But, well … you looked shit.'

'Well aware,' I reply. Actually, I'm embarrassed they all saw that. People are going to worry that I'm not up to the game. Don't have what it takes this close to the final.

'Good to see you,' says John, clapping me on the arm.

'And you know Lily,' says Winston.

'Yep,' I say, and she gives me a fake smile.

'I wish it could have been under better circumstances,' she says.

I barely acknowledge her.

'I'm starving,' says Blake, either ignoring or oblivious to the chilly atmosphere. He loads his plate with sandwiches, even though I know he had a late lunch barely two hours ago.

'Lily, this is Blake Pedlar, another one of the team.'

'Sure, nice to meet you,' says Blake. 'I've heard a lot about *you*.' There's a slight frown on his face and I shoot him a warning glance. I do not need him telling Lily about the state I was in when he first met me.

'Why don't we sit down?' suggests Winston and he takes a seat.

I've got a rare craving for sugar, so I follow my body's

lead and just start helping myself to cookies, pastries and cake. The works. I need to refuel. My body has been through one hell of a workout, but I'm not going to let any of them know how shit I'm feeling. I can feel Lily's eyes on me. She doesn't miss anything. Never did.

I turn and look at her, my gaze impassive. Take in her lithe body clad in black Lycra. While not as out-and-out stunning as the flaming-red number she had on last night, she's nailed the sexy-ninja look. It's a natural urge – that's what I tell myself – imagining peeling that tight black T up her body, revealing the rosy skin beneath. Kissing my way up as I freed each inch of her chest from the snug material of her top.

Focus Tate. Get your head in the game.

I can't let Lily distract me. I decide I'm going to let them do the talking. I've only one thing to say and I'm not wasting my energy on small talk.

Winston gets straight to it. 'Tate, I know you don't like the idea, but we've been advised that the threats against you need to be taken seriously, so we've hired Lily to provide extra protection for you.'

I take a large bite of cookie and focus on the sweetness on my tongue. There's silence around the table. Everyone is watching me.

'No, thank you,' I say politely. 'Like I said, I don't need a bodyguard.'

'Tate,' Winston starts. 'This is not up for debate.'

'I beg to differ.'

'Why not?' asks Lily, surprising everyone with her

question. I turn to meet her interested gaze. Her eyes, warm brown like bourbon, meet mine. For a moment, I pause.

'Because I don't need one, and it will make me and the team look like we're scared.'

Scared, weak people lose games. I think again of how close I came to not making the draft. If it hadn't been for my dad or Blake's support, I might have lost everything. Everything I'd worked hard for and dreamed of for years. After my mom left, it was just me and Dad, and I needed to prove that everything he sacrificed on my behalf was worth it – and show Lily what a mistake she made walking away. We succeeded without her.

'But you've seen the threats,' she persists in a quiet, steady voice. The first person round here to actually enter into a conversation about it with me, rather than what Winston's done, which is presented as a fait accompli. Lily is at least treating me like an adult who has a mind of his own. Almost as if she cares.

This thought strengthens my resolve. Lily Heath never cared. She walked away. Left me without a backward glance. Yeah, she called with some bull about her dad being ill. I'm sure he was, but she ghosted me after that, and let's just say, sending someone texts when they don't reply gets old real quick. At the time, it made me lose sight of the bigger picture. The game. My dad. Our dream. I grit my teeth and swallow hard.

'You get stalkers who are mentally unwell, or fans who just care a bit too much all the time in this business. It's nothing new. I've had them before when I scored, when I didn't score, when I fouled, when I didn't foul – it goes with football, fame … you name it.'

'Tell me.' She leans forward. 'If you thought it was more than a threat, would you consider a bodyguard?' she asks.

I shrug. 'Possibly.'

Something flashes in her eyes. Triumph? But she conceals it well, keeping the concerned look on her face. It mirrors the one she wore last night when I was flat out in the lobby. I know it's part of the whole anaphylaxis deal but when she left my suite last night, after escorting me up with the doc, that awful sense of doom overpowered me, and I almost begged her not to leave me. Not to leave me again, like she did before. I was wrecked when she left. I don't plan to ever feel weak and needy like that again. It's against everything I've worked for. I don't need anyone else. All I need is football.

Her voice softens. 'Last night. We think someone tried to kill you.'

'What are you talking about?' I ask.

'Last night, there were traces of peanut oil on your plate.'

'What?'

'We tested the food on your plate.'

I stare at her.

Tierney nods. 'We were specific with the catering team before the event, that under no circumstances could there be any trace of peanut in the food. I had a lab test for peanut allergens on the food left on your plate. There's no doubt it looks like sabotage.'

'Come on,' I scoff, looking round the table at the faces

earnestly staring back at me. 'It could easily have been an accident. It's a kitchen. They prepare hundreds of meals there, every day of the week. Someone just made a mistake.'

'A potentially fatal mistake,' points out Lily, 'which catering knew the seriousness of.'

I shrug.

'And what about your EpiPen?'

There's silence around the table as this sinks in.

I could have sworn I tucked the EpiPen in my pocket but then it could have fallen out of my jacket. It was draped over the back of a chair for most of the night. I hate wearing a suit. I wince because I feel stupid. I never go anywhere without it – just like I promised her all those years ago. I've stuck to it and I'm careful. I have back-ups at home and in my locker.

'Look, I don't know what happened to it. I had it when I left home. I know I did. I must have dropped it someplace.' I hold up my hands. 'Maybe I got a little careless. It's the first reaction I've had in years.'

I don't add that it frightened the hell out of me.

'Tate, this is non-negotiable,' says Winston. 'You're not just a ball player. You're like a son to me. And if anything happens to you, it's gonna kill the whole team.'

'That's foul play,' I say. Winston is one of the good guys. The team is family.

But I fold my arms and nod. I know when I'm beaten.

'And there's one more thing,' adds Winston, lifting his chin, a clear sign he's going to be bullish. He didn't get where he is without playing hardball sometimes. And this is clearly going to be one of those times. 'Lily is going to be with you twenty-four-seven.'

We'll see about that, I think. I'm gonna show them how wrong they are.

'But we don't want any speculation as to Lily's identity in the press. I don't want to spook the sponsors or the league.' Winston pauses and looks directly at me. 'So Lily is going to pose as your fiancée.'

I almost swallow my tongue.

He carries on. 'We decided that it would play better and make a great story. Your short-term relationships are well documented, Tate. The press team felt it would be a better angle if you were seen to be engaged. It would explain why she's with you all the time and has full access to the team hotel and stadium.'

I'm staring at him, but there's more.

'The press team have booked an appointment at Tiffany's tomorrow for you to make it official.'

I gape at him.

'Tiffany's?' I croak. This is all getting out of hand. I'm on the back of a horse galloping to the finish line of the Kentucky Derby without a clue how I got here.

'To buy the engagement ring, man,' says Blake with a huge grin. 'You lucky bastard.'

My mouth is open, but all my words seem to be at the bottom of a well, a very long way down.

'Right.' Winston throws down his napkin and rises to his feet. 'If you'll excuse me, I've got to meet my lawyers.'

I watch his shoulders sink for a minute.

When everyone else stands up, I point to Lily's stature.

'Question.' It's a dick move, but I'm much bigger than her. I'm genuinely curious. 'You're clearly good at your job, but how are you going to protect me. There's quite a size difference between us.'

She's silent and her gaze holds mine. Ice-cold and stony.

Then a smirk plays around her lips. 'Come at me,' she says.

'I can't do that,' I say. I would never take a hand to a woman. Under no circumstance. It's everything I've been brought up to despise.

'Yeah, I guess you're not feeling up to much after yesterday. It wouldn't be a fair fight. For you.'

I narrow my eyes as the insult sinks in. 'I'm just fine.'

She raises that fine eyebrow, holds my gaze and mouths, 'Chicken.'

There's silence in the room, apart from Blake, who sniggers. Shane is trying to hide a smile while Winston, who'd been nearly out the door, turns back with interest.

'I'm not going to embarrass you in front of these gentlemen,' I say, even though I could just pick her up, wrap my arms around her and hold onto her.

'You couldn't embarrass me, JB,' she says and walks right up to me and pats my cheek. Anger burns a hole in me. She called me Jock Boy, before she got to know me, when she was so sure she didn't want to go out with me. She shortened it to JB after our second date. Her dismissive, derisive gesture underlines just how little of a shit she could give about me – now, or then. Even the brief feel of her soft skin on my cheek adds insult to injury. She grins up at me, challenge sparkling in those dark-brown whisky eyes, those mocking, plump lips.

Fine. I take one step forward and before I can even process it, she twists her body, like something out of *The Matrix* and has me in a hold with my hand behind my back. I'm left in no doubt that if she wanted to, she could break my arm or force me onto the floor.

Around us, there's dead silence. Awed silence.

Something has changed. This is a Lily I don't know. She's harder, tougher. But she's forgotten I'm a ball player and I'm used to getting out of tight scrapes. When she drops my arm, I twist my body and pick her up, my arms around her waist, clamping both her arms to her sides. She's nose to nose with me and suddenly I realise that this might not have been my smartest move.

Lily stares into my eyes, and I see a flash of uncertainty in hers. Her mouth is inches from mine, her lips parted in wary suspicion. I hear the involuntary hitch of her breath, and the corresponding expansion of her ribs as if she's been taken by surprise. Her face is still, but I can see the angry pulse beating in her neck. Her body is flush against me, and I can feel her soft breasts pressed up against my chest.

'Put me down, Tate,' she says in a menacing voice.

I meet her imperious gaze and hold it, staring back at her. I wonder if the rest of the room can feel the charge between us. Around us everyone is silent and watchful.

Finally, I slowly lower her to the ground, not letting go until her feet are flush on the floor.

'Okay. I think we're quits.' I hold out my hand.

She pauses for a minute and then takes mine. I have a

longing to bring her hand to my lips and kiss her knuckles, but I stop myself.

'Very well done, Lily.' My voice is husky as I shake her hand then let it go, but I'm careful to make my tone a little mocking. 'You sure know how to bring a man to his knees.'

She gives me a tight smile and then nods. This isn't over. I've got a feeling I'm going to pay for teasing her.

Winston clears his throat. 'Right, then. I think we'll leave the two of you to talk and make the necessary arrangements.'

'The appointment at Tiffany's is at eleven tomorrow,' Shane chips in. 'The press team will be tipping off a tame contact. Try to smile, Tate,' he says with a grin. 'We want people to believe that Lily sees something in you.'

Lily and I exchange a very quick glance. Once upon a time, she did. Now I ask myself what changed? What made her hightail it back home without so much as a backward glance?

Just like what my mom did to me and Dad.

'Have fun kids,' says Winston.

All I can do is grunt and watch as their feet file out of the room. Blake stops in front of Lily.

'I think I might just have fallen in love with you,' he says and pecks her on the cheek. 'See you, Tate.'

With that, he follows the others out of the room.

Chapter Six

LILY

I turn my back on Tate and cross the window that overlooks the city below, just for a second wondering what the hell I'm doing here. I should have walked out when I realised Tate Donaghue was the detail on my assignment. It was never going to work. Tate's always going to want to be in charge and play the one-upmanship game. He's never forgiven me for calling quits first all those years ago. Even though he clearly saw our relationship had an expiration date. I'm pretty sure taking him down in front of everyone, while proving a point, was neither politic nor endearing. No wonder he made me pay for it afterwards. For a second back there, I thought he was going to kiss my hand, which would have been even more patronising.

The temptation to play him at his own game and kiss him on the mouth idles in my brain for a few seconds more than it should. Don't go there, Lily, I tell myself. Even though it's too late. My brain is whirring with the memory of our first kiss...

Tate pursued me after our first meeting, even going as far as leaving a tube of arnica in a bag on my dorm door to heal my bruises which was cute, but I'd heard all about his reputation and I had no plans to become another notch on a bedpost that was clearly in danger of collapse.

I was at a party when I spotted him and immediately did a reverse turn and headed into another room, which was a mistake. I'd read enough paranormal romances to know that you never run from an Alpha male, werewolf or otherwise. Because of course, Tate took that as a challenge and hunted me down. Every time I moved rooms, he was there. I didn't like running, it wasn't my style, so of course, I approached him.

'I know I'm irresistible. But I'm not interested,' I told him, annoyed at myself for enjoying the game.

'I've worked you out,' the cocky bastard replied, grinning at me with those beautiful sparkling blue eyes.

'I doubt that very much,' I said at my haughtiest, which I might say is pretty up there given it's backed up with several generations of aristocratic blood.

'You're scared.'

'Scared?' I scoffed. 'I'm not scared of you.'

'Prove it. Go on a date with me.'

'I don't need to go on a date with you to prove anything.'

'Chicken.'

Determined not to respond, I sat down on one of the kitchen stools and sipped at my beer, looking around the room at everyone but him, although I was very aware of him when he sat down next to me. I tried not to smile.

He pulled out his phone and fiddled with it for a moment and then music started to play. He'd only gone and linked his phone to the portable speaker on the side.

The lyrics, '*you're beautiful*', bounce around the kitchen and Tate has turned his chair to face mine and is singing along to the chorus ... about seeing my face, about never being with me.

Around us everyone turned to see what was going on.

It was so cringy, I turned crimson pink, but at the same time I wanted to giggle because he was so ridiculous and over the top.

'Stop it,' I hissed.

'Make me. Go on a date with me.'

'I hate you,' I told him, even though I knew I didn't. Even then.

'No, you don't. You're just scared of me.'

I'd been brought up by my dad to be afraid of no one. To be self-reliant and not make the mistake of 'feeling' too much for anyone. It was protection for when they couldn't or wouldn't stick around.

Who did this jerk think he was? I wasn't afraid of him. To prove it, I stepped right into his personal space, put a hand around his neck and pulled him towards me and kissed him like I meant business.

I had every intention of walking away after kissing him.

Unfortunately, the minute his lips touched mine, the kiss went from zero to scorching in seconds flat. Tate knew what he was doing, and my willpower where he was concerned proved non-existent.

'One date,' I told him, finally pulling back, horrified by how breathless I was. That was some kiss. 'You'll get bored when you've got what you want. You jock boys always do.'

'Maybe I will, maybe I won't,' he responded lightly, but there was something in his eyes that told me I was more than a challenge now.

———

Back in the present, I take a few breaths. That was then. This is now. Keep things professional. Whether he likes it or not he's stuck with me. And he needs me, I'm sure of it. There's something about these threats I don't like – a nasty, malicious streak to them which worries me. Like a child revelling in being naughty. They may well be coming from a crackpot but that doesn't mean they aren't genuine.

Right now, Tate has no choice but to have me alongside him. Given our history I'm not sure how I build a relationship with him. One thing's for sure, I can't trust him. My dad taught me that lesson when he abandoned me and sent me off to boarding school. He wasn't being cruel, he was trying to insulate me from pain in the future because in his career he'd seen the absolute worst of humanity and knew what humans could do to each other. He also knew that people, like my mum, could die. He was trying to protect me. Once I was old enough, he drummed into me that trusting people was dangerous, they invariably let you down. They'd tell you what you want to hear to get what they want. Tate's a very good actor. I once believed he loved me as much as I loved him. It hurt so much when he proved my dad right. Tate had told me what I wanted to hear to talk me into bed because I'd been so adamant I wouldn't fall for him. He just had to prove that he could make me.

'What are you plotting?' he asks, jolting me out of my thoughts.

I turn round, reluctantly impressed by his ability to still read me so well.

'Not so much plotting as strategising. Trying to work out a suitable compromise.'

He sits down and leans back in his chair, folding his arms and studying me. I swallow and lift my chin, not enjoying the scrutiny. Once upon a time, those lips would have curved with a tender smile while his eyes would have roamed across my face, like he was reading a book and enjoying the words. Now his expression is stony, as if he no longer sees anything worth his interest.

'Whether you like it or not,' I tell him, 'we have to try and make this work.'

'What's my incentive to make it work?'

'You get to stay alive.'

He takes a long, slow breath. 'Look, I think the boss and senior management team are overreacting, and I don't like being lied to or blindsided.' I narrow my eyes but then he holds his hands up in surrender. 'But they're worried, and there's a lot going on, so for the time being, I'll play ball. It doesn't mean I have to like it. What do I have to do?'

'Follow my instructions. Listen to me. Keep me and

Tierney in the loop of all events, advise us of any changes. Your schedule looks busy.'

'It is. The next couple of weeks are all about football, training and sponsor events.' He stands up and helps himself to a fresh cup of coffee from the coffee press on the side. 'Want one?'

'Thanks.' I nod as he pours me a cup, but then he picks up a cream jug.

'I take it black,' I interject.

He puts it down slowly. 'Of course you do. Is it part of the new hard-woman image? Or were you always like this and I just didn't notice?'

There's a strained moment between us, as if we are both acknowledging all the things we no longer know about each other. It's a weird feeling – losing all that we had before.

His eyes narrow and he stares at me, as if he's trying to see into my head.

'What?' I ask.

'Nothing,' he says and folds his arms, his body language making it obvious he's creating a barrier between us.

I try to focus on the notes I'm making on my iPad, rather than his movements or the rolled back sleeves exposing slightly tanned forearms as he lifts a mug to his mouth. I'm certainly not noticing the lift of his T-shirt over the planes of muscles in his back.

I suck in a breath and force myself back to my notes. 'You've got a solid weekly routine. Pretty much a creature of habit. Usually lots of dates, but nothing that lasts – or is worth noting at least.'

He lifts a brow.

'You make me sound boring and predictable. You never used to think so.'

I tense my jaw, refusing to take the bait and wait him out.

His mouth quirks, dangerous and cocky. 'I can be very spontaneous when I want to be. I like to make the most of opportunities that arise.' He lifts an insolent brow. 'Women like ball players.'

'I'm sure they do,' I say, deadpan.

'But I don't have time. So you don't need to worry about us spending quality time with a girlfriend.'

'I wasn't worried,' I say in a snippy tone. Why would I care if he has a girlfriend? He's a job that's all. Admittedly, a very attractive job, which is making parts of me sit and beg for attention that they are not getting. The pile of unfinished business between us has quadrupled.

'And I wasn't saying you were boring, I simply noted that you have set patterns of behaviour. A regular grocery day. Visits to the gym on the same days and times each week. A weekly meet-up with friends. Favourite bars and restaurants. They're all potential targets.'

He sits down and hooks an ankle across his other knee, leaning back looking totally relaxed, whereas I'm wound up so tight, I can feel the familiar painful knot in my right shoulder, near my neck. I raise my hand to rub at it and roll my shoulder trying to loosen it. It's a tell when it comes to my stress levels, unfortunately one that Tate knows well. He used to massage that knot before I would compete.

'You look like you could do with a shoulder rub,' he says.

'I'm good, thanks,' I say. 'You can help by being cooperative.'

'Where's the fun in that?'

I huff out my exasperation. 'Look, whether you believe how serious the threat is or not, I have a job to do.'

'And so do I.'

For a moment we glare at each other across the table, and then he twists his mouth.

'I can't vary my routine. At the moment, my main focus is on football. It doesn't matter if I'm in New York or Texas, I have apartments in both, I run every morning. Do weights for an hour every day in the gym, and mix it up with half an hour of stretching or flexibility exercises. I'm a pro-footballer. This is my life. The other stuff I can forgo – like going to a bar sometimes with the guys, a few of them live in the neighbourhood.'

During this brief bout of cooperation, I gradually tease the minutiae of his life out of him, trying to establish whether he has any more set routines or patterns that someone could identify, then hide out in waiting to take a strike at him.

After half an hour of asking questions and probing into his movements, I've enough information to come up with a plan.

'I'll accompany you in public at all times and when you're at home.'

He raises an eyebrow. 'You're going to move in with me.'

'You have another suggestion?' I ask, trying to curb my sarcasm.

'My apartment has top-notch security. Unless someone decides to blow the place up or set fire to it,' he says, 'but that seems a bit extreme. A flamethrower to light a candle.'

'My team has assessed it, there are a couple of weak spots but we're in the process of plugging them. We're not taking risks.'

'How long have you been doing this job?' asks Tate suddenly.

'A while,' I reply, wondering what triggered the question. 'I know what I'm doing.'

'Yeah, I'm well aware of that. How did you get into it?'

'It was after I left college. You know my dad had a heart attack. After that, I went to work for the security company he founded with my godfather.' This is an entirely acceptable white lie because it was my cover when I was initially recruited by MI6. Even though I've left the service, I'm much more than a bodyguard and usually any protection details are considerably more high-risk than this one. Looking after Tate Donaghue is way below my paygrade and I smirk to myself. What would he say if I said that out loud? How much would it damage his ego?

'Now that I've satisfied your curiosity, can we discuss tomorrow?'

'What?' he says. 'Our happy trip to Tiffany's?'

'Just think of it as taking one for the team,' I say with a smile chockful of syrup and insincerity.

We agree a plan for the following day. I'll go to his New York apartment, and we'll travel by cab to Fifth Avenue for 11am. Then he has a sponsors lunch event, for which the press department will need to wangle an invite for his 'fiancée'.

'How did you get here?' I ask.

'I got a lift with Blake.'

'In that case, I can drive you back? I can do my own sweep of your apartment.'

'Is that a rhetorical question?'

'You can say no.' I shrug.

'No, it's fine,' he says wearily, surprising me with his sudden acquiescence until I realise he must be exhausted after yesterday's episode. His whole body went into shock and being pumped full of epinephrine can't have been much of a picnic.

'If you want to play chauffeur, I won't stop you. It looks like I'm stuck with you for the time being. But don't get used to it.' He raises those eyebrows again and for a second the fight is back.

'Trust me, I won't,' I say, my voice as dry as the Sahara, determined to believe it. That was the mistake I'd made before he sneaked under my defences.

As I drive the BMW SUV up to the glass-fronted lobby, Tate is standing outside, one shoulder propped against the glass, a takeaway coffee in one hand, his phone in the other. He looks as if he doesn't have a care in the world, too damn cute for his own good. I take a moment to study him as he's bent over his phone – from a purely objective point of view, of course. It's January, but he's in a white Henley shirt that sculpts all the honed lines of his body, and I swallow at the thought of what's under the soft white cotton. Smooth skin, taut muscle. I remember the joy of touching him, taming all that masculine strength while he moaned under my hands.

He comes towards the car, not even looking around him as he keeps half an eye on his phone. Does he have any idea how vulnerable he might be?

I'm desperately trying to be professional and fight my unreasonable anger because, if I'm honest, I'm scared for him. I know how easily a life can be lost and I don't think he's taking this threat seriously.

He gets into the car and I glare at him.

'Sorry, should I have got you a coffee?' he says.

I purse my lips, but manage to take a deep breath before I calmly reply.

'While there's a very active threat in place, it might be good to take a few precautions, such as waiting inside until your protection detail is on hand and not wandering off to buy coffee.'

'Look, I know you're taking all this very seriously. But what if we're dealing with someone who hasn't spoken to another living soul for ten years – apart from the life-size cardboard cut-out Storm Trooper in their front room – who lives with fifteen cats and has kept every issue of *National Enquirer* since time immemorial?'

I feel stupid. Tate is reassuring me. I need to be objective about this.

'If it is,' I say, 'I'll be delighted. But until we know what we're dealing with, I'll do my job.'

I give him my best I-mean-business look, but fail to stop

a yawn escaping. I'm done arguing with him for today. Jetlag is catching up with me. 'Can you direct me to your place, or put your zip code into my phone?'

'I can direct. I do know this route quite well.' There's an edge of sarcasm to Tate's voice, which I ignore. Silence settles in the car as we wend our way out of the underground car park below the apartment complex.

I focus on the job and not how small the car feels with him in it, scanning our surroundings for potential dangers. I don't like the hemmed-in sensation of the single-lane road in the bowels of the buildings, it's like something out of a sci-fi film. There's nowhere to move out of trouble.

Tate starts fiddling with the seat configuration, pushing himself back to accommodate those long, muscular legs. I try not to look at them or the denim constraining his taut quadriceps. As scholarship athletes, we both knew a lot about anatomy. I might not be able to remember the names of every muscle, but I can't shake the knowledge of their shape and texture from memory. The feel of them on top of me, beside me, below me. I swallow. Tate fills the space next to me. Those broad shoulders almost brushing mine. His clean, spicy aftershave with its hint of cedar teases my nostrils, but can't disguise the essential scent of him. He's so close I can see the bristles peppering his cheeks like iron filings. His hands rest loosely on his big thighs and a hot flash of heat rushes through me at the thought of those hands on me. He's all man, and then some.

Eyes on the road, I remind myself and scan my mirrors, on the lookout for any cars tailing us. But there's no movement in the car park behind us.

As we pull out onto the main road, I notice a car on the side of the road, the driver immediately signalling and joining the slip road behind us. I take note and keep an eye on it. Another car gets between us and I relax a little. When we turn right, the car's behind us again but hanging back. I slow down, trying to catch the number plate. Tate has his head down, scrolling on his phone, but looks up every now and then.

'You need to take the next right,' he says. 'And after that the first left.'

'Okay.'

I take the right and so does the car behind us. I indicate left and slow for the traffic lights, sliding into the left filter lane ready to cut across the oncoming traffic. The other car indicates left, too.

The person in the car behind us has dark glasses and a baseball cap. It's impossible to see their face, and I don't like the anonymity.

'Hold on tight,' I warn Tate.

'Wh—?'

There's no time to warn him further. The lights change and I ram my foot on the gas. We lurch forward just squeezing into the gap on our right. How we miss it I don't know. Tate slams back into his seat, his knuckles white as he grabs the armrest at his side. Horns blare. The engine revs in protest as I accelerate out into the main flow of traffic. The car behind us is left with nowhere to go but filter, as planned. I watch in the rear-view mirror with satisfaction as the driver's forced to turn left and I put my foot down, weaving with precision in and out of the traffic.

'Fuck,' says Tate and I turn to glance at his face, which is dripping with coffee – a brown stain covering his sweatshirt and jeans. He's about to say something, but when he sees the grim expression on my face, he closes his mouth.

I look at the spilled coffee.

'Sorry about that, but we had a tail.' I hand him my phone. 'Open up the maps app and put in the Four Seasons.'

'I thought we were going to my place.'

'Change of plan. My hotel is closer. I've just lost whoever might have been tailing us but if we head to yours, we might meet up again. No one knows where I'm staying.'

Chapter Seven

TATE

The elevator glides to a stop and Lily gently hustles me out, like she's a mother hen rounding up her chicks. It's a weird contrast to the brusque control she exerted back in the car. She was all action, few words and no emotion. I suddenly feel like I have absolutely no idea who this woman is. And I'm desperate to take control again.

'Fuck, I think you've been burgled,' I say as we step into her room. It looks as if her suitcase has exploded, and the sight reassures me, giving me an anchor. It's the first familiar thing about Lily. Like, finally I'm seeing the real her again. Back in college her room was always like a yard sale, clothes strewn everywhere, open books piled on random clear parts of the floor and countless pairs of discarded shoes. Here in her hotel room, clothes are draped over every piece of furniture in the lounge, her uniform of black cargo pants and Ts on one side and a rainbow of glamorous dresses over the back of the large sofa. Shoes are tossed here, there and everywhere. Heels, sneakers and boots. And then there's the underwear. I immediately perk up and pick up a black lacy bra that's been abandoned on one of the easy chairs.

'You never used to wear underwear like this, unless it was a special occasion,' I say, holding it up with a smirk. Inside I feel a bit sick wondering who's seen her in this. To me, it's the kind of underwear you buy with sex in mind.

She snatches it from me. 'I wasn't expecting guests.'

I look at a pair of matching panties on the coffee table and raise an eyebrow.

'I was unpacking in a hurry.'

'Unpacking?'

'I was looking for something at the bottom of my case.' The way she says it, and her sudden, defensive posture makes me wonder what on earth it was she was looking for and why she looks so uncomfortable.

'Did you find it?' I ask, deliberately lowering my voice. Sensing the opportunity to have a bit of fun.

'Huh?' she says. 'Oh, yes.'

'This thing you found, would it be battery operated?' I ask.

The blush on her face is a picture, but she gives me that super snotty glare I remember so well when she was pissed, looking down her nose at me like I'm a bug she already should have squashed. She carries it off well, as she draws herself up to her full height.

'I could use a drink,' she says. 'You want something? Although you're still wearing your last drink.' She indicates my top, which is never going to be the same again. Now that I'm aware of the clammy fabric sticking to my skin, I can't stand it. Taking the hem, in one quick move I rip it off and use the clean back to pat down my chest.

The noise I hear makes me look up and she turns away rapidly but not before I saw the wide-eyed expression on her face. She immediately walks into the corner of the desk and curses as she rubs at her knee. It takes me right back to my old college room, and her hands exploring me for the first time, her eyes full of wonder and heat.

'I can get you a robe,' she says crisply.

'I'm good,' I say to mess with her.

I see the tightening of her mouth as she turns away. I grin to myself, seems like the professional bodyguard is just a bit rattled. I was beginning to wonder if the girl I remember is still in there.

'I could murder a bourbon if there's one in your fancy bar,' I say. 'But I'd like to clean up first. Take a shower and see if I can at least salvage these jeans.' I start to undo my belt.

'Why don't you go into the bathroom?' Her tone might be calm, but the words are hurried. 'It's through there.' She points to the bedroom door on the other side of the room. 'There's a spare robe. And help yourself to toiletries.'

'Thanks,' I say and head towards the bathroom.

It smells feminine and sexy. There are skincare lotions and potions on the shelf below the mirror above the sink. Two robes hang on the back of the door, one of which has been used, the other is still tied around the waist.

Then I catch sight of myself in the mirror. I've got coffee freckled all over me.

I step under the bucket head of the shower into hot water and turn it up a notch or two, letting the scalding rivulets run down my face. There are plenty of potions in here, which makes me smile. Underneath the no-nonsense surface, someone likes looking after herself. I help myself to a liberal handful of her shower gel. Huge mistake. The orange blossom smell is all Lily. It's like she's in here with me. I close my eyes and for a moment I allow myself to think of her lithe body, naked, slippery and wet. Her dorm shower, so small we were jammed together with no space to move. Kissing her under the water, her hands on my cock. The memories are all it takes and suddenly I'm hard, my dick like wood. All the frustrations of holding off sex because we were going to wait until after the championship, after her cheerleading auditions. We were both driven, goal-orientated, and we were doing it together. Now all that seems like a fuck of a waste of time. I made her come every which way but the one that counted the most and she'd walked away on the very night we'd promised ourselves to each other.

Clearly it was just about sexual attraction. We always had great chemistry. None of it meant anything to her. I have to remember that. What we had between us was a mirage – it didn't exist, just like my dad always told me. Lily walked away just like Mom did, and I was the dumb schmuck who believed she might be different.

Once I've cleaned up, I towel off and wrap myself in a robe, which is a size or two too small. Clearly, not too many ball players stay here. The front barely meets so I put my damp, boxer shorts back on, grateful they escaped most of the coffee, and go back into the lounge.

She's on the phone but looks up and tucks the phone into her neck as she pours Wild Turkey into two cut-glass crystal tumblers while giving clipped answers to whoever is on the other end, her face grave and stern. Looking up she hands me one of the glasses and gives me a tight, unsmiling nod.

'I think that's the best idea. I'll liaise with Winston. Okay. Thanks.'

Ending the call, she puts down the phone and takes a slug of bourbon.

'You got everything you need?' she asks.

'Sure, apart from clothes.'

'I'll see if housekeeping can do a quick laundry turnaround,' she says, and I can tell her mind is already working out the next move. 'I need to change. I might as well get these things cleaned with yours.' She holds up the sleeve of her cream cashmere jumper adorned with coffee splashes.

Who knew a to-go cup held so much liquid.

'Will you be okay?' she asks, and I realise she's looking at me, her eyes slightly narrowed.

'Me?' I look around, but the truth is, I'm starting to get an adrenaline come down. 'Of course, I'll be okay.' Does she think a near-miss in the car is going to bother me? I'm made of sterner stuff. Or at least, I always thought I was. To be honest, now I'm thinking about it, I'm feeling a little nauseous and I've got that itchy, can't-sit-still feeling. I take another hefty sip of bourbon, which doesn't do much for the nausea.

'You sure, you look a little grey.'

'I'm just fine. Why don't you go get cleaned up?' I'm unnecessarily terse.

'Okay,' she says, giving me another uncertain look.

The minute she walks out, I lift my shaking hand with the glass to my mouth, but I can't take a sip. I have to put it down. Both hands are shaking badly. I refuse to sit down. Instead, I open the balcony door, despite the fact it's freezing outside, and take a lungful of the icy, early-evening air. I feel like shit and my legs are wobbly. Gripping the handrail of the balcony to ground me, I stare out at the view. I have a love-hate relationship with the city. I love the fancy restaurants, the twenty-four-hour lifestyle, its fast pace, but I miss the friendliness of small-town living, where everyone knows you and no one is impressed by you because they remember when you were a snot-nosed kid crying over a dropped ice cream. Where people care about you because they know you, not because you're someone famous.

None of this is helping. I've still got that sense of doom and the shakes are getting worse instead of better. The doc warned me I might feel like this after my reaction. I go back into the room and over to the bar and try to pour myself another bourbon, the bottle chinking against the glass as I splash the liquid over the edge. I manage to get enough of a shot in the glass and scoop it up to knock it back with my trembling hand when Lily returns.

'Tate?'

Fuck, I feel like I've been caught by the school principal.

'Yeah.'

'Why don't you sit down? You look bushed.'

'I'm okay,' I growl, though I'm clearly not. I immediately feel even more shit because Lily looks like an innocent angel. Her hair is bundled up in a towel, which accentuates the dainty features of her face, scrubbed free of make-up. She looks soft and rosy, her skin creamy and smooth. My heart misses a beat, this is the girl I fell in love with, and in her fluffy robe, with bare feet – toenails painted a very pale pink – she looks sweet and defenceless.

Although, I'm not falling for that again.

I swallow. 'Sorry. You're right. It's not every day you realise someone really is trying to kill you.'

I sit down on one of the dark, forest-green velvet couches and I'm surprised when she comes to sit next to me on the couch rather than on the one opposite. There's no point trying to hide my shakes, but I try for a bit of bravado.

'That was quite some driving,' I say, tossing back a good slug of bourbon, which burns a smooth path down my throat. 'You do some kind of advanced course? Is it all part of the training?'

'My dad taught me evasive driving skills in a Land Rover on the estate in the school holidays when I was fourteen, the year before we moved to the States, but of course I did a refresher when I joined the firm.'

'I've said it before, but you had a weird upbringing.'

'And you didn't?' She tosses it in and I'm shocked.

'What is that supposed to mean?' She has no idea what's she's talking about. 'My dad went above and beyond for me. I wouldn't be where I am today without him. I owe him everything.'

I lapse into silence, thinking of all the sacrifices my dad made to make sure I could always play football. He'd be devastated if anything happened to me, and I didn't make the final. Shit, if Lily hadn't been there today, what could have happened? Would I have even noticed a car behind us if I'd been driving. Or what if I'd been with Blake? I could have got him into trouble, too.

'Sorry,' I say. 'I should be saying thank you. You really think someone wanted to harm me?'

Lily gives me a gentle smile, and damn if it doesn't make me feel just a little stupid inside.

'I don't know what they planned but we still need to keep our wits about us and take all necessary precautions.'

'Right,' I say.

'Would you like something to eat?' she asks.

'No. Another drink will do me fine.'

She places a soft hand on my trembling hand, steadying it.

'Shit, I'm sorry I can't stop shaking. What a loser, huh?'

The feel of her hand is hot on my skin, like a gentle burn, warming and painful at the same time. I focus on it because if I don't, I'm going to make a fool of myself and say something like, I'm glad you're here and don't ever let go.

With a shake of her head, she grips my hand tighter,

lacing her fingers between mine. 'Stop trying to be the big bad ass. Your body has been exposed to a huge dose of adrenaline.'

'Again,' I put in.

'Are you feeling nauseous? Shaky?'

I catch my lip in my teeth. No point denying it, she can see it right under her very pretty little nose.

'I don't think the bourbon is helping.'

'Do you ever do yoga?' she asks.

I snort. 'Yoga? Hell, no. I'm more of a Pilates man.' I pat my core.

She smiles. 'Yoga is a different discipline, and it might help those feelings of anxiety and dread.'

'Who says I'm anxious?' I immediately say, but it's a relief that she's named these weird, swirly, itchy feelings. She's right. I'm anxious as fuck. My skin feels too tight for my body, and I want to scratch it off.

She takes the glass out of my hand and with both hands gently tugs me to my feet.

'Let me show you a few stretches and breathing exercises. I think they'll help.'

Her hands are warm and soft as they close around mine. Her touch anchors me, settling me at once, and her quiet confidence calms me. She's reaching to me on a different level, like I need looking after. I'm overcome by a rush of gratitude as she pulls me over to the rug by the windows.

'Kneel down on the floor on all fours,' she says.

'Whatever you say.' I cock an eyebrow, trying to add levity to the situation and how I'm feeling.

'Just do it, JB,' she says and gets down on all fours beside me.

'I like it when you talk tough.'

'Stop it,' she says. 'You're using distraction, and I'm not buying.'

I get down on all fours.

'Hands under your shoulders, knees under your hips.'

I move into the position, but not before I shrug off my robe leaving me topless in just my boxers. It's a bit of a power move when I'm feeling just a tiny bit vulnerable, but knowing I affected her just a little when I took my top off earlier makes me want to take a few risks. It's been ages since I've done anything out of my comfort zone, I realise. For the last eight years, all I've done is live and breathe football. Everything has been geared towards that. The food I eat, the exercise I take, the places I travel. It dominates my life, but that's how I got to the top. And it's why I'm so important to the team. They're relying on me. I rely on them. They're brothers.

One of her hands lands on my shoulder gently pressing and shifting me so that I'm more in line. Her hand touches my hip. 'Pull back a little,' she says. 'And let go of all those thoughts. I can almost hear them. You're so tense here.' Her fingers massage the hard knot just a little.

She's right, my mind is spiralling. I concentrate on her soft voice to anchor me.

'Spread your hands and your weight evenly. Feel the ground beneath you.'

I feel the stretch in my shoulders.

'Tuck your toes under.'

I follow her instructions, but I'm struggling to get them. My muscles are tight – it doesn't feel right.

'This isn't possible,' I say. Surely, she doesn't want me to stand upside down. That's what it feels like she's asking me to do. I tense. Any second now she'll tell me that of course I can do it, I'm just not trying hard enough.

'Lift your bottom to point skyward.'

'What?'

On all fours, she moves in front of me, sadly her robe is belted tightly and moulds her slim form like a mummy.

'Watch.' Her body flows with the same elegant grace I remember when she was out on the field with the cheerleading squad. She tucks her toes under and lifts her bottom in one fluid move. I can't stop watching her as she lifts the heels on each leg one after another and still manages to look incredibly graceful, even in the uncomfortable-looking pose.

'Now you try,' she says with a sunny smile, rising to her feet with barely any effort at all, as if the move has given her an injection of positivity. 'And don't worry, it doesn't have to be perfect. Just do what you can.'

With my head facing down, I wrinkle my nose. Do what I can? That's not good enough, it always has to be the *best* I can.

I try again, and this time I have a better understanding of what I'm trying to achieve. I lift my butt up 'to the sky' and feel the stretch on my hamstrings but it's a nice pull, makes me feel like I'm working, and for once, I'm not so worried about whether I've got it exactly right.

'That's really nice, Tate. Lovely. Just take a few deep

breaths.' She stands and comes over to my side. I feel ridiculously pleased with myself and her praise. Her hand rests very gently on my hip and I can smell the scent of her shower gel. I immediately picture her in there again. Oh, Fuck. How the hell am I going to get out of this? I need to make sure she stays exactly where she is. The strain is starting to tell on my legs.

'You can come down now.'

'I'm okay,' I grunt.

'No, Tate. You don't want to overdo it,' she says, touching my bare skin again, pushing lightly to press me back down. 'This is for you, no one else. No one is watching. Needing anything from you.'

For me? The thought slides into my brain like a slice of light. Don't I do everything for me? My dad always told me everything he did was for me. To help me. So that I could play football. Everything was about making me stronger, faster, better on the field. So that I could be the best player.

I slowly sink to my knees and let out a long slow breath feeling lighter inside.

'Feeling better?' she asks.

'Mmm,' I mumble, exploring the sensation of the sunshine coming out inside me. Is this good? Can I afford to be self-indulgent like this and take this time for myself?

'You are allowed to feel better, you know.'

Lily's eyes hold mine, assessing, and there it is again, that slight lift of her chin like she's a boxer ready to step into the ring. That's the Lily I remember, never one to back down.

I'm aware of a subtle change as we continue to stare at

each other, my eyes locked on hers like a tractor beam. There's a charged silence in the room, the low lamplight casting soft shadows – and outside, the lights of the city twinkle in the night. Something's changed, I'm no longer interested in teasing her, I want her. Her mouth on mine, those delicate hands on me. I drop my gaze to her lips, which are parted, and I see the hitch in her breath. My dick aches with longing for her touch. I see her swallow.

Two steps and I could undo her robe. I take a step forward, slow and careful, my eyes dipping to the exposed V of skin on her chest. There's a flash of heat in her eyes but she doesn't move or say anything. I run a gentle finger down the inside lapel of her robe. Soft, soft skin, the slight swell of breast, the scent of her – it's all intoxicating. I want to lower my head and graze my lips along her collarbone. Lily's chest rises as she takes in a deep breath and her head lifts to look at me, this time bewilderment, confusion and pain are in her eyes and it makes me pause. All my rage and anger, the sharp desire and urgent need, dissipate. I find myself wanting to offer comfort and tenderness. The need is still there, but it's different and it scares the shit out of me.

She closes her eyes, and for a moment I kid myself it's like she's receiving benediction. Then her lips part beneath mine and I inhale her soft sigh. I'm anticipating the slow, slow, kiss, the tender caress of mouths, like coming home, it's all sweetness and softness. I lift a hand to her face, my fingers caressing the smooth skin of her cheek.

I feel her stiffen beneath my touch. Her eyes dart to mine.

'We can't do this,' she says and her eyes harden with resolve.

A jagged edge of pain reminds me of all that was lost. She left me back in college and I nearly lost myself, I nearly threw everything away. Football saved me. I have the biggest game of my life ahead of me, I would be crazy to allow any distraction right now, let alone with Lily Heath.

Chapter Eight

LILY

The door softly closes behind us, sealing us into the awed hush of the store. It reminds me of the quiet on a snowy day when all the noise is absorbed and is a stark contrast to the loud confusion outside. Even Tate who must be used to all that attention visibly relaxes.

Expensive parquet flooring is softened by cream rugs and around the room angular art-deco-style counters in brass and marble are bathed in soft, warm light, their contents sparkling like the thousands of diamonds they are. Arched windows line either side of the huge space, filled with iconic scenes of New York dazzling in an azure sky. The effect is doubly impressive thanks to the ceiling of mirrors reflecting the light and colours of the city.

A small, slim man in a dark suit rushes up, his face lit up with a polite deferential smile which manages to be neither overly obsequious nor pompous.

'Mr Donaghue, welcome to Tiffany's. It's an honour to

have you here today and this lovely lady must be your fiancée.'

Was it really only yesterday that this was all agreed, I think, trying to get into my role.

The store assistant is good, very smooth and sincere, immediately making me feel like we're in very capable hands. Only I can see the sudden clenching of Tate's jaw.

'Yes, this is Lily Heath,' he says.

'A pleasure to meet you, Ms Heath.'

I nod regally. And it's not hard to genuinely smile at the guy, because he oozes niceness. 'Thank you.'

'Oh, my God, you're British. *Fabulous*.' The man's face creases with joy. 'I just love London. And may I say how much I love that dress.'

'Thank you.' I smooth my hand down the fabric. He has excellent taste. I love this dress, but then I also love jeans and T-shirts and my beloved selection of cowboy boots. I'm a bit of a chameleon when it comes to clothes.

Another woman, polished, with a bright white smile, approaches with a couple of photographers in tow.

I hear Tate hiss out a breath.

'Hi, Nancy, from the press team. You might remember me.'

'Nancy.' Tate nods, and I can tell from the tightness of his jaw and the tension in his shoulders that he does remember her and his memories aren't that great.

'We'd like to get a couple of photos of the two of you, if that's all right?' she says. 'If you could just stand together and look…' She gives us an encouraging smile as her words falter. Probably because Tate is as stiff as a board in his demeanour.

Tate duly moves to stand closer to me and awkwardly puts one arm around me, but let's just say there's enough space between us to drive a bus through.

'That's it,' Nancy says, clearly a little nervous. I feel sorry for her, so I relax a little into Tate's body which is a mistake because it's solid and comforting. We're in this together.

As Nancy steps back a minute to talk to the photographer, I glance again at Tate.

'Smile,' I murmur, and I'm so close to his face I can feel his warm breath against my skin. It lights a small glow inside me and inexplicably I want to wrap myself around him and take all of that warmth from him.

'You're supposed to be excited. We don't want your fans to think you've knocked me up.' I smirk, and add huskily, 'In which case, you should be so lucky.'

'I don't know,' he whispers. 'Yesterday you were being nice to me, you held my hand. Who knows where we might get to tomorrow.'

'I felt sorry for you. You'd clearly had a scare.' I lift my hand to cup his face, sliding my fingers against his freshly shaven, smooth skin, with a faux concerned expression. A mistake because it triggers an intense desire to skim his cheekbones and slip my hands into his thick black hair and pull his mouth to mine.

His eyes darken and as the photographer starts snapping, he leans into my touch, it gives me a brief sense of victory, but then he laughs and drops a kiss in my palm. 'You keep believing that.'

I have to close my eyes at the tender touch, tantalising my nerve endings sending them in a tizzy of hope and excitement. Bastard body betraying me.

'Perfect,' Nancy pipes up as the photographer takes a final shot.

'Now, have we had any ideas on the type of ring you're going for?' our enthusiastic sales clerk says. 'Let me take you up to our third floor which is our engagement room.'

Shit, I really hadn't thought this far ahead. Excited fiancées marrying very rich sportsmen have probably already decided on how many carats and what kind of diamond they want, along with the type of setting. I berate myself for not being better prepared.

We ascend a magnificent, brightly lit staircase dominated by a huge, bronze statue of Venus dappled with a patina of Verdigris. It's awe-inspiring, and obviously, the goddess of love is symbolic, which makes me feel a bit grubby. Even if the motives behind our actions are justifiable, pure, surely we're committing some kind of love blasphemy. It doesn't feel right.

The Love and Engagement Room, to give it its full title, is a long thin space full of glass display cases, the contents of which are twinkling like shooting stars in a meteor shower.

Another smartly dressed sales assistant glides towards us.

'Good morning. I'm Lacey. I'll be here to help you today. Have you any ideas of what you'd like?'

'We haven't really thought about it,' Tate and I say, at exactly the same time.

We glance at each other and smile at our obvious ineptitude. He reaches for my hand and gives it a quick squeeze and suddenly we're comrades, united in our awareness of how awkward and ridiculous this is. I squeeze his hand back, happy to let him take the stereotypical lead.

'Why don't we take a look?' says Tate. 'Do you mind if we have a wander see if anything takes our fancy?'

'Absolutely. Just let me or any of our assistants know if you'd like to try anything on and, of course, we have a sizing service, it usually takes two or three days but…' she gives an eager smile, 'I'm sure we can turn it round quicker if necessary.'

We both nod. Still hand in hand, we move over to one of the several glass-topped counters dotted around the room.

The bright white light of diamonds sparkles everywhere, and at any other time I might be entranced, but I suddenly want to cry. I daren't speak, not that I could, as the words are stuck in my throat behind an outsized lump. This was supposed to be a bit of acting, a bit of razzmatazz, all part of our cover story. And I thought it would be fun trying on expensive rings. Now I'm just haunted by a strong sense of wrongness.

'Anything caught your eye?' asks Tate, as we do another studious circuit of the diamond jewellery displays.

I shrug, and then realise that I ought to look a little more enthusiastic. I know Tate's loaded, but I don't want him buying me an actual engagement ring just for show.

'Who's paying for this,' I whisper. 'And can we send it back?'

Tate snorts out a tiny laugh. 'That's what you're worrying about?'

'Yes,' I say indignantly in a hushed voice. 'I can't keep it. And certainly not if you're paying for it.'

'Don't worry, I checked with Winston. He's picking up the tab. He's getting a hefty discount because of the publicity. Consider it compensation,' Tate gives me a crooked smile, one I remember well, 'for putting up with me.'

My heart melts just a little as I catch a glimpse of the boy I used to know.

'If this were real,' he says, 'what would you choose?'

'Something simple, elegant, not too blingy,' I tell him.

'Okay, but I do have a reputation to uphold you know,' he teases. 'You're going to need a big rock.'

An assistant waltzes by, obviously earwigging, and Tate adds, mischievously, 'I'm looking forward to seeing a ring on your finger … and nothing else.' He shoots me a look full of suggestion, and the assistant covers her hand with her mouth and blushes.

She's not the only one. A zing heads southwards lighting up my nerve endings. Damn, the man still has that effect on me. An ache of frustration burns between my thighs. Tate and I got naked plenty of times, but we never went all the way. We were in love, we thought it was forever – or I did – and we decided to wait until the end-of-season game. Now I wish we had got on with it, at least the thought of sex with him wouldn't hold that mystique. I've had sex plenty of times, and good sex at that, but I still wonder what it would have been like with Tate.

'Cut that out,' I hiss into his ear as if I'm whispering sweet nothings.

'I was trying to be romantic.'

'If that's your idea of romance…'

'Sorry,' he says, looking contrite. 'It was … inappropriate. Truce? This is supposed to be fun … at least for you. I'm supposed to be putting a brave face on and hoping my bank balance isn't about to be decimated.' He winks at me and I remember how playful he could be.

'Decimated, you say?' I tilt my head and give him an impish smile. 'Okay, then, let's see how much damage I can do.'

I focus on the case of rings in front of me and one stands out in particular. I walk around the displays, but it's the one in the second cabinet that draws me back. A single solitaire, an emerald-cut diamond set in platinum. Simple and elegant.

Tate shadows me and when I'm about to do my fourth circuit, he cups a hand under my elbow and leads me back to the second cabinet. 'Which one?' he asks.

I give him an uncertain look. 'I don't know how much it is,' I say. 'It might be really expensive.'

'I thought we were going for decimated,' he murmurs. 'I can afford it, babe.' He sounds indulgent and amused, and all the assistants smile at each other.

'We'd like to try this one,' he says and points to the siren ring.

'Excellent choice, madam,' says Lacey, appearing from thin air.

She is already unlocking a drawer and pulling out a velvet tray, on which she lays the ring. Then she looks up and eyes Tate as if he's the ultimate romantic hero.

Tate turns to her. 'Would you mind?' She backs off to give us some privacy, although everyone is surreptitiously watching us. I can feel their eyes burning into our backs. It's definitely a red-letter day for the staff at Tiffany. Big football star gets engaged before the biggest game of his life.

'Let me,' says Tate, picking up the ring.

My hand as I hold it up is shaking slightly. He takes my finger and slowly slides the ring onto it, his touch a caress. The contact is intimate, almost reverential, and I can't help a quick involuntary intake of breath. Tightness grips my stomach and suddenly I'm full of regret. I don't want to be here. Don't want to take part in this charade. It should be something special and we're making a mockery of it. Once I had dreams of happy ever after with Tate. Nausea rises up in my throat and I feel cheap and shitty.

He lifts my hand, tilting it this way and that, so that the facets of the gem catch the light and sparkle. His thumb caresses the palm of my hand as I stare down at the rock on my finger. A hollow, hungry sensation fills my stomach. I've avoided emotional entanglements because they don't suit my lifestyle, but standing here, this gorgeous diamond solitaire weighing heavy on my finger, I realise that it's an approach I've stuck to because of Tate. I was badly burned by his confession to his father that he was merely filling time with me. This ring is a symbol of what might have been, and it hurts a million times more than I could ever imagine.

I make the mistake of looking up at Tate. His tousled dark hair, framing those brilliant blue eyes, which are focused on me with such intent I miss a breath. Everything hurts but I don't even flinch when he leans in to kiss me. My lips part and my whole body trembles with the ache of longing and loss. As his mouth touches mine, my heart expands with both pain and joy.

Tate's hand slides up my back as his lips softly trace mine, bringing balm to my soul, soothing away the jagged edges of hurt that have been buried beneath the surface for so long. I wrap my arms around his neck, as much to hold on as to help me stay up. My body is magnetised to his, north to south. As we draw closer together, I inhale the scent of him and a million memories flood into my head like shimmering butterflies. I lose myself in the kiss, it's like coming into harbour after a long voyage, when you thought you'd never see home again. My feelings are perplexing: big, complicated emotions at odds with the calm and simplicity of the moment. Inside I'm serene, like there's a sense of completeness that I didn't even know I had missed.

The sudden realisation of what's happening wrenches me out of my reverie. What are we doing? This is all show. Our bodies don't seem to have a lick of sense between them. Yes, I want him. Lust. Desire. But I can't afford to get back into that murky mix of emotion and craziness. I stiffen, my lips freezing at his gentle onslaught, and instantly he draws back, his eyes dark with emotion and a flash of something I can't quite identify. Confusion. Anger. Fury?

There's a sigh from Lacey, and I catch sight of a woman in my peripheral vision holding up her phone.

I look back at Tate, his mouth has flattened, all the warmth and softness gone. His blue eyes are as fierce and icy as the cool sparkle of the diamond on my finger. I pull my hand out of his.

'I don't think I can do this,' I say to him in a low voice, my heart beating with an uncomfortable, uneven rhythm in my chest.

Tate's jaw tightens 'Seriously? You get to walk away at the end, Lily. You're good at that, I seem to recall.' He strikes a hit, anger reverberating in his voice. Obviously Tate Donaghue's memories are very different from mine.

Chapter Nine

TATE

P ulling Lily with me, I force our way through the crowd of waiting fans – who are all calling out their congratulations – to where my car is parked. Opening the door, I practically push her inside the back seat ahead of me.

She glares at me as she slides across the seat, and I can see she's about to speak.

'I know, I know you're supposed to be in charge here,' I tell her. 'But from a purely practical perspective, I'm bigger than you.'

She pinches her mouth. 'True,' she concedes, 'but I don't have to like it.'

The car pulls away and Lily closes the glass window between us and the driver.

'We need to agree some ground rules,' she says. 'About kissing and PDAs.'

'Right,' I say. And even though I'm still smarting from her rejection, her primness amuses me.

'I'm serious. There need to be boundaries.'

'I agree,' I say, and lean back, folding my arms, prepared to be entertained. 'You're in the driving seat.'

I let my gaze rest on her lips, which are pouty with irritation, and she narrows her eyes. 'No kissing on the lips,' she says.

'Okay.' I say with a nod. 'I think I've got that one.' She made it pretty damn clear back there, after all.

'And no kissing … you know, anywhere sexual.'

'Such as?' I quirk an eyebrow at her.

'Funny,' she says, her jaw tightening. 'Just stick to pecks on the cheek.'

'What about touching?' I ask, starting to enjoy myself. 'Can I put my arm around you? Hold your hand? Touch you in the small of your back?' I immediately think of that silky red dress she wore, the way it dipped to reveal the long, smooth, sexy line of her back.

'Try and think about what normal couples do in public,' she says with a snap.

'I'm guessing not Kourtney and Travis, then,' I suggest.

'Think more William and Kate,' she says.

I wince. 'Lily, I have a reputation to uphold.'

'Just do what you would normally do with a girlfriend, then,' she snaps, then adds, 'in public.'

The car drives into the underground car park below my apartment block. I thank the driver, who is a little put out that we insisted on taking the luggage up ourselves, and open up the trunk to take out Lily's cases. As of today, she's moving in with me.

God help me. It feels like temptation is being waved in my face with her tantalising scent, the softness of her skin a mere touch away, the silkiness of her hair waving around her delicate face. I need some me-time or a very long, cold shower.

I use my code to programme the lift and we stand in silence, side by side, as it ascends. I study her in the mirrored wall. Today she looks drop-dead gorgeous in a dress that subtly highlights her narrow frame, elegant limbs and pert breasts. Everything is covered up in a way that makes me want to unwrap her like a special gift I've been looking forward to forever. The lift takes its sweet time reaching the top floor.

Eventually, we land on the top floor and the doors open. In another life, I'd sweep her into my arms and carry her straight to bed. Unfortunately, this life has other ideas.

Lily shoots an arm out in front of me, barring my way.

'What the—?' I bat her arm away, then see what's down the hallway.

My front door is covered in red paint. Someone has daubed a message on the white wall of the corridor in big red letters.

I'M WATCHING YOU, DONAGHUE

What the fuck?

The paint has dripped down the walls like blood, which strikes me as a ridiculous third-rate movie cliché. But somehow, I know the intent is serious.

'Tate, stop.' Lily steps right in front of me. 'Let me handle this.'

She's taking no prisoners. Her face is set and severe. She means business.

I watch as she opens the fancy purse she's been toting all morning and takes out a gun. I'm shocked at how smoothly she handles it, as if it's an extension of her body. It seems so at odds with the carefree girl I knew, and I look at her with fresh eyes.

'Wait here,' she says.

'No fucking way,' I whisper.

'Just stay here.'

'No.'

She huffs out an irritated sigh. 'Stay behind me, then.'

She approaches the door slowly, having kicked off her shoes outside the elevator, and moves with sinuous, silent grace. They've made a mess of my door, the red gloss paint has dried in tacky furrows and there are spatters of paint all over the carpet.

The door is still closed, which is some relief, but someone has clearly tried to get in, there are gashes in the paintwork around the lock.

Lily is already looking up, studying the security camera, the lens of which is coated in a layer of red paint, as is the one by the elevator and the door to the fire escape, I notice.

'Give me your key.' Lily holds out her palm.

'No,' I say, and side-stepping the paint on the floor, I insert my key in the lock.

'Tate!' She grabs my hand. 'Wait.'

'Seriously. This is the work of dumb kid.' I'm angry at the damage to my home. FFS.

'A *dumb kid* who managed to bypass the security and get this far?' Lily's expression is stony. 'You don't know they haven't got into your apartment. Or that they're not lying in wait.' She lets out a long breath. 'Now. Please move out of the way.'

She pushes me to one side, then crouches down beside the door. It's still locked.

She holds out her hand and I give her the key, watching as she inches the door open, her gun at the ready. She peers around it and then carefully rises to her feet. Light streams in from the floor-to-ceiling windows in the living area through the double doors on the right.

It takes a good five minutes before Lily's satisfied that this floor is clear. Then she mounts the open staircase up to the next level.

I walk into the kitchen and switch on my fancy-ass coffee maker, which has taken me six months to master but it's worth it. I make myself a coffee and pour in some creamer. I'm tempted to yell up the stairs and ask Lily if she'd like one, too, but decide to let her carry on doing her job. Something tells me she wouldn't take kindly to her focus being diverted, and this is what she's being paid for, right?

I make myself useful by getting on to the maintenance team to sort out the door, and then, while I'm sipping a second coffee, Nancy Drew returns with a perturbed look on her face.

'Find anything?' I ask.

'No, 'she says.

'Want a coffee?'

'Yes please.' She frowns. 'It's worrying that they got to your floor.'

'But they didn't get in.'

Her mouth purses. 'Do you have a number for the building's security?'

Over coffee, she goes into command mode, phoning her boss, Winston, and the building's security asking if they can review the feeds and share them with her. I leave her to it and head up to my home gym to work out a few kinks, amongst other things.

I'm sweating, my biceps straining under the weight they're bearing, and I feel like shit. The team doc was right, it's going to take a couple of days to get over the anaphylactic shock and ensuing chemical blast, but I'm not giving up yet. I've got a game to prepare for. The biggest of my life. Dogged determination has got me this far, and I'm no quitter. Unfortunately, there's a car due in half an hour to take me to training. I thought I'd be okay with a bit of strength conditioning beforehand.

'So, this is where you're hiding.' Lily walks in carrying a glass of water. Barefoot, and now dressed in jeans and an oversized sweater, which has slipped off her shoulder. She looks completely at home already.

Grateful for the interruption, although I'm not going to

show it, I put down the weight and turn round to face her, pleased to note that she's not unaffected by the sight of my toned chest and abs, judging by her eyes zoning in on that part of my body.

'I'm not hiding, I live here,' I say, stretching my arms above my head. 'Found the perp yet, Agent Heath?'

'Very funny.'

She sits down on the bench opposite me and I feel duty-bound to pick up another weight and start a bicep curl, even though I've already done reps on this side.

'I've reviewed the security footage,' she says, little furrows forming in her forehead making her look like an earnest schoolteacher.

'And what conclusions have you come to?' I continue flexing my muscles, amused by her surreptitious glances their way.

'That whoever did this, knew their way around the building. They knew where all the cameras were, the weak spots. They used a selfie stick to paint out the cameras so that they couldn't be seen. They knew the code to the lift. Just like they knew that you were at the stadium yesterday. You weren't scheduled to be. This is someone close to you, related to the team in some way. Someone you know.'

I lay down the weight, careful and deliberate and give her an icy look. 'Don't go making trouble where there is none. The team is tight. You're wrong.'

She sighs. 'I know you don't like hearing this, and you have a loyalty to the team, but I have to consider the balance of probabilities.'

I glare at her. I refuse to think about it. 'My focus is on preparing for the game.'

'I know, and I'll do my best to make sure any security detail doesn't interfere with that.' She gives me a half-smile. 'I hope it's okay, but I've taken the guest room on the second floor.'

'Sure, sleep where you like. You always could.' The words slip out before I can stop them. It's getting harder and harder not to refer to the past. She was like a cat back then, able to sleep anywhere, anytime, especially in my single bed when there really wasn't much room. She'd curl around me in whatever limited available space there was.

'I never did tell you why I slept so well with you or why I couldn't watch the Harry Potter film,' she suddenly says, reading my mind. She links her hands together over her knees.

'No, you didn't.' We'd settled down to watch the movie one rainy afternoon, then Lily left to go to the bathroom and didn't come back.

'Occasionally, my dad had me sleep in a cupboard, or a treehouse, or a tent. Part of the self-sufficiency training. His view was that sleep was valuable in self-survival. If you can sleep anywhere, you can face anything the next day – because you never know what life will throw at you. He was referring to my mum leaving. Teaching me to be resilient. Prepared for the worst. Which is why I never knew when I might be woken.' She pauses and looks at me, with a sad smile. 'Sleeping with you always made me feel safe and I always knew what the day would bring, until the day it didn't. And I've no idea why I'm telling you this now.' She stands up and brushes down her jeans.

'Wait—' I say, but I'm interrupted by the sharp buzz of the front doorbell.

Lily and I exchange a glance.

No one is supposed to come up here without the front desk phoning up first.

Chapter Ten

LILY

I grab my purse as we come down a floor and approach the front door.

'Who is it?' calls Tate from a safe distance down the hall as I refuse to let him use the peephole. If you want to kill someone, shooting through a peephole seems a pretty sure-fire way to do it.

'Hey, Mr Donaghue. It's Ray.'

'Who's Ray?' I mouth at Tate.

'Doorman,' he whispers.

'You've had a delivery from Tiffany.'

'Aren't you supposed to phone up?' Tate asks, looking at me.

'Of course, Mr Donaghue, I'm so sorry. I clean forgot in all the excitement.'

I roll my eyes. Tate starts towards the door, but I put a hand on his arm and shake my head.

'He might not be alone,' I mouth.

Tate's jaw tightens, but he lets me creep ahead and lean into the peephole.

'I hate this,' I hear him mutter from behind me.

Through the peephole, I can see that Ray, in his smart concierge uniform, is alone. I step back and nod at Tate to take charge. He opens the door.

'Mr Donaghue.' Ray hands over the parcel and his eyes slide to me in my pretend fiancée-getting-engaged outfit I'd put on after the gym. His round face lights up and he pats down the wispy hair barely covering the top of his head. 'I'm really sorry about this mess.' With his thumb he indicates the door. 'Security says they came up in the back elevator. If I get my hands on them.' He clenches both fists and shakes his head, looking like the archetypal boxing coach in every film you've ever seen. 'Bums. Got nothing better to do with their lousy lives.'

Ray nods at me. 'You must be Mrs Donaghue-to-be. Many congratulations to you. I saw it on TMZ.' He beams at us both, the vandalised door forgotten.

While Tate was in the gym, every social-media platform has gone viral with numerous pictures of me and Tate in Tiffany. The *pièce de résistance* is the shot taken in the store, where Tate is sliding the ring on my finger accompanied by the headline: 'The Kiss' – which must have been sent to every last news outlet by the press team.

'Sure was a surprise to read about it. You two keep a low profile,' he says, with a smile.

'We've been very discreet,' I tell him. 'You know what the press are like, we didn't want to jinx things. Tate's spent most of his time at my place.'

'Of course,' he says.

'Thanks, Ray,' says Tate.

'Yes, thank you,' I add, suddenly aware that there's a nation of genuine, earnest citizens who want good things for Tate and that they're happy for him. And we're lying to them.

'I take it this is the ring,' says Ray, holding the box up with dewy eyes. 'They get it sized for you today?'

'They did. Great service,' says Tate, taking the box from him.

Ray looks on expectantly as if he's hoping Tate's going to get the ring out there and then and put it on my finger.

Tate changes the subject with the speed and finesse of one of his own moves on the pitch.

'How are the grandkids? Little Davey still playing the guitar you got him for Christmas.'

I'm guessing that Tate is in the same uncomfortable camp as I am, deceiving good honest people doesn't sit well.

'Hell, yeah. He's driving his mom mad but he's learning real fast. He's a quick study. I'll tell him you were asking after him.'

'You do that. Remind him that if he's hungry enough for something, he can make it happen.'

'Sure will, Mr Donaghue. We'll all be rooting for you, next week. Got a big party planned. All the family coming over.'

'Thanks Ray. Sure means a lot. We'll do our best to bring it home.'

'No doubt about it. You got this.' Ray nods to Tate and

walks back along the corridor to the lift, then halfway down he stops and turns. 'Again. Congratulations. Great news. I hope you're going to be as happy as me and my Dorrie have been for the last thirty-eight years.' He waves and gets into the lift, his smiling face the last thing we see before the doors close.

'Shit,' says Tate, passing the Tiffany package from hand to hand like it's a fidget cube. 'This sucks. I didn't know I'd feel like this. Lying to the fans.' His jaw is tense.

'I know,' I say. 'This situation. It's nobody's choice but we're not harming anyone.'

'There's no boyfriend or partner who's going to be shocked to see you in the press?' Tate asks.

I shake my head and say firmly, 'No.'

'Or that you're engaged?'

'A few friends might be surprised, but my closest friends know what I do.'

He opens up the package and takes the contents out.

He holds out the turquoise blue box to me and we both stare down at it. I catch my lip in my teeth.

To my surprise he flips open the lid and takes out the ring.

'Might as well do this properly. Who knows if I'll ever do it for real.' He takes my hand, all business, and slides the ring onto my finger. It fits perfectly and my stomach flips at the sight of the exquisite, emerald-cut diamond. It's absolutely gorgeous, although I still can't believe that Tate paid that exorbitant sum of money for it. When I found out how much it cost, I wanted to downgrade to a much smaller diamond of less than a carat, but Tate insisted that this ring had been my first choice and I had to have it. It was difficult to argue in front of the sales assistant, who probably wasn't going to back me up.

'It's a beautiful ring,' I say quietly. 'Thank you. Even if it is only temporary. I'm going to enjoy wearing something so lovely.'

Tate runs a finger along mine and I think he's going to say something, but then his phone beeps.

'The car's here,' he says. 'I need to grab my bag.'

We arrive at the stadium at the players' back entrance, which is manned by two burly security guards. Apparently, today's quite an occasion as it's the last training session at the stadium before the team fly to New Orleans, so there's a bit of a party atmosphere with the whole team, families, wives and girlfriends assembled.

'Hey,' says Shane, who is there to meet us. 'I'll take Lily up to the box.' He smiles at me. 'Don should be fine here. We've got the best security.'

I glance at the broad-shouldered guys with impassive faces. Sure, they look the part, but I'd be happier escorting Tate down to the locker room myself.

I slip an arm through Tate's and clutch his rock-hard bicep, like the best clingy girlfriend. 'Can't I see the locker room?'

Tate and Shane talk over each other.

Tate saying no, while Shane nods and says, 'Sure.'

'That's not necessary,' says Tate. 'I need to focus on practice.'

Just to wind him up, I say. 'But darling, I want to see where you work.'

One of the security guys sniggers and Tate rolls his eyes. He leads the way down under the stadium. It feels like we're in a coal mine as we twist down the dimly lit corridors until we come to a museum-like area, full of glass cases holding pennants, old uniforms and trophies – which I'm guessing are minor ones and not like the big shields and silverware upstairs.

Tate heads towards one of the doors.

I hesitate. I feel I ought to go in to check it before Tate enters. I slide in front of him.

Tate snorts. 'Be prepared to get an eyeful.'

I pause.

'Chicken,' he murmurs into my ear.

Turning to face him, I tilt my head. 'Maybe I'm worried about their privacy. Seen one, you've seen them all.'

He raises an eyebrow. 'You sure about that?' he says, reminding me that that is not the case. He has the most impressive dick I've ever seen.

I swallow and glance back at the door. I don't like leaving him, even though I know Tierney's team are responsible for stadium security and they've been doing this for a long time.

'Lily, there will be at least twenty other guys in there. No one is going to attack me in the locker room.'

I purse my lips. He's probably right, but I hate not doing my job properly. I don't know Tierney's team.

A group of players appear, including Blake Pedlar.

'Hey, Lily,' he calls with a big grin on his face. 'How you doing? Still with this bozo? Let's see the ring. I hear you guys have been shopping. It's all over social media. There's still time to change your mind.'

He winks at me. He's the only other person apart from senior management that is in on the fake engagement.

'I tell you if it doesn't work out, I'll always be your plus one,' he adds.

'Thanks Blake.' I smile at him, pleased to see a friendly face.

'I'll see you after the game,' says Tate and I feel a bit guilty for bothering him. I can see he's trying to get in the zone.

'Good luck,' I say.

'Come on, man. Don't you get a lucky kiss?' asks one of the other players. I recognise him from the team sheet, which I've been studying. Mike Tomlin. With his stocky barrel-chested build, the missing teeth and heavy beard, he looks more like a wrestler and has a wicked grin on his face.

'Yeah,' joins in Blake, shooting me a mischievous wink.

Tate gives him the side-eye but plays along. 'Yeah.' He looks down at me, quirking an eyebrow in challenge. 'It's a football tradition. A guy's got to get a kiss from his girl. On the lips. In public.' I know he's referring to our conversation in the car. 'It's good luck.'

Unfortunately, for the sake of the charade, they all have to believe that Tate and I are an item. And I just know, from the cocky gleam in his eyes, that Tate is going to put on a show for them. I look up at him.

Bring it on. I can give as good as I can get.

When he lowers his lips to mine, his tongue teasing the entrance, I meet him and wind my hand into his hair. As soon as his tongue touches mine, a thrill shoots through me and I realise I've made a massive tactical error. I thought, with an audience, I wouldn't get swept in but when Tate gives me an open-mouthed kiss, it sears me from my mouth to the soles of my feet. My heart takes off with a giddy gallop, and I have to suck in a breath to steady myself. Shit, his hands come out to hold my arms, and I need that support to keep me upright. What is it about this man that triggers all my senses and makes me turn into mush at his touch? Is it because he's so fiercely masculine and I'm so used to fending for myself I can relax with him? I've no idea. I just know that I like the way he makes me feel, and I shouldn't.

I allow myself one more kiss and then pull back. He grins down at me and touches my lips.

I'm not allowing him to have the last word and I capture his finger between my teeth and give it a little nip, with some tongue, too. His eyes widen and he laughs.

'I like the way you wish me luck. What will you do when we win?'

'Wouldn't you like to know?' I play along with a sultry smile for the benefit of our audience, but the warmth between my thighs makes it clear that my body has a very specific interest in knowing.

'Until later, Princess.' He salutes me and saunters off

with the other players through the door painted with the Bullington shield.

I ease out a sigh, which could be construed as a whimper, and Shane glances at me.

'The man's a jerk,' I say.

'Looks like you're handling him okay.'

I give Shane a scornful look. 'Of course, I am,' I lie.

Chapter Eleven

TATE

'Go home and stay home, Tate,' Coach snaps. Over his shoulder, Doc gives me an annoying, smug, 'Told ya' look, which I could well do without.

'Sorry Coach.' He's torn a strip off me and he's right. I fluffed a dozen catches – just didn't have the speed or the momentum on the field. I've let them all down.

I all but crawl out of the locker room, all in and dispirited.

'Jeez, Tate. What the fuck is going on?' Great. Dad.

'Hey, Dad.'

'"Hey Dad", is all you got to say to me.'

'How was your golfing break?'

'A serious mistake, I'm thinking. What was that?' He points towards the field although we both know exactly what he's talking about.

'Everyone has an off day.' I don't need this now. I'm weak as shit. The doc has given me strict instructions: fill up on protein, limited exercise and rest.

'Other people do. Not *The Don*.' His face is flushed and his eyes small, filled with ugly rage.

'What do you want me to say?' I'm tired to the bone. It's been a hell of a couple of days and I'm as mad at myself as he is, maybe madder.

'I could do with an explanation for a starter. I get to hear from the *National Enquirer* that The Don has lost his mind. You got engaged! Now. Are you fucking nuts?' His voice rings with apoplectic rage. 'This is what we've been working towards your whole life. What have I told you about women? Suck you dry. And what do you do? You prove me right.'

He's been banging this drum as long as I can remember, and I'm weary of it.

'There's something I need to tell you.'

'No, Don. There was something you should have told me before today.'

I look around making sure the corridor is empty. 'Dad, it's a publicity thing.' Can I bring myself to tell him my fiancée is actually my bodyguard?

'What?' He scowls.

'I'm not really engaged,' I say, low and urgent.

'It sure looks that way on all the socials.'

'It's a ruse. I couldn't tell you before. It's complicated.'

'Well, put a stop to it, right now. It's killing your game.'

'It's not that simple.' I'm going to have to come clean to him. 'Winston's been getting notes, threats towards me. Some crazy says they're going to kill me.' I try to make light of it. He doesn't need the worry of knowing they've made one attempt already.

'I'll be first in line if you don't pull your head out of your ass. There are always crazies.' He shakes his head as he paces back and forth.

'Winston's hired a bodyguard. Being my fiancée is her cover.'

My dad steps back. 'Someone's making threats to The Don.' He laughs. 'Come on, you can look after yourself. Who's going to mess with you?'

'You and I know that. But unfortunately, Winston is taking it seriously.'

'The man's a pussy. Has no idea how to run a fucking football team.'

If he wasn't my dad, I'd probably point out that for a man who has no idea, he's doing pretty well for his team to get to the biggest game of them all.

'He threatened to kick me off the team if I didn't go along with it.' As soon as the words are out of my mouth, regret piles in.

My dad really goes off on one and looks like a slightly deranged Rumpelstiltskin, hopping around as he mouths obscenities about Winston, Shane, the coach – and then he adds my mom into the mix. 'I bet *she* had something to do with this.'

'Don't bring her into it, Dad.'

'She never wanted you to play. Always messing with your chances. I remember her saying you could miss practice to go to the prom committee. And the time she wanted to take you to the doctors instead of play in the Fresno game.' This is a familiar tirade and it's fruitless to point out that I had actually fractured my leg that particular game, and had to be carried off the field. My dad is on a well-trodden roll and it's pointless to interrupt because I'll get the same old, you-wouldn't-be-where-you-are-today without me spiel.

I'm grateful to him. It's true, I wouldn't be where I am today without him. I'm the luckiest guy in the world, I get to play football and I love it, but every now and then, Dad gets carried away. He always apologises afterwards – it's his passion for the game and his desire for me to be the best I can, he tells me. But sometimes I wonder what we'd be like if I hadn't risen to the top flight of the game. If we'd have gone to bars together, on camping trips, celebrated birthdays together like other families did. Normal life seemed to evaporate after Mom left. Not that I'm complaining. Hard work, persistence and determination is what got me here and I wouldn't be anything without my dad.

His rant draws to a close and he gives another disappointed shake of his head.

'You need to show them who's boss, Tate. After this season, you can go any place you want. You know Brad is already in talks with you-know-who.'

I hang on to my irritation. Brad is my agent, and he talks to my dad more often than I do. But Brad knows my feelings about loyalty, which is why he's been avoiding me of late. Whether we win or lose, I won't walk away from the Armadillos, no matter how much money is on offer.

Then Dad's off again, and a wave of exhaustion rolls over me, nearly felling me. I grit my teeth and fight against the need to close my eyes. Showing any weakness in front of my father right now will probably send him over the edge. It's a huge relief when I spot Lily approaching with Winston and Shane. Dad doesn't even see her. He rounds on the two men and starts firing questions about the game plan and the strategy for the coming week.

Lily takes one look at me, and somehow separates me from the mêlée, guiding me away without anyone noticing.

'Car's this way,' she murmurs taking my arm, leading me down the corridor. 'Shane had it brought round.'

Seconds later, we're at her car, its hazard lights flashing, and a security guard emerges from the driver's seat holding up the keys. Lily takes them from him, has a brief interchange and then opens the passenger door and urges me inside. I collapse into the seat with relief. I've been running on empty for the last hour. She pulls the belt across me and clicks it into place like I'm a kid, and for once it's nice to just be, just to let everything happen around me. I close my eyes and savour her fragrance and the swish of her silken hair across my cheek.

I wake up on the couch in my apartment a couple of hours later, with a vague memory of leaving the car and getting up here. I'm swathed in a blanket and my head is supported by a couple of pillows. Blinking into the softly lit room, it takes a minute for my eyes to adjust. It's a grey, gloomy day, and outside the lights of the city's skyscrapers shine in neat recognisable columns. The sight reinforces the order of the world and reminds me where I am. It's soothing, as is the sight of Lily, curled up on the opposite chair, one hand tucked under her chin reading a book in the lamplight beside her. It casts a golden glow over her hair. She really does look like an angel, and I take a moment to study her absorbed in her book, her eyes thoughtful. She's as beautiful as ever and I have to swallow down a lump of something I refuse to identify.

Sensing my regard, she looks up and smiles. 'Hey, there.'

'Hey,' I say, my voice a little raspy with sleep. 'How long was I out?'

'A couple of hours. You needed it.' Her soft smile reminds me of so much I want to forget. For a second, we're back in the past. I can almost imagine it's just the two of us in my room in college, and the last eight years never happened. My heart pitches just a little and fear rushes in. I don't want this.

I scowl. 'You've been talking to the doc.'

She sighs. 'Tate, it may surprise you to know that he is actually a medical professional and might just know what he's talking about, along with your coach, who both agree that you need a couple of days' rest.' She holds up a hand. 'Two days. That's all. You can do light resistance work. No cardio.'

'You my jailer now?' I snarl, because I need to be mad at someone.

'Want something to eat?' she asks, ignoring my jibe. In answer my stomach growls and Lily shoots a cocky smile my way. 'I'll take that as a yes.'

I bite back the laugh. Lily always gives as good as she gets. She's still got that feisty never-give-in attitude. The one that drew me to her when we first met.

It's nice just to lie here, cocooned in the half-light, comfortable on the couch and I notice the quiet and the peace it brings with it. I listen, and at first it's disconcerting. I always have the TV on, ESPN usually, turned up loud so I can hear the sports announcers, shouty and punchy, caught up in the moment. If I'm in the bathroom or kitchen, there'll be more of the same on the radio.

I listen, the silence is full of muted noise; the whisper of wind around the windows, the river flow of traffic washing through the streets below, muffled sounds from the kitchen, along with the faint rustle of the fabric of my clothes and the blanket. Now I'm aware of it, I can hear my own breathing – it's soothing. Being in the quiet is like being unplugged for a while. Normally my whole life is logged on to football, the game blasting on every channel. When was the last time I took a break? Went to the beach? Went hiking? My life is a whirl of plane flights, hotels, gyms, training, interviews and gala dinners. Don't get me wrong, I'm not complaining. This is my life and I chose it, but with rare time to think I just wonder about maybe taking a holiday. My life is measured out in training sessions and games, off-season conditioning, pre-season camps.

Lily returns, bringing with her a plate of beans on toast, which smells surprisingly good.

'Here you go, champ. Slim pickings in your kitchen apart from a gazillion protein shakes, which all look disgusting. Do you ever eat real food?'

'It's all nutritionally based,' I say.

'Yes, but what does it taste like?'

I shrug, then inhale. Who knew beans could smell so amazing? I realise I'm ravenous.

I haul myself into a sitting position and Lily hovers next to me with a tray bearing flatware, a paper serviette, a large glass of milk, and the toast and beans. As she places it on my knee, I have a sudden flashback of having the flu at college.

'You're ill, Tate.' I remember the look of concern in Lily's eyes as she ran a hand over my flushed face, and the nice but painful feeling it gave me. I'd wanted to lean into her cool touch and rest my forehead against hers. Instead, I'd lifted my chin and gave her an I've-got-this grin, I was far from feeling.

'Can't let the team down,' I said, even though my head felt like it was stuffed with crumpled old newspaper and my throat was as raw as if I'd snacked on razor blades. 'I have to go. It's just a cold.'

I'd already spoken to my dad, who'd called earlier with some advice about strategy that he thought I should talk to Coach about. When I'd told him I was feeling rough, his response had been to ask me if, 'I was some weakling that was going to let a few little germs stop me'.

'Fair enough,' Lily had said. 'Although I'd have a word with Coach Silverman, first.'

'What do you mean?'

She'd lifted her shoulders in one of those elegant shrugs of hers and turned her candid gaze on me.

'I'm just wondering how he'd feel if you infected the

whole team with your bug, just before the next game. It's an important one, isn't it?'

'They're all important,' I said glibly.

'Fair enough,' she said and didn't look up when I left with my kit bag slung over my shoulder.

When I got to the stadium, I went straight to see Coach Silverman. I was planning to talk to him about my dad's advice – always tricky, as Coach sometimes suggested my dad should butt out – but I owed everything to my dad.

Coach Silverman took one look at me and, before I could even open my mouth, said, 'Go home, Tate.'

'What?'

'Go home. You're not well.'

'How do you know? It's just a bit of a cold.'

'Jeez. You kids. Do you even know how to look after yourselves? Your eyes are red-rimmed, you look like you're carrying a fever and the flu is doing the rounds. You're no good to me or the team if you can't give a hundred per cent.'

'I can give a hundred per cent.'

'There's a difference between wanting to and being able to. Go home to bed. Drink lots of liquid and take some over-the-counter flu meds.' He paused and then raised one finger, which was always what he did when he brooked no argument. 'And the team does not want your germs. I've already sent Richardson and Beck home. This conversation is done.'

When I got back to my room, Lily had been shopping. There was a quart of orange juice by my bed, a box of

Tylenol, a bar of chocolate and two tins of soup, along with a note.

Ice cream in the refrigerator.

I reverse out of the memory and glance down now at the tray on my lap.

'You always were a good nurse,' I tell Lily. The memory of how she used to be with me is making me an ass. I don't want her to know I appreciate her looking after me. It's the last thing I want from her.

But it's as if I've pulled the cork out of a shaken champagne bottle. Images burst into my head like effervescent bubbles of memory. Lily tucking me up in bed. Heating up soup. Pouring me a glass of orange juice and sitting with me but not talking, just checking periodically whether I needed anything. She was so easy to have around when I felt like shit. She didn't make it about herself, she just let me be me. She was there when I needed her. A rare skill, I realised. My Dad always believed in tough love and that exercise was the best medicine. Once, I remember him advising me to go for a run when I had food poisoning, insisting that it would get it out of my system quicker. I'd stopped in the park to puke and then collapsed on a park bench to recover…

'Sorry,' I say now to Lily. 'I mean, I'm grateful. You're good at looking after people, is all.' I take a long slug of cold milk.

Lily shrugs. Either she's indifferent, or looking after people is second nature to her. I'm hoping it's the latter.

'But Lily,' I hold her gaze, 'I always wondered something… Who looks after you?'

Sudden intimacy crackles between us as we stare at each other. Something flickers in her eyes, but then it's snuffed out.

'Don't let it get cold,' she says with a weak smile, and then she walks out of the room.

Interesting. The Lily I knew never backed away from anything.

Chapter Twelve

LILY

In the kitchen, I lean against one of the cabinets, my shoulders slumped in rare defeat. My heart is more than a little sore, it aches with a kind of grief that I thought was long buried. I'm not sure I can do this. There's too much water under the bridge. I can't sit in there with him looking all sleep-softened and rumpled, with that milky moustache begging to be kissed away. Not when I'm still sizzling from the stadium kiss. I'm overwhelmed by this weird, alien compulsion to look after him.

No. I *do not* want to crawl in beside him under that blanket. I *do not* want to feel his lips on mine again. I *do not* want to nuzzle into the warmth of his neck just beneath his chin.

I straighten up. I need something to distract me before I jump the man's bones. Where has all this angsty pent-up sexual energy come from? Parts of me are buzzing with heat and want, a burning desire to be touched.

I go through the cupboards in search of proper food and

distraction. I need something practical to do. As I find bare space after bare space – apart from one cupboard stacked with tins of protein powder, I push the doors shut with disgust. Ugh. I shudder.

I make a quick phone call, then march into the living room.

'I'm going out. Can I trust you to behave yourself?' I demand. 'Tierney's team have someone out front watching the building. If anything, and I mean *anything*, doesn't feel right, call Tierney and he'll have someone come straight up.'

Tate looks up, justifiably surprised by my mood.

'What's got you in such a snit?' he asks, bemused. 'And since when has there been a car outside?'

'Since day one. And you've got no food in the house,' I say tightly.

He smirks more widely. 'I didn't invite you here.'

'No, and I don't want to be here, so we're both on the same page. Unfortunately, we're stuck with each other.' I give him a sweet smile. I'm enjoying the bickering.

'You can leave any time you like.'

'You know I can't.'

'So, what's got your panties in such a bunch?' he asks, interest glowing in his eyes.

'Nothing,' I say, but I can't help looking at that mouth, the full, slightly sulky lower lip. He goes still, watching me. Our eyes hold. He's still got that cute milk moustache and I long to lick it off, tangle my tongue with his.

'I won't be long,' I say instead. 'Don't open the door to anyone.'

I snatch my purse up before he can say anything and march out of the apartment, slamming the door behind me.

It takes the whole of my swift march down the block to calm me. I take in deep lungfuls of icy air, then long, slow breaths out. I've been taught how to lower my heart rate and manage my body's response to critical situations, but today it's like the world has tilted off its axis. I can't quite recapture my equilibrium.

My intention was to storm the nearest grocery store, do a smash-and-grab raid on a few basics and get back to the apartment ASAP. But, as I near the store, the storm in my head settles. I'm taken back to the time I returned from college, when my dad was in hospital and my heart was smashed into irreparable pieces. Alice, our housekeeper, half in love with dad, recognised how broken I was and set about fixing me in her calm, unemotional way. Every day she'd insist that I helped her in the kitchen, cooking ridiculously elaborate meals for the staff. The gamekeeper, stable hands and estate manager had never eaten so well. At the time I didn't realise that it was as much to occupy her as it was to comfort me.

I learned not only to cook in those months while Dad recuperated, but also that it was therapeutic. A way of nourishing body and soul when you most needed it. For Alice, it was her way of showing love to my dad, which thankfully he finally recognised. They've been married for five years now. I often wonder that if Alice had been on the scene earlier, my childhood might have been a bit less eccentric and more stable.

I grab a basket and survey the produce. I don't even

need to think about what I'm going to cook, it would seem I can't help myself. Tate always used to love spaghetti and meatballs. He'd joke that it would be his death-row meal, and if it was ever on the menu any time we went out to eat, he would always order it. He said his mum used to make it for him when he was a kid, before she left. Funnily enough, it's one of the things Alice taught me to cook first, and it's my go-to, my signature dish.

I seek out the ingredients I want, working my way through a mental list, until my basket is full and I'm at the counter ready to pay.

I'm loading everything into brown-paper carriers when I decide that this food needs a decent accompaniment. 'Where can I buy wine?' I ask the checkout girl, remembering that in New York, grocery stores don't have an alcohol license.

'There's a liquor store down the street.' She points with her thumb.

I've only been gone half an hour, but by the time I get back to the apartment, I've done some serious damage with my credit card, treating myself to a nice bottle of Barolo and a couple of bottles of beer, because I'm not sure if Tate drinks wine. He never used to. The store kindly offered to deliver the booze because I'm carrying way too much.

'Back so soon, Mrs D-to-be,' says Ray with a huge grin as I walk into the lobby of Tate's building. He's clearly pleased with his little abbreviation. 'Let me get the lift for you.'

He's so sweet and it gives me a pang of guilt. Tate's fans who want to see a happy-ever-after are doomed to disappointment. The only thing in the man's life is football. Always has been, always will be.

'Thank you,' I say and smile back at Ray, not wanting to disillusion him.

'Someone's cooking in tonight. That's what I like to see.' He gives the grocery bags an approving nod. 'I can tell you're going to look after Mr Donaghue real good. My wife is a great cook. It's true what they say, that the way to a man's heart is through his stomach.' Ray pats his generous belly and winks at me.

If only he knew. God bless his romantic soul.

'There's a delivery coming in about half an hour. Some wine,' I tell him, indicating my full arms. 'Couldn't carry everything.'

'No sweat. I'll make sure it gets to you. You have a good evening, now,' he says, as the lift doors close behind me.

I buzz the door outside the apartment and wait for Tate to open it, standing back from the peephole so he can see it's me. I needn't have bothered. He opens the door and walks off without waiting for me to walk through.

'Tate!' I yell. 'I could have been anyone.'

He carries on walking and heads back into the living room without even acknowledging me.

I stomp after him. He's already back on the couch and there's a ball game on the television. I roll my eyes.

'Tate,' I say with earnest entreaty. 'You need to take this seriously.'

'Ray told me you were on your way up. Wished me a nice evening. Does he know something I don't?' Tate raises an eyebrow.

I purse my mouth and walk off into the kitchen carrying my booty.

Ten minutes later, I'm all unpacked with my ingredients lined up ready to go and my current favourite Spotify playlist primed.

Tate reappears and comes to lean against the kitchen island, his muscular arms folded against his broad chest. He fills the space with his presence, and straight away my body buzzes with awareness. His scent, the size of him, and that invisible static that fills the air whenever the two of us inhabit the same space. Does he feel it running across the fine hairs of his skin the way I do? Like I'm magnetised and he's my North Pole.

'What are you doing?' he asks in that slightly crotchety bored-teenager way, and I realise he's in need of entertainment.

'I'm cooking. Dinner.'

'For me?' He gives me a look. 'I didn't know you cared.'

'I don't. It's to give me something to do.'

'I don't remember you being able to cook,' he says. 'In fact, you were pretty crap at it as I recall. You could burn pizza.'

I turn, hands on hips, radiating indignation. 'That was your fault for—'

He grins at me and raises that damn eyebrow again, pleased with himself for getting a rise out of me.

I turn my back on him to hide the flare of memory, raising my eyes to the ceiling because I can't begin to look at the kitchen counter. But it's no good. I can hear the oven timer going off. Me panting his name in a desperate chant over the insistent beeps. His big strong hands supporting my thighs, his fingers caressing my bottom as he spread me out, wide and open, then tasted and teased. His mouth relentless and ruthless. Oh God, how much I loved it. It was the first time I lost my 'pussy cherry' and he took so much pride in it, ignoring my shyness and initial embarrassment as I desperately tried to hold back my moans of pleasure. I blush now as I recall his constant filthy encouragement and praise, making me feel even more turned on.

My core clenches at the memory of the ecstasy as he tormented me to the brink of orgasm, over and over. I close my eyes. A mistake, because I can see his delighted grin as he kissed me, the taste of me on his lips. Proud because he'd reduced me to a breathless mess and while that damned beeper carried on, he gently cleaned me up, closed my legs and hugged me, promising soon that we'd go all the way.

Stupid tears prick at my eyes. His sweetness. The trust. That consuming feeling of love and lust so intertwined. I didn't know where one began and the other left off.

Blindly, I open cupboards looking for a measuring jug. For some dumb reason it's on the very top shelf, as if a bloody giant normally cooks in this place.

'Can I help?' The low timbre of Tate's voice purrs around me, twisting up my already hyper-charged senses. Even as I raise my hand, Tate comes to stand behind me, his body caging me. He reaches around me, the warmth of him sending a shiver through me.

I swallow. 'If you could…' The words desert me and I wave a hand at the jug. My arm parallel to his. He leans forward, his body almost flush against mine. The temptation to lean into him is tortuous.

'This?' He lifts one of the tumblers next to the jug. I shake my head.

He leans another inch closer, his breath against my cheek. 'This?' He picks up another glass. 'Or this?' Now his chest is against my back, his hips cradling my waist.

My mouth has dried. I close my eyes, my chest restricted and tight, I can't seem to get a breath in or out.

Then, with another soft, hot breath against my skin, he takes the measuring jug.

I nod, a little frantically and he grasps it and takes a step back. I want to cry out at the loss of contact, even though he's a mere inch away and my nerve ends are still singing.

'Thank you,' I croak, stepping to one side and taking the jug from him.

'My pleasure,' he says. I can hear humour in his voice, but also the slight rasp that tells me that perhaps he's affected, too.

'Anything else I can help with?' There's no mistaking the suggestion this time.

'All good,' I say. I suspect my bright, briskness might be a dead giveaway that inside I'm all shook up.

He retreats to all of two steps behind me and takes up his position leaning against the kitchen island again. It's the narrowest point of the room, and I'm going to have to keep brushing past him between sink, fridge and hob. But I can hardly ask him to move in his own kitchen.

I look at the mountain of vegetables I need to chop. Onions, celery, carrots, plus the tomatoes.

'Actually, you could chop some onions for me.'

I hand him two glossy brown onions, my fingers grazing his, and I risk a quick look at him. His eyes are a little smoky as he looks at me.

'I'd forgotten how cute you are when you get flustered,' he says, with an amused grin.

I shove a knife, handle first, towards him. 'Chop,' I say smartly.

'How do you want them done?' he asks, surprising me with the question. I can't imagine he ever cooks, even though the place is beautifully equipped with the best kitchenware. The gleaming knives, with bright sharp blades, are chefs' quality. His interior designer really went the extra mile.

I busy myself opening the meat, while I hear the crisp curl of onion skin as Tate peels off the outer layer next to me.

Then to my utter surprise, I hear rapid chopping and I turn to find his fingers are a blur, expertly slicing and dicing the onion. I'm transfixed by his efficient, precise grace, finding his unexpected proficiency uber-sexy for some very bizarre reason. This is a man who knows what he's doing.

He turns to find me staring and probably fan-girling more than a little. My mouth is partly open and I'm looking at him with stunned admiration.

It takes a single step and he's in front of me, his finger under my chin giving it a light nudge to close my gaping mouth. Our eyes catch and a second later his thumb grazes my lips. The gentlest of touches, the opposite to the fierce blaze in his eyes.

'I've never been able to eat pizza without thinking of you,' he rasps, his eyes boring into mine. 'Hot, wet and all mine.'

Oh God, I suck in a shocked breath. Heat erupts between my legs and I let out a strangled gasp.

'I need to know if you taste the same,' he whispers, his thumb sliding over my mouth.

I can't look away. My chest heaves as I try to breathe in weird, stuttering breaths.

Tate's other hand slides under my sweatshirt, his fingers hooking into the waistband of my black cargo pants. His eyes never leave my face and his unblinking gaze is intent and direct. I can see the darker blue flecks around his irises and all I can do is stare mutely back at him. I can't say a word because I'm so scared at what I might say, because my head, heart and libido are all at war, but my libido is definitely winning. It's pretty much a guarantee that the words, take me, God, yes please, go down on me now, are likely to come spilling out.

Now one finger slides across the top of my zip down to the seam of my trousers.

'You were so wet. Tasted like honey.' His voice is a growl now.

My skin flushes, the heat inside me like an inferno.

He strokes the seam of my trousers, and a sigh escapes me. I can't help it.

One corner of his mouth lifts, satisfaction glittering in his bright, focused eyes.

I don't move. I can't. I'm desperate for more. For that hot mouth of his. His thumb pushes against my lower lip settling on my teeth. With my tongue I suck the pad into my mouth, and I might as well have shouted game over. His responding smile is slow, sensual and slightly terrifying and he slides his fingers along my cheekbone. He knows he's got me.

He loosens the button at my waist, and with both hands slides down my trousers and my panties, before picking me up, hands looped under my thighs, and lifts me onto the cool surface of the island. The move is quick and efficient, and I'm immediately aware of the contrast between the ice-cold marble of the counter and his warm, strong hands.

I feel like I'm in a trance, watching all of this, a willing spectator in thrall to him. He pulls my legs apart. All the time looking at me. I don't flinch once, and it's all the answer he needs. My heart is thudding hard in my chest as I put my hands on either side of me. His gaze sharpens, a touch feral. A thrill shoots through me, excitement and anticipation fizzing together.

He pulls me forward to the edge of the counter and slides his hands along the top of my thighs, then gently pulls them apart. For the first time his gaze ducks. I lift my chin a tiny bit embarrassed at baring all, even though there's no way I can stop. I'm desperate for his touch, to feel his mouth on me. I feel slick and wet.

He rubs a finger against my clit and then looks at me again before popping his finger in his mouth.

I close my eyes and drop my head, not sure I can take the intimacy. No one has ever stripped me bare like this, not since him. I feel his hand on my chin again. I open my eyes.

He runs his hand down my neck, down the V of my

cleavage, down again to settle on my waist. With both hands he holds me and then eases me back, so that I'm open and on show.

'You're so wet for me, Lily,' he murmurs, a smile on his lips as he bends to taste the soft skin, kissing his way up my inner thighs. I tremble in anticipation, excitement mounting but he's slow and sure, nipping and nibbling at my skin and sending tingles swirling everywhere. His mouth, when it finally reaches my vagina, is hot and warm and I can't help the sigh of pure pleasure that escapes.

'Yes, Tate,' I murmur, and his eyes flicker up at me as his tongue licks my tender flesh, the nerve endings alight. My head falls back. My whole focus is on the heat of his wet mouth, and the pleasure, unbearable and intense at the same time. Agony and ecstasy.

'Tate,' I cry, trying to hold on. But he's relentless, pushing me to take as much as I can. I make mindless moans and it's all too much. I'm losing control and I don't care. I have no shame, no inhibitions, especially not when he slips one finger inside me and then another. He pumps me, his fingers gliding in and out, while his tongue does unspeakably beautiful things to me. His hand on my waist is holding me fast and when I try to rock, his grip tightens.

He takes his time, his tongue leisurely teasing and tasting, his fingers maintaining their determined, controlled rhythm. I'm a prisoner to his will as he works me with fingers and mouth, fingers and teeth. I'm utterly powerless against the force of pleasure drowning me.

'Yes, baby,' Tate groans, before his tongue latches onto my clit. I can feel the texture of him. It's so sensitive, the pleasure almost pain. I scream and I try to wriggle free because it's just too much. Too much. Too much. But Tate holds me firm, his tongue brooking no retreat. And then I feel it, a slow shuddering wave that expands and expands inside me and with a long low moan I fall back as the orgasm's explosive wave sweeps through me.

I lie there feeling like I've been run over by a snowplough. Between my legs, my nerve endings are throbbing; sensitive and on fire. Tate gives me one last kiss on my mound while he holds my gaze.

I have to close my eyes to blot him out, and it takes me a good minute for my hammering heart to settle and my breathing to slow. I struggle to my elbows, but Tate is immediately there and gently pulls me upright. He tilts his head surveying me, the grin has widened and it's full-on cocky now.

I'm momentarily embarrassed, still fully on display. But before I can wriggle down off the counter, he gently slides me down, pulls up my panties and trousers and pulls up the zip.

He leans forward and whispers in my ear.

'Anything else I can help you with?'

Instead of telling him that this shouldn't have happened, I say, completely deadpan, 'As you're so good with a chopper, you can do the rest of the vegetables,' before handing him a large carrot.

Chapter Thirteen

TATE

There's a silence between us, tension burgeoning by the second. I'm focused on chopping fucking vegetables because I've no idea what to say to her. Just when I think it's reaching snapping point, she throws down the wooden spoon she's just picked up.

'Fuck! Fuck! Fuck!' She throws her head back and she looks up at the ceiling. 'That shouldn't have happened.'

I can't agree. It was heaven right here on earth. There's a gleam of tears in her eyes, which is the worst thing, because I know Lily doesn't cry.

'Hey,' I touch her shoulder. 'We're two consenting adults. No one needs to know.'

She whirls round and glares at me. 'No one needs to know?' she echoes at the top of her voice. 'We know!' She gulps, I can see her throat working. 'This isn't supposed to happen. This isn't me. I'm a professional. I have a reputation for getting things right the first time.' All fired up, her eyes are flashing with angry tears. I want to scoop her up, and as much as I want to be inside her right now, because she's so fucking gorgeous, I also want to comfort her. And that feeling scares the crap out of me.

'It's cool,' I try to be calm, logical. 'Think of it as an itch we never got to scratch.'

She stares at me for a moment and then gives a half-laugh. 'I think you got your analogies a little mixed. We still haven't scratched that itch.' As soon as the words are out of her mouth, her eyes widen, and she looks at me.

'Maybe it's time we did,' I say, because fuck it, why the hell not. 'Get it out of our systems once and for all.'

'We can't,' she says, but her voice is quiet, as if she's not completely invested in the words.

I know we shouldn't but…

'We can. Why not, Lily?'

'Because you're my client.'

'And that's the only reason?'

'There are lots of other reasons, Tate,' she says with a reproving stare.

'Name them.'

'We don't like each other.'

'I like you just fine. I think I just demonstrated quite adequately how much I like you.'

'Tate,' she warns, her cheeks flamingo pink.

I touch her skin as if it sizzles my finger. 'And I think you liked it a lot, too.'

The shade of colour on her face deepens and my desire for her ratchets up another notch. I want her beneath me, skin to skin, body to body. Those soft breasts of hers up against my chest. Her hips cradling me.

'You want it too,' I say, unable to believe that she isn't as hot for me as I am for her. 'Tell me you don't want me.' I pin her with a fierce, challenging stare.

'That's not the point.'

'Excuses. Give me a good reason, apart from the client bullshit, why we shouldn't sleep together. You want to. I want to.'

'And then what?' she asks, lifting her chin.

'Then, when this is all over and done, we walk away. Just like before.' Except this time. I won't let my heart get involved. I'll get this itch scratched once and for all and then we can both move on. 'Admit it, Lily. There's unfinished business between us. Don't you wonder what it would be like.' I lower my voice. 'Taking all of me, hard, inside you.'

Her mouth opens and I see her chest rise as she breathes in, but I can see the deliberations in every expression that subtly flicker on her face.

'We—'

A loud explosive bang reverberates through the apartment.

'What the—?'

Lily's sexually hazed trance is shattered in an instant. Talk about killing the mood. She's already on the move, grabbing her gun, which seems have appeared from nowhere. From the hall I can hear the strident screech of the fire alarm.

'Stay there, Tate,' she throws at me over her shoulder as she races towards trouble.

Smoke is billowing from beneath the front door, and I

can hear an unfamiliar crackling noise and then I see it, the lick of flames fanning beneath the wooden sill.

'Fire extinguisher?' she shouts above the sound of the unremitting alarm pounding our ears.

'Don't have one,' I yell back.

'Towels?' she barks.

'Closet upstairs.' I'm already on my way up the wooden open-tread staircase to the next floor. Lily's right behind me.

'Call nine-one-one,' she says, grabbing the towels the minute I retrieve them and heading for the bathroom.

She runs in and hurls the towels into the shower, turning it on full velocity.

I call the emergency services. 'Fire department,' I snap into the phone. While I'm giving them the details, Lily has scooped out an armful of wet towels from the shower and is running back downstairs, leaving a dripping trail of water behind her. I follow, feeling a little useless, because she clearly knows what she's doing as she rolls the towels into loose sausages and wedges them against the gap under the door.

The crack and pop of flames on the other side of the door is now clearly audible, and the varnish on the inside is beginning to bubble up and blister, like some hideous disease spreading and multiplying at a furious rate. The heat radiating through is intense and sweat breaks out on my forehead, my clothes sticking to me.

'Shouldn't we open the door and try and fight the fire?' I say, as smoke starts to seep through the door's hinge and jamb, grey-blue creeping through the crack and then burgeoning and blossoming into the air.

'No!' she yells above the increasing noise. 'It'll give the fire oxygen. Feed it, and we could get a huge backdraft right in our faces – and possibly set light to the whole apartment. The door will give us at least sixty minutes' burn time. Close all the doors on this floor.'

She's right. The only escape route is out through the door into the corridor to the concrete stairwell. The emergency protocol is to stay put and trust in the fire-safety features of the building.

How does she think so fast? I'm all fingers and thumbs trying to catch up. Lily Heath is one BFD in an emergency. Happy to have been given something to do, I close the door to my study nook, the downstairs bathroom and the formal dining room. Unfortunately, there isn't much more to close, and the main living space is, despite Lily's best efforts, starting to fill with smoke.

She coughs a little and puts a wet hand towel to her face, handing me one.

'We need to find a safer place,' she says. 'Smoke is the biggest killer.'

Easier said than done. This is a very open-plan apartment.

'We can go up to the master bedroom, then we've got a bathroom with running water.'

'Got any more towels?'

'Yeah.'

'What are we waiting for?' We run for the stairs and I feel the slight catch at my lungs. The insidious creep of the smoke is worse than I realised. I can hear her breath whistling as she runs past me into my bedroom, straight for the shower room. Before I've cleared the door frame, she's back with another soaking towel in her arms. She steps in front of me, slams the door and rolls the towel into gap below it.

'Now what?' I ask, my heart pounding like the pistons on a freight train.

'We wait,' she says, cool as the proverbial cucumber, although there's soot on her nose and her eyes are red and streaming.

My heart is hammering, but now I've got time to find my mad. 'What the fuck is going on?' I ask, pacing up and down the length of my bedroom before swinging towards the balcony.

'Don't open the door,' says Lily, her voice firm but gentle.

I take my hand off the handle. It's second nature for me to go and stand out on the big balcony when I'm in need of some thinking time. I miss the heat and space of Austin, but I like the cold, crisp air of New York in winter.

'Who's doing this? I don't understand. It doesn't make any sense. Why would anyone not want me to play in the game?'

'That's what I keep asking myself,' says Lily. 'But then, with some folk there's just no logic.' Despite her words, her brow remains furrowed as if she's still thinking things through.

'What do you think happened?' I ask. It makes me wonder what Lily Heath has been doing for the last eight years.

'A firebomb, detonated at your door, I'm guessing,' she says. 'The fire department will know.'

She's already on her phone.

'Hey, Ray, it's Mrs D-to-be. Just letting you know that we're safe and holed up in the bedroom on the upper floor.'

Mrs D-to-be? Great. Now she's best friends with my doorman.

She's nodding. 'We're fine. It's out in the lobby.'

I can hear Ray's agitated voice and Lily soothing him.

'Ray, it's okay. Did you get a good look at the delivery person? It's not your fault, I cleared it. Don't worry. We'll get to the bottom of it.' She hangs up and pushes a hand through her hair.

'What happened?'

She frowns. 'It's my fault.' I can see she's beating herself up about this.

'I don't recall seeing you setting fire to the door.'

'I didn't take enough precautions. I was … not thorough enough. It won't happen again.'

'You gonna explain how it's your fault?'

'I told Ray that there was another delivery coming. I arranged with the wine shop to deliver some wine and beer. They said they could do it in twenty minutes or so, depending on how busy they got. Someone either hijacked their delivery or took advantage of the fact a delivery was due.' She rubs at her forehead. 'Someone must have been following me and I didn't see it. Or they were hanging around outside. Either way,' she sighs and looks at me, 'I took my eye off the ball. Let myself get distracted.' Her lips tighten, her expression both sad and resolved. 'From now on, it's purely professional between us.'

Her words give me a ten-thousand-volt jolt as I remember the sexual charge between us just before the fire.

I shrug. 'If you say so.' Difficult to think about sex right now when someone is trying to kill me. Shit. *Someone is trying to kill me.* It hits me like a truck. The threat is real. Someone out there wants me dead or doesn't want me to play the biggest game of my career so far.

'We're going to have to move you to a safe house.' Lily catches her lip between her teeth and I can almost see her brain working at a mile a minute working out next steps and strategy.

I sink onto the bed, my head in my hands. 'I can't believe this.'

Chapter Fourteen

LILY

'Is there anything I can get you, Mr Donaghue?' The blonde simpers at him and I would bet my life she's just reapplied her strawberry lip gloss.

She's the second member of cabin crew to ask this since we boarded the plane five minutes ago.

'No, thanks. I'm all good, but I'll be sure to let you know,' Tate replies smoothly, giving her one of his kilowatt smiles before settling into his first-class seat for the three-hour flight.

I wait until they finish their mutual appreciation of each other and then shoot him a bored glance, and he grins.

'Doesn't it get boring, all this fawning over you?' I ask, taking out my Kindle.

'Don't know what you mean?'

'Seriously?'

'People are just nice to me. They like me.' He gives me his usual cocky smile.

I turn away and see the plane's captain coming down

the aisle. Oh, dear God, now *he's* coming to see Tate. He stops beside our seats and extends a hand right across me.

'Tate Donaghue, the honour's all mine. I'm delighted to be flying you down to New Orleans today.'

'Thanks, Captain Frederickson.' Tate shakes his hand.

'You feeling confident about the big one?' asks the captain. 'I've got two hundred bucks riding on the game in your favour.'

'I'll do my best,' quips Tate and they share a manly chuckle.

'You headed in early. I thought the team weren't arriving for another couple of days.'

'Advance party,' says Tate. 'Wanted to spend some time with my girl.' Suddenly remembering the script, he hooks an arm around my shoulder and squeezes me. That's the line that's being fed to the media for our disappearance from New York.

He's also doing it to annoy me. Since our … our episode in the kitchen, Tate's been using any excuse to touch me, as if he's determined to prove that he *can* affect me.

'Excuse my manners,' says the captain. 'You must be Tate's fiancée. Congratulations to the both of you. I'll be sure to get one of the stewards to bring you down some champagne. Is there anything else I can get you?'

'We're all good, but thank you.'

'The pleasure is all mine. Actually, would you mind signing something for my boy.'

'Not a problem.' Tate whips out a sharpie to sign the baseball cap the captain has produced from inside his jacket pocket. 'What's his name?'

'He's Josh. He's ten and he loves his football.'

Tate signs a personal message and pushes it back into the captain's hand. 'You be sure to tell him I said hi,' he says. 'Do you want to take a picture to give him?'

'That would be awesome,' says the captain, whipping out his phone. He takes a couple of selfies with Tate before pocketing his phone. 'So, Tate, what do you think of the Snakes offensive...' He proceeds to spout a load of incomprehensible football jargon, not in any hurry to move until one of the stewards approaches him and murmurs in his ear.

'Right. Right. Guess I'd better get this bird in the air.' He takes his leave.

The stewardess, another one, gives Tate a smile and leans over me. 'Is there anything I can get you, Mr Donaghue?'

'No, I'm all good thanks, Patti,' he says, reading her badge.

She lets out a little giggle and blushes. 'You let me know. Just use the call button situated above you.'

'Like he's never been on a plane before,' I intone under my breath.

She gives me a filthy look and saunters off.

'It's sad they think you're so incapable you need help all the time,' I say, and instantly regret sounding so bitchy.

'I'm very capable,' says Tate, lowering his voice to, what I'm rapidly coming to call in my head, his sex tone. Deliberate as I know it is, his low timbre still sends annoyingly gooey shivers rippling across my crazy nerve endings. All the hairs on my arm and the back of my neck stand to attention, flowing like sea anemones at the mercy of the current. 'Happy to show you how capable I can be.'

The cabin crew start the safety talk, demonstrating how to put a seatbelt on, but as usual barely any passengers are taking any notice of the standard spiel.

'Have you ever joined the Mile High Club?' Tate asks.

'Cliché much?' I splutter out a laugh and shake my head. 'Does that line ever work?'

'You'd be surprised,' he jokes, and I roll my eyes at his fulsome grin.

'Well, try it on someone else,' I suggest.

He grins at me. 'You're no fun.'

And, despite everything, I like his good-natured response. Tate is pretty easy to be with. For all his fame, he's self-deprecating and has always been able to laugh at himself when I take the piss.

'What *do* you do for fun?' he asks, surprising me because he's studying me as if he's genuinely interested.

'Jump out of planes when my neighbour gets really boring.' I give him a cheesy smile.

He laughs, before his eyes narrow and he gives me a considering stare. 'Have you ever jumped out of a plane?' There's a note of disbelief in his voice as if he's not quite sure whether I'm being serious. This is fun. I like keeping him on his toes.

'Yes, actually. I have.' There's a flash of surprise and awe on his face. And I'm ashamed to say, it goes to my head. I add. 'A few times.'

'What else can you do? Are you like a Navy Seal? You

know, can you hold your breath underwater for a really long time?'

I laugh. 'I'm in security, not *The Avengers*.'

I'm not sure he can handle what I can really do.

'You carry a gun. You ever killed anyone?'

I lift a shoulder. 'I'll take the fifth on that one.'

He looks in my eyes. 'What made you go down this route?'

I was lost and looking for purpose in life after I realised that you didn't love me the way I loved you.

He's probably not interested in that answer.

'Family business,' I say. 'My boss is my godfather.'

That much is true, although there's never been much familial relationship with Pennington. He was my father's best friend in the SAS. I didn't realise until I was older that my father had worked for MI6. At twenty-two, when the recruiter came knocking, I was ripe and ready. And I had a gaping big hole to fill where my heart had once been.

The cabin crew are doing the last safety checks before take-off and we fall silent. Hopefully, this conversation is over. It's a relatively short flight, but I'll have time to read the fire department report emailed over this morning on the damage to Tate's apartment. Luckily, solid, building fire regulations kept us safe and the firefighters arrived quickly and put out the blaze, which hadn't spread beyond the area around the door.

From what I can gather, the delivery boy was hijacked and the bag taken off him. The firebomb was small. Not designed to do much damage.

That puzzles me. Are these serious murder attempts or

menacing threats? Also, none of the attempts so far have been particularly well thought through.

Tate's phone buzzes and he glances at it. I can see it's a message from his dad. His jaw tightens and he switches the phone to airplane mode.

The plane taxis along the runway and I stare out of the window. I love everything about flying. Always have done. Although I'd far rather be in the cockpit at the controls because the thought of sitting idle for three hours is painful. Tate, sitting next to me in the window seat, leans back with his hands resting calmly on his knees, but every so often he rereads the message on his phone's screen, and a scowl darkens his face.

I lean towards him and whisper in his ear with a throaty purr. 'So how many times *have* you joined the Mile High Club?'

His eyes fly open. 'What?'

'Once, twice, three times?'

Tate stares at me as if he's trying to catch up.

I look him up and down. 'Yeah. I mean, how'd you fit? Those toilets are pretty cramped. Talk me through it. How do you manage?'

He's still staring at me. 'What?'

'You know.' I prod him and tilt my head. 'Do you stand? Like upright and hold her. I'm assuming it's a she. You've got the upper body strength, I guess. But your height, I don't know. It must be tight, I imagine. Don't you bang your elbows? Or get stuck between the door and the loo?' My eyes widen with sudden horror. 'And aren't you worried that door might fly open by accident. That would be one hell of a photo opportunity.'

Despite the obvious irritation brought on by whatever is in his dad's message, Tate cracks out a laugh. 'You've given this considerable thought.'

'A little.' I feel the slight lift of the plane. 'Or maybe the guy sits and the lady straddles. But then would there be enough room for your knees?' I lean down and assess his knees, patting them. 'I think you'd be too big.'

'Are we talking about airline toilet sex, or something else?' quips Tate with a smile. We're airborne now and he's breathing easier. The colour has returned to his knuckles.

'You didn't answer the question,' I say, pleased that I've taken his attention off the message from his dad.

'Which question, there were a slew of them there. Who knew you were so interested in my sex life.'

'I'm not, big guy. I was worried you were a nervous flyer.'

'I'm not the least bit afraid of flying,' he shoots back. 'I spend half my life on planes.' He narrows his gaze and surprises me with his next question.

'What are you afraid of?' he asks.

'Me?' I ask brightly. There are plenty of things I have a healthy fear of – it's what keeps me alive.

'That's a stalling tactic, if I ever I heard one, Lily Heath.'

'In my line of work, fear is always there. It keeps the adrenaline pumping. The day you don't feel fear is the day you don't come home.'

His eyes meet mine, and I feel like he can see right

through me. 'You'd have made a good lawyer or a politician,' he says with a half-smile. 'That was a neat avoidance of the question. I asked what you are afraid of, not what you fear. Technically, there's a difference. We all fear lots of things. But being afraid is different, it lingers long after a threat has gone.'

'Maybe you should be the lawyer, you're very good at semantics,' I tell him.

'Still ducking the question, Lily.'

I stare at him for a few seconds before I have to look away.

I'm afraid of falling in love. I'm scared of having my heart ripped out again.

The plane has levelled out and a new stewardess appears with two glasses of champagne. 'With compliments from the captain and all the crew. Congratulations on your engagement, Mr Donaghue.' Her eyes slide to the ridiculous diamond on my finger. 'Lovely ring,' she says and smiles at me. 'Someone has excellent taste.'

'She does,' says Tate, nodding at me. 'She chose me.'

I almost snort my recent sip of champagne out of my nose.

The woman grins and rolls her eyes. 'I'd say you're lucky to have her.'

I lift my glass towards the woman in sisterly solidarity.

Tate puts his hand on my knee. 'Yeah, she's special, she has to be to put up with me.'

I almost choke again as I recall him saying exactly these words eight years ago to a put-out mean-queen from the football groupie squad, who'd asked him what the heck he saw in me.

'I hope you'll be very happy together,' the stewardess says, before continuing up the aisle.

'I've realised there must be a lot of broken hearts out there, and a lot of ladies wanting to scratch my eyes out,' I say light-heartedly, because I don't actually care.

'Not really,' says Tate. 'I've always made it clear I'm not a relationship man. Three dates, max.'

'Seriously?' I have to ask. 'That's your rule.'

He actually has the grace to blush. 'It's not a rule but it's … a boundary. I don't have time for relationships. I focus on my game.'

'And do you tell the women you sleep with that they have a sell-by date? And is that before or after they get into bed with you?'

He raises an eyebrow at me. 'I'm not a slut, you know. I only sleep with women who know the score. I never lead anyone on. I'm the good guy. I'm honest with them. A lot of guys aren't. They take advantage of their fame and money to get sex whenever they want. I'm not like that.'

'What changed?' The bitter question pops out before I can stop it.

'What's that supposed to mean?'

If I say any more I might reveal that he broke *my* heart, and I'm not going to give him that power.

'I guess you have to be pretty dedicated to the game to get as far as you have.'

'Yeah, but it will all be worth it, when we lift the trophy and I have that ring on my finger.'

'And then what?' I ask.

'What do you mean?'

'What next? What's the next goal? More money? More fame?'

He frowns at me. 'I'm focused on the one goal at the moment. Plenty of time later for the future.'

I nod, but the question has stirred me more than it has him. What do I do next? What do I want? I've seen the close-knit team around Tate. He's got friends, allies and supporters. It makes me question what and who I've got in my life. It strikes me that I'm pretty aimless. Maybe lonely, too. My goals last as long as each mission. They're life and death, but if I wasn't leading those missions, someone else would be. My job is, by its very nature, expendable. It just happens that I haven't expired in the course of it so far. Dad and Alice might mourn me if I did, but they certainly won't miss me. You have to have someone in your life to miss them. My job doesn't allow anyone into my life … although, for the first time, I wonder if I chose it for that very reason.

———

I realise trying to keep Tate incognito is going to be difficult, even with a baseball hat and dark glasses, his height and breadth makes him stand out in a crowd.

As we're waiting in the baggage hall, a young man approaches us.

'You Tate Donaghue?'

'Sorry man, I wish,' says Tate, lapsing into a very credible southern drawl. 'If I had his money.'

'Sure,' says the guy in baggy jeans and an outsize T-shirt, giving him a disappointed shrug and backing off.

Maybe we'll get away with this.

Winston has arranged a car for us, and there's a black-suited chauffer who's almost as wide as he is tall waiting for us bearing a sign that says 'Lily English', as we'd agreed. My name has been plastered all over the tabloids and internet, so I wasn't taking any chances on any eagle-eyed fans spotting it.

'That's us,' I say to the man.

'Come right this way, ma'am.' He beams.

We follow him out to a huge limousine and he takes care of our luggage, putting it in the trunk, as I remember to call it, and we slide into the back seats.

'So far so good,' I say.

'Lily, relax. No one knows we're here.'

'Apart from the captain, the air crew, neighbouring passengers,' I say. 'Including a well-known senator.'

'I don't think he'll say much.' Tate shrugs. 'Let's just say that lady he was not-so subtly groping certainly wasn't his wife.'

'Hmm.' Even so, through our tinted windows I scan the other cars around us.

The driver shuffles into the front seat and he looks in the rear-view mirror, his eyes going as wide as saucers as recognition kicks in.

'That you, the Don?' he asks.

'Shh,' says Tate. 'Me and my lady are trying to grab some quiet time before the media circus begins. I'd be grateful if you didn't mention who you had in your car for a few days when the rest of the team gets here.'

'Sure thing. But can I say it's a real honour to have you

here.'

'Thank you, sir. What's your name?'

'Benji. Mr Donaghue.'

'Please call me Tate. How long you been doing this job, Benji?'

'Nigh on six years. I get to meet all sorts of folks. I had Sandra Bullock in that very seat, a few weeks back.'

And just like that, Tate engages him in easy conversation. By the time we arrive at the hotel Benji and Tate are fast friends and Tate has handed over his baseball cap – signed by the ever-present Sharpie.

It gives me considerable food for thought. In his twenties, cocksure and arrogant, Tate had been a big deal on campus, doing pretty much as he'd pleased, encouraged by his overbearing father. I smile to myself. I'd made him work hard to earn that first date. He'd been so damn confident I'd fall at his feet, just like all the other girls.

Chapter Fifteen

TATE

Nine years earlier

'Hey Tate, great game.' A beer bottle taps mine and Cindi Bartlett raises it to her glossy pink mouth, giving me a long, lingering look before she sucks the neck of the bottle right between her lips and then lets it slip out with an audible pop.

'Thanks.' I grin at her, and I raise my brows very slightly. She grins back and this time she circles the opening of the bottle with her tongue. I like that Cindi is a girl who knows what she wants and goes out to get it. Despite standing in a circle of people, she's eying me like she'd like to lick up every last drop of me. There's no game-playing with her. My dick hardens. Having had a couple of rounds between the sheets with her, I'm not averse to a further bout.

'What are you doing later?' I ask, not worried if anyone hears. Not that anyone does, because everyone's baying at each other over the loud music, swilling beer and partying. We've won another game. We're returning heroes.

She lays a hand on my arm. 'Taking you home.'

'Just so you know, I've got training in the morning.'

She shrugs, clearly a little disappointed. This is my shorthand for 'I'm not staying over'. This will be our third hook up, but I reckon I've given her a clear warning. She should know by now that I'm not interested in a girlfriend, or anyone who's going to tie me down. It's common knowledge.

'Sure,' she says and knocks back the rest of her bottle. 'I'm going to dance. See you later.'

I nod and watch her walk off, her hips shimmying in the tight white denim skirt that skims her ass cheeks.

'Lucky bastard,' says Andy, one of my teammates and a good friend.

'I can't help it.'

'You treat them like shit, you know that,' he says disapprovingly. He's been with Joanie since high school. She comes up every other weekend. To be fair, she's great and I really like her, it's just not my scene.

'Everyone knows what I'm like. I don't make any promises.'

'I wish someone would make you work harder for it,' he says. 'I'd like to see you fall head over heels.'

'Never happening,' I tell him, because it won't. 'I don't believe in true love and all that crap. Love isn't real. It's some jumbled-up emotion that vanishes when things get tough or difficult.'

Andy claps me on the back. 'Another beer. It's your turn.'

I wheel away towards the bar, it's hard work shuffling through the crowded bar. I spot an opening to my left and change direction to take advantage of the clear yards of space, at the same moment I bowl into someone, a woman, and her full plastic cup of draft beer flies up in the air and she goes sprawling across the floor.

I try to grab her to break her fall, but she lands with a heavy thump. I immediately step forward. 'Hey, are you all right? I'm sorry.'

I crouch down to help her up and she shakes a cloud of blonde hair out of her face, indignant blue eyes glaring at me, her long limbs spread-eagled across the floor. She's wearing a short plaid skirt and a little white crop top revealing a tanned and toned midriff. My mouth goes a little dry.

'Bloody hell,' she snaps. 'You must be a ball player.'

Ouch. It doesn't sound like she's impressed. Most people usually are. I throw her my best aw-shucks smile 'You got me. Nice accent by the way.'

She huffs out a breath, blowing away the last few strands of soft blonde wavy hair covering her face. Pretty. Real pretty. Eyes sparkling with humour and something else. Pretty pink lips shaped in a pretty mouth. Oh yes, she's pretty, even though she's glaring at me like she'd like to shoot fireballs at me.

'The game finished an hour ago. Didn't you get the memo?'

Shit, she's really cute, and feisty with it, but that breathy

British accent socks me right in the gut. She grasps my hand and whoah! Yeah, just static. I pull her up, already trying to work out how quickly I can get her into bed.

Our eyes meet and I see hers darken a tad. Did she feel it, too?

'Hey,' I say. 'Are you okay? Did I hurt you?'

She shakes her head although she's rubbing at her elbow.

I set her back on her feet and, although her build is slender, delicate – like her arms could snap like twigs – she's much taller than I realised. She's got to be a least five-eleven in bare feet. Now she seems a little stand-offish, and I wonder if I misunderstood that five-thousand-volt jolt of sexual awareness, but then she licks her lips and I'm a goner. I smile at her and something deepens in those almost deep brown eyes of hers. Yep, we've got a connection and we're broadcasting on the same frequency.

'You took quite a tumble.' I take her arm and turn it to get a better look. Her skin is smooth and tanned. I can't help sliding my fingers up to the edge of the bruise which is already blooming on her soft skin.

'Shit, I'm really sorry. I should have been watching where I was going.' I stroke her arm very gently because I can't help myself. 'You should get some arnica on that. I have some in my room.' I will swear to my dying breath that that was not a come-on. I just hated to see that I'd hurt her and left a mark on her.

'I'm sure ice will be equally effective,' she says with a smile.

'I owe you a drink at the very least, and I can grab you some ice. Can I get you another beer?'

She raises an eyebrow.

'Are you on your own?' I glance around in case there's some guy about to come barrelling around the corner laying claim to his girl. I might be a lot of things, but I don't cheat, I don't poach and I'm honest about my allergy to peanuts … and my attitude to commitment. Good-time girls apply here. Anyone else, I'm bad news and that's the way I like it. I don't have room in my life for anything permanent. Football is my life and I plan to be top of the draft picks next year. I'm happy for a minor distraction but I'm not in the market for anything more than that right now or, let's face it, ever. My parents didn't make it, I don't want to go through that misery.

'I'd love a fresh beer, given you sent my last one flying when I was barely a sip in,' she says, her voice deep and smoky. 'Thanks.'

'You're British?' I say, stating the obvious.

'I am. You're American?'

'What gave it away?'

She laughs, exactly like she's supposed to. I hold out my hand. 'Tate.' My introduction is a formality, because pretty much everyone knows me on campus.

There's a slight hesitation as she swallows. 'Lily.' Then she shakes my hand. My old man always says you can tell a lot about someone from their handshake. Lily's handshake is at complete odds with her appearance: firm, no nonsense and businesslike. We could have been completing a merger, rather than doing the first dance towards bed. Because that's where we're going to end up tonight, of that I'm pretty sure. The electricity sparking between us could light up the Empire State Building.

We walk over to the bar together, and even though I'm not the first in line, one of the servers catches my eye and immediately comes over. 'Hey Tate, what can I get you?'

I place the order for our beers, and also ask for some ice and a towel to put it in.

'Coming right up, Tate.' The bartender doesn't hesitate.

'Does that happen all the time to you?' Lily asks.

'What?'

'That,' she says, indicating the fan-boy server.

I shrug. 'I guess.'

Our beer arrives and I pay for it, then I wrap the ice in the towel and cup it to her elbow.

'You don't need to do that.'

'I'm not sure you can manage holding it and your beer, whereas I can do both.'

She considers me. 'True.'

'How's your ass?' I ask with a suggestive wink.

'It's fine, thank you very much,' she says, rolling her eyes and smiling.

She's got a smart mouth and the measure of me. And I like it. I like her. A lot. Although she isn't giving anything away.

'So, what do you do…?' There's a pause. Damn, for the life of me, I can't remember her name. She smirks at me and doesn't supply it.

There's a brief silence and then she takes pity on me. 'I'm here on a cheerleading scholarship.'

'I haven't seen you around before.'

She smiles again, like she knows something I don't. 'I've been here since the beginning of term.' The way she says it makes me think there's a private joke I'm missing.

'My loss,' I say, with a flirtatious smile.

With a very direct look straight into my eyes, she says. 'Yes, it is. But you can't win them all. My elbow's feeling better.' She steps away. 'Thanks for the beer, although you did owe me.' With that she starts to walk off.

'Hey…' I call after her, still not able to remember her name. 'Fancy a d—'

'Nice meeting you, Tate Donaghue.' She lifts her beer in salute and walks away. She knew my name all along. Amused I watch her go.

'Don't tell me she blew you off,' says Andy, coming over. 'And where's my beer?'

'Shit, sorry. I got … distracted.'

'I wouldn't have thought she was your type,' says Andy.

'Why not?'

'One, she didn't fall at your feet—'

'Actually, she literally did.'

'And two, her tits aren't big enough.'

I turn back but Lily's disappeared into the crowd. I hadn't even noticed her breasts. I'd been too busy trying to read those smiles of hers and trying to keep up with her quick-witted teasing.

'Lily,' I murmur as her name suddenly pops back into my head.

'Lily?'

'Yeah, English chick.'

'Oh, I know the one. I think she's in Stacey's dorm.'

'Is she?' I arch a brow in interest. Andy laughs and digs me in the ribs.

'She turned you down, hound dog. I'd say Cindi's a sure thing.'

Suddenly the thought of sleeping with Cindi doesn't seem quite so appealing. All I can think of is Lily and those long limbs of hers wrapped around me.

'Know anything else about her?' I ask. Stacey is his lab partner. Besides being a ball player, Andy has plenty of smarts and is a science nerd.

'Nope, and if you've got any sense, you'll forget about her. She's not going to give it up. From what Stacey says, she's pretty innocent.'

'Is that so?' I swig my beer. Let's see how long that lasts…

A couple of hours later, I'm sneaking into the girl's dorm. If I get caught I'll be in so much trouble. Definitely suspended from the team for a game, if not two. But for some reason I want to impress the indifferent Lily. It's not just that she's the first girl that I've not been able to charm at the get-go. It's that sizzle between us, which I know I didn't imagine. The corridor is quiet, and I pray I don't get caught as I creep down with the torch from my phone trying to find number twenty-one.

When I find the right room, I carefully tie a plastic bag to the handle and try to imagine her reaction when she finds the tube of arnica there in the morning.

Chapter Sixteen

LILY

Present Day

The car pulls up outside the hotel and I frown. There's a crowd gathered around the lobby entrance. Whether they're here for Tate or not, his presence is soon going to be public knowledge if we get out of the car now.

'Is there a back entrance? A service door?' I ask Benji.

'Sure,' says Benji, but before he can put the car into reverse, someone spots the limousine, and the crowd's attention is pulled towards us, a couple of photographers leading the pack as they charge towards us.

Benji calmly puts the car into reverse, backing away from the zealous paps, and takes us back onto the road. Thank God for tinted windows.

'They don't know it's me,' says Tate. 'I could be anyone.'

'You could,' I say, but I'm not so sure.

'The back entrance is down on the right,' says Tate.

'How do you know that?' I ask him.

'I've been here before. If our usual hotel is full, the girl in travel books us in here.'

'What?' I slap my forehead. Am I working with complete idiots? The whole point of coming here was to hide from people. 'Why in God's name didn't anyone tell me that before?'

'No one knows we're in New Orleans already.'

'Apart from a whole planeload of people.'

He leans over and pats me on my knee. 'Don't worry, Lily. I've got you to protect me.'

I grit my teeth and have to forcibly stop myself from grinding them into dust.

Benji drops us off and unhappily allows us to wheel our own cases into the back entrance, which is currently filled with metal cages of dirty laundry.

We wend our way down several corridors before finally coming to a big fire door.

'The lobby's through there,' says Tate.

'You stay here, while I check things out.'

To my relief, the lobby is quiet now. Although there are a few people hanging about, a couple with cameras around their necks.

I walk up to reception. My hair's in a ponytail, and I'm wearing jeans, a T-shirt, a casual jacket and sunglasses and no one looks at me twice. They're all on the lookout for a six-foot ball player.

I check in and then explain the predicament to the receptionist. Luckily, the service door is close to the lifts, which are on the opposite side of the lobby and away from reception. I figure I can get Tate from the service area into the lift relatively easily. It's not ideal, but I seem to be up against the odds all the time.

I take my case and leave it by the lift and then go back to Tate. 'The lift is out on the right. I'll text one character when the lift is here. Come straight out without drawing attention to yourself. I'll take your case.'

'Yes, ma'am,' says Tate.

I sigh and haul his case out into the lobby and over to the bank of elevators.

I press the button and wait. It takes a good couple of minutes for the arrow to indicate that an elevator is on its way. When the number two slides past, I text Tate.

The doors open as he comes to stand next to me. We have to wait for a whole group of people to disembark and we're about to step in, when suddenly there's frenzied barking and a little dog is jumping around Tate's heels.

'I don't believe it,' says Tate as the dog dances at the entrance to the elevator preventing the doors from closing. 'Shoo, Teddy, shoo.'

The dog's yips increase in volume, its plume of a tail waving with ecstatic excitement.

Everyone in the lobby is staring at us and then, someone who I recognise as Winston's wife – Pammie Radstock – squeals from the reception desk. 'Tate! Tate Donaghue.'

With Pammie is a tall, Scandinavian-looking guy, whose physique marks him out as some kind of athlete.

'Hey, Pammie,' says Tate, having successfully disentangled the dog from his feet. 'Fancy seeing you here.'

Chapter Seventeen

TATE

Lily is not happy – a very long way from it. Her shoulders are hunched up by her ears and she's stabbing at the keypad on her phone like she wants to kill it.

'Hey, it's not that bad. No one knows what room I'm in.'

'That's true. The room was booked under an assumed name. They only need to burn the whole hotel down this time.'

'You're such a drama queen,' I tease, trying to get her to lighten up.

She rocks her head back and glances up at the ceiling. 'Or they could set off the fire alarm, wait for everyone to evacuate and shoot you.' She nods. 'Yeah, that's what I'd do.'

'Well, at least I don't need to worry about a bad guy abseiling down the building and shooting me through a window. I can rest easy.'

She sighs. 'Habit. I always try and put myself in the

other guy's shoes. Although I have to say, whoever is trying to kill you is seriously incompetent.'

'And that's supposed to make me feel better?'

She winces, her brow furrowing and paces over to the window. She's like a big cat in a cage.

'Why don't you sit down and relax?' I suggest.

'Good idea,' she says with a touch of sarcasm. 'What do you suggest we do? Game of chess? Tiddlywinks?'

'I need to go to the gym. Unless you've forgotten, I've got quite a big game on, but you've probably put the kibosh on that.'

'I mean, it's probably not a great idea,' she says, and I can see she's as frustrated by this situation as I am.

'Come on.' I'm frustrated. I can't take my foot off the pedal now. I need to be stronger and faster than ever. 'Surely, we've got a few hours on whoever it is. They're probably still in New York, don't you think.'

'I don't know.'

'No one knew we were coming apart from a few people on the team. Even if it's got out that I'm here, it's going to take someone half a day to get here. A hot, sweaty bout in the gym would do us both the power of good. If there's anyone in there, they'll ignore us.'

She bites her lip.

'I promise I'll do what I'm told, and you can bring your gun.'

It's fascinating watching her weigh up the risks.

'Okay, but you have to do exactly what I tell you.'

'I'm liking the sound of this more and more,' I say with a suggestive grin, because I don't want her to know about the doubts that are circling like vultures. They're always there at the back of my mind. What if I don't train hard enough? What if I let the team down because I didn't put the hours in? What if I could do better?

She ignores me. 'Be ready in five minutes in case I change my mind. And don't forget the doctor said light resistance.'

Lily goes full-on SWAT team on me, as we go down in the elevator for three floors. Then she insists on us taking the last two flights of stairs, checking the stairwell before I'm allowed to set foot in it. Clad in black Lycra, she seems more ninja-princess warrior than ever and I can't help giving her cute ass more than a second look as she walks down the stairs ahead of me.

The gym, at three in the afternoon, is as empty as I was banking on. We stroll in and I head straight for the weights.

'I'm going to go on the running machine,' she says.

I look over at the set of treadmills, side by side. 'Think I'll join you. Run a bit of frustration off.'

'You and me both,' she says dryly and marches over to the equipment.

I can tell Lily's fit from the shape of her body in the Lycra crop top and leggings, which highlight the muscles of her long legs and hug her toned ass. I'd love to grab a handful and slide my fingers to cup that roundness.

I set up the machine next to her and start my own steady run. She sets a fast pace, but I'm running along beside her, matching her stride for stride. She's gorgeous to watch, fluid in motion and supremely confident, head held high and facing forward with quiet determination. I can see the rise and fall of her steady breath. She's completely in control of herself. She doesn't so much as acknowledge me, she is fearless and focused. I wonder what happened to her to make her become this composed, isolated woman. When I knew her, she was warm, vivacious and funny. She's still as outspoken. One of the things I always liked best about her.

We run in tandem for about twenty minutes. Tension I wasn't aware of has released my shoulders and the slight knot in my stomach has eased. She changes the pace and slows to a walk and I match the speed.

'That all you got?' I ask.

She gives me the sort of look that says, 'pleeease'.

'I've got plenty more in the tank, buddy,' she says, her eyebrows lifting in amusement. 'Want to race?' She throws me a sassy side-long, shit-eating grin.

'I'll beat you,' I say.

She gives my body a slow appraisal. 'You think so.'

'Challenge accepted,' I say. I'm known for my speed on the field.

'First to two kilometres?'

'Okay,' I say, as if it's no great distance. I run most days but it's more of a conditioning thing than fitness training.

It takes us a minute to work out the detail. We agree that we'll set the distance on the treadmill to a 2.1K start, which gives us time to get to our running speed with the race starting properly, as soon as we pass the first 0.1K.

'What's the furthest you've ever run?' she asks settling

in with a gentle trot and gradually increasing the pace on the display, 'apart from forty yards.'

The forty-yard dash required by scouts for the teams was an area I excelled in. I recorded the fastest time the year of my draft.

'I can run plenty more than that. What's the furthest you've run?' I ask, genuinely interested because she's in good shape and, belatedly, I remember that she did some track-and-field at Radley.

With a nonchalant smile she says, 'Done a couple of marathons. And an ultra 50K. Did a triathlon last year.'

'Stamina, then. But have you got speed?'

'You're about to find out.'

She ups her pace now, and I increase mine to match hers and then we hit our starting point.

I glance over and she's comfortable, taking long smooth breaths, her arms pumping. She's gorgeous to watch. Her technique is perfect, her feet seem to bounce lightly on the treadmill, and she has an impressive economy of movement along with laser-focused determination – as if she can see the finishing line. I can't help thinking she looks like a goddess, all sleek motion and determination. It's hot. Seriously hot. I continue to match her pace, and for a while we run in tandem. Then she tosses a grin my way and speeds up, for fuck's sake. I've been too busy watching her instead of concentrating on my running, and although I'm faster and stronger than her, I do need to put in some effort.

I up my pace with ease, striding out and feeling the kick in my muscles. My feet thunder on the treadmill and suddenly I'm in the zone, running hard.

Next to me, Lily notches things up and her pace quickens.

The race is on, and I'm surprised that I'm having to work this hard. She's fast and strong but I'm faster and stronger. I kind of like it that she thinks she could even beat me. Even so, I'm not going to give her an inch and I hit the 2K finish well before her.

Shit, though. I very nearly blew it. Too busy thinking with my dick instead of my head. Which is exactly why I should be exercising caution around Lily Heath. I've got a game in a couple of days. That should be my focus. But there's no rule that says I can't wind her up a little. I'm in need of a bit of entertainment and she's the only person around.

Her treadmill starts to slow, moving into the cool-down zone, thirty seconds after mine, I shoot her a cocky grin, wondering how much fun I can have with her.

'What do I get for winning?' I ask as she slows to a walk, her forehead covered in a light sheen, tiny blonde curls plastered to her neck and forehead. I look down at her snug leggings before working my way up to her mouth, which is a mistake because I was trying to tease her, but my body did not get the memo and blood is rushing to a place it has no place going to.

'You can buy me dinner sometime,' she says with a dismissive curl of her lips and grabs one of the gym towels to wipe her face.

'Did you just ask me out on a date?' I ask, my chest still heaving, sweat dripping down my face.

'No, dinner. A very expensive d…'

Her voice falters as I strip off my T-shirt.

I can't help the jolt of satisfaction when her eyes rove over my hard-won abs and broad pecs.

For a moment she's gratifyingly silent, sending an immediate message to my dick which jumps to attention. She raises her arms to tug at her ponytail. The movement draws my attention to her high, firm breasts. Her nipples, which I've been trying to avoid staring at, are standing proud through the fabric of her sports top. She catches the line of my gaze and I swear her nipples tighten a little more. We stare at each other.

Everything inside tells me I could reach out and cup her breast, kiss that hot moist mouth and caress her through the Lycra of those skintight leggings. But I know I can't.

Despite this, the words spill out. 'Do you know what I want to do right now?' I ask, my voice low with lust, even though I know I shouldn't be doing this.

'No,' she replies, her voice tight. 'And I don't want to know.' She holds my gaze, her chin lifted a little. Her cool words should make me reign things in, but the competitive side of me wants to see how far I can push her before she cracks and loses her cool with me.

'I want to put my hand between your legs and find out how wet you are down there.'

'Do you?' she asks, before adding with a haughty stare, 'and you think that's appropriate behaviour?'

I shake my head, but part of me is resentful. Doesn't she feel this pent-up lust, too? I want to find out if she's as wedded to being as professional as she claims. I haven't forgotten that night in my kitchen.

She bends to tighten one of the laces on her sneakers and I have to push it one more time.

'But I can't decide between that or reaching out my hand and teasing those nipples poking out through your shirt, like you always used to love me doing.'

I hear her little gasp and I grin.

'So ... what do you say?'

And then the fucking door bangs behind us and a middle-aged guy enters the gym.

Lily expels a heavy breath. 'I say you need a shower. A cold one.'

Ponytail bouncing, she strides ahead of me towards the door, giving the other guy a nod.

Thankfully, our room is a suite and we've got an en suite bathroom each. I step into a cool shower and turn the temperature down degree by degree. It might reduce the swelling, but not the desire and the pent-up, itchy, scratchy feeling that makes me want to run another couple of miles. Although I was winding her up downstairs, it showed me how easily Lily Heath could distract me. I might still find her as sexy as hell, but I need to focus. Spending this much time in close proximity with her for the next few days is going to be a challenge. I can't afford to give less than one hundred per cent to my game training and my mental attitude. At least when practice starts in a couple of days' time, I can burn off some of this energy.

Chapter Eighteen

LILY

I might have been outvoted on this recreational trip, but I'm vetoing the convertible sports car, even though I'm very tempted. Tate has persuaded Winston's team that he'll be perfectly safe going out of the city with his bodyguard. As they're paying my wages, I have no choice but to agree.

'It'll be fun,' he says, his eyes twinkling.

'If I had my way, you'd be doing lengths in the pool,' I retort.

'I hate swimming, and I did four hours' training this morning. I deserve a break.'

Although I'm still feeling put out that I was overruled, I am equally relieved that I don't have to be holed up in the hotel room with Tate and his pheromones, which are pumping out at full blast. Last night, I got myself off within two minutes of getting into bed, but it wasn't enough. And I'm clearly not the only one feeling like this. The sexual tension is getting to Tate, too; it's making us both as skittish as colts saddled for the first time.

'Wait,' says the rental car sales guy, Darryl – who I swear is no more than twelve years old – his hands faltering with excitement when Tate hands over his driving licence. 'You're The Don! Tate Donaghue. Wow man. Wow. Just wow.' The tips of his ears poking through his sandy hair turn bright red.

Tate gives him what I now recognise as his modest, 'aw-shucks-I'm just a regular Joe' smile.

'Hi, Darryl.' He puts out a hand and shakes the guy's hand. 'Nice to meet you.'

'Doncha want anything fancier? I mean … you got the…' He falters to a stop.

Tate shakes his head and leans forward to say in a conspiratorial tone. 'My fiancée doesn't want us drawing attention to ourselves. She wants me all to herself.' He winks at the young man, whose eyes widen as he nods in collusion.

'Sure, man.' Darryl's head is still nodding. 'I understand.'

I highly doubt it – he has that wide-eyed innocence that suggests he's never got past first base.

'Now, how about you recommend a place we could drive to, where we can get ourselves a decent lunch?' asks Tate, and young Darryl is only too delighted to be of service. His face lights up at the prospect of helping 'The Don'.

I wander off, leaving them to their conversation, glad to escape the little glow of gooey warmth I get when I see Tate being so damn sweet to his fans. I don't want him to be nice. It's bad enough that my body is betraying me, I don't want him to have any redeeming features. It's getting harder and harder to see him as the hard-hearted, goal-orientated football player who chose the game over me.

Ten minutes later, Tate is behind the wheel and driving us out of the city. There are times you have to pick your battles, and letting him drive seemed an easy compromise after I'd put the kibosh on his convertible wet dream. He's a good driver, confident and relaxed, not shouting at the other drivers or pushing the gas and then braking constantly, which means I can relax and enjoy the scenery. Principally, my view of him, because we're still downtown. I can't help it, my eyes are constantly drawn to his handsome profile. Maybe we should have gone for the open-top, after all. In this confined space, I'm hyper aware of him. The dark hairs on his arm resting nonchalantly on the centre console so close to mine. In a long-sleeved white Henley, which emphasises his tan, and the jeans moulded to those strong, muscular thighs, he looks good enough to strip.

Tate has plugged something into the satnav. Jean Lafitte.

'Who or what is that?' I ask.

'It's a small town, named after a notorious pirate who made good when he did his bit for the army during the Revolution – that would be the one where we kicked you guys out.' Tate turns sideways and gives me a cocky grin.

'It was a long time ago,' I quip. 'I'd have thought you'd have got over it by now.'

'This guy was a bad guy and operated in the Barataria

Bay area, and that's where we're headed. Easy drive and, according to Darryl, we can't get lost.'

'Promises, promises,' I say.

'Of course, I forgot you're an ace navigator, too.'

'My dad taught me how to read a map and use a compass at a pretty early age. It was around the first time he dumped me on the moor and told me to find my way home.'

'Jeez. Why didn't you talk more about your nuts upbringing before?' Tate asks.

'Because it didn't occur to me at that age that it *was* nuts. Anyway, you can hardly talk.'

'Me? What do you mean?' Tate raises an eyebrow in genuine bemusement.

I stare at him. Really, he's not aware?

'Well, your upbringing after your mom left was hardly normal.'

'You're kidding me, right.'

'No, Tate. I'm not.' I think about elaborating, but it doesn't seem like he's ready to hear it. Not just now. It was obvious from what I overheard at the stadium at the training session, that Tate's dad is still very much in the picture.

'So why Jean Lafitte?' I ask, to change the subject. To be honest I'm looking forward to a day out and the sun is shining. After the winter temperatures of New York, New Orleans is positively balmy. I could almost be on holiday, although it's been a while since I've had one of those. I'd forgotten what it's like to have nothing to do, no place to be.

Normally, my life is run on a tight schedule with strict parameters.

'According to our Darryl, they have some great seafood restaurants. Proper Cajun food. I thought we could stop for lunch,' Tate says.

'Now you're talking my language. I've always wanted to know what gumbo is.'

'It's good, like a stew, but there's also Jambalaya, which you should try. Or some Cajun prawns.'

My mouth is watering already.

Once we get out of the city, the roads quieten, although there's plenty of traffic on the highway. I check the mirrors periodically.

Because of all the water in the marshland area there are few main roads, so navigation, as Darryl promised, is pretty straightforward. We arrive in Jean Lafitte in just over half an hour.

We park up and Tate glances over at me, and his expression is that of a kid just let out of school for the summer. I guess he's under quite a lot of pressure at the moment, what with the upcoming game and the recent threats, and I am determined to be as laid-back as I can be today, realising that this is a rare taste of freedom for him.

'Now what?' I ask because we haven't exactly planned this trip. Spontaneity doesn't feature much in my life. 'Your call.'

He lifts his shoulders. 'An adventure. We're in pirate country.' His eyes twinkle with irrepressible fun.

'An adventure?' I tease, because I'm amused by this

boyish side of him. Even when we were together there weren't that many times when we kicked back like this. There was always training, classes and study to fit in. Today feels positively decadent.

'Obviously, it's not that much of an adventure for you because you're probably used to hiking through the jungle with a knife in your mouth and whip in one hand,' Tate teases. 'Ducking poison arrows.'

I laugh. 'I think you're muddling me up with Indiana Jones.'

'Nah, please let me have my Lara Croft fantasy.'

'As long as you don't expect me to wrestle an alligator or anything,' I say.

We smile at each other and suddenly it all seems so easy and natural. We're having a day out.

'Visitor Centre?' suggests Tate.

'Good plan.' We follow the signpost towards the sprawling one-storey wooden building, with a white picketed veranda, walking side by side like a real couple. I have to admit to feeling that little frisson of excitement, with a new place to explore and with someone else, for a change. I haven't felt it since I went to Europe the year after I graduated from university, visiting cities like Paris, Berlin, Prague and Budapest – as well as the amazing beaches in Croatia and the lakes of Slovenia. I travel a lot, but I never get to see much. It strikes me Tate is probably the same.

'When was the last time you took a holiday?' I ask. 'And where did you go?'

'What, now you're my hairdresser?' teases Tate.

'No. Just making conversation. Pretend you believe I'm interested.'

He rolls his eyes. 'I'm always travelling. When I'm not, I like to stay home, either in Austin or New York.'

'So, which is your real home?'

'They both are. Mainly Austin during the season. New York when I'm here. And it's convenient for travelling. I can do a layover if I'm travelling long-distance.'

'You must have a hell of a lot of air miles,' I observe, 'if you can keep an apartment in New York.'

'I earn a hell of a lot of money.'

I look down at the huge ring on my finger. 'So you do. Apparently, I'm marrying you for your money and you're marrying me for my title.'

'Your dad still a duke?'

'Yeah, until he dies,' I reply. My aristocratic background works well in some ways and not so in others. I play up the socialite Lady Lily, so that people don't see past the façade. Very useful in close-protection work, like now.

'Hang on. I'm marrying you for a title.'

'Yes, a genius brain at one of the tabloids has worked out that if we had a baby boy, a male Donaghue, he would be the fifteenth Duke of Landsfforde. Don't tell me you haven't seen the composite pic in the *Daily Planet* of a baby-you wearing a crown?'

'Pretty sure the *Daily Planet* was in *Superman*.'

I nudge him in the ribs. 'Okay smarty pants. I don't know what it was called but I saw the piece in a paper at a news kiosk at the airport.'

'I never read those things. Most of it they make up. If I

read half the stuff that's printed about me, I'd spend my life chasing my tail or trying to find the two dicks I supposedly have.'

'Enough said.'

The visitor centre is busy with a long line of other tourists either waiting to or talking to the desk clerks. Both Tate and I are quite content to wander around scanning the brochures and maps.

'Fancy the Wetland Trace?' asks Tate, picking up a leaflet and waving it at me. 'It's a boardwalk through the swamp. There are a couple of different routes we can take.'

'Lead on,' I say, giving the information a cursory glance. It sounds exactly what we both need. Some physical activity to burn off some of this restrained, jumpy energy.

It doesn't take us long to find the boardwalk, which is almost deserted, and we amble along the wooden boards a metre above the water. The hushed silence is made less oppressive by the birdsong filtering through the gloomy swamp cypresses with their tattered-rag foliage. A dart of colour catches both our attention, and we see a bright purple-blue bird with a bright red beak land on one of the logs nearby. We watch it for a little while before it takes flight again. As we keep walking, we see spindly white egrets flying with elegance and blue herons while the more solid pelicans fly past with a great rush and wash of wings.

'Alligator,' says Tate pointing. He's right. There, sprawled along a log just above the water line, is a long scaly body with what looks to me like a very smug smile. Although to be honest, it seems unbothered by us and reminds me of an old man sitting, whiling his time away in the sun. Next to him, a huge turtle is balanced on the same log. They both seem indifferent to each other. It all seems very laid-back.

'Glad we came?' asks Tate as we saunter along and he checks over his shoulder at the deserted boardwalk. 'No bad guys.'

'No bad guys,' I agree.

'Must be hard work being on your guard all the time.'

'No harder than always having to train and watch your food intake and think about your next game.'

'Not hard if you love what you do,' he says. 'It's everything I always wanted.'

'Yeah, don't I know it,' I mutter under my breath, bitterness seeping around the edges of my words.

Thankfully, Tate's attention is caught by the sudden movement of the alligator slithering into the water and I'm not sure if he didn't hear me or has no response.

***

Grease drips down my chin, but I don't care. Because these are the best damn shrimps I've ever had in my life.

The crowded restaurant is on the edge of the bayou, and we were lucky to get a seat. In fact, if the server hadn't recognised Tate we might well have been turned away.

He has the usual effect on the wait staff, who bob up and down every five minutes making sure he's got everything. But as usual, he's completely charming and natural with all of them, even the elderly waitress who insists on prodding his biceps and making sure they're real.

Tate leans over and swipes at the side of my mouth, but the quick move appears to be in the friend zone as far as he's concerned, for which I'm truly grateful. This morning in the hotel room, I was worried that I was going to spontaneously combust if I so much as brushed past him, but thankfully being out in the open air has given me a bit of breathing space. I'm still conscious of him, but I've been able to relax a little. It's like I'm with Tate the person and not Tate the footballer. Although that brings its own challenge. Far too many flashbacks of the time we spent together on campus, in that sultry honeymoon period where he first told me he loved me. The memories make me mad at myself. How did I get it so wrong? He'd been so convincing. We'd talked about the future – laughable, I realise now, because he never had any intention of us staying together.

'You still with me?' asks Tate suddenly with a frown.

'Er… Yes. Sorry, enjoying the food. It's so good.'

'Certainly is.' Like me he has his napkin tucked in the collar of his T-shirt.

'I need to give Darryl a good tip when we return to the car. This was a great suggestion.'

I nod in agreement.

'What time do we have to return it?'

'By eight this evening. The rest of the team fly in the day after tomorrow, and after that we'll travel as a team and have police escorts taking us to and from the stadium – and all the other places we have to be.'

We spend the rest of the meal talking about all the events that are coming up in the next week to celebrate the game. Music events. Press previews. Gala dinners. Plus, training and strategic planning.

By the time we leave the restaurant it's after three, so we decide to continue south to the next town and visit the harbour there before meandering slowly back to the city.

I hope it is slow, because suddenly I really don't want this day to end.

Chapter Nineteen

LILY

When we pull out of the car park, I notice a white SUV swinging out behind us. I watch it for a little while, but given there is only one road out of town and everyone else is headed the same way, I'm not overly worried. Before long I've lost sight of it behind a stream of other cars all travelling along the highway.

We spend a little time on the harbour in a cute town called Belleton, where we watch an airboat crossing the channel before stopping for a takeout coffee. A couple of people eye Tate as if they're trying to figure out why he seems familiar, but we don't linger.

From there we get back into the car and leave the main road, travelling on some little backwater roads, crisscrossing channels of water, skirting swamps and circling the edges of lakes. There's water everywhere, reflecting the low sun that is starting to sink, and we stop frequently to take pictures before it gets dark. The sun starts to go down at five-thirty and as the light fades the sounds of the frogs and birds seem to intensify as they echo across the water.

When we return to the car for the last time, the sun is almost level with the water on the horizon, lighting up the sky with a rainbow of pinks, oranges and golds, which in turn are reflected on the water. As I turn my head to catch a last glimpse of the sunset, I notice the white SUV turning into the road. The hairs on my arms stand up and I watch it in the wing mirror. We're on quite a remote lane heading down a dead-end road, with the bayou right next to us.

'How far from the main road are we?' I ask.

'No more than a mile,' says Tate. 'As the crow flies, but unfortunately there are no bridges, so in reality it's a couple of miles because we'd have to double back.' He points to the satnav screen, which is more blue than white. We're surrounded by water. The only way to return is to turn around and go back the same way.

'I think maybe we ought to head back,' I say, keeping an eye on the white car. There's no point alarming Tate. I'm weighing up the risk. No one knows we're here or even headed this way. I try to relax, and outwardly I look like I've achieved my goal. Inside, I'm totting up all the possible permutations for this situation to go tits-up. My hand slips into my purse and feels the comforting weight of my gun. This is what I'm trained for, although I wish I was driving. I'm pretty sure Tate has never done an evasive-action driving course.

'Sure,' says Tate easily. 'We'll get to the end and turn back.'

I could insist we turn right here, but I don't want to

alarm him, and whatever we do we're going to have to drive past the white car. I pray that I'm being overly cautious, although in this job there's no such thing and I don't believe in coincidences.

I nod my agreement and keep a watchful eye on the other car, which is maintaining a discreet distance. The road peters out into little more than a track and there's barely any space to turn around. In the distance on the other side of the open water, I can see the occasional roof among the trees, but apart from that there's very little evidence of any human habitation. A quick shiver of foreboding runs down my spine. I don't like this. It's too remote and suddenly I'm horribly aware of how very vulnerable we are.

As Tate is halfway through a three-point turn, manoeuvring the car round to head back the way we've come, the white car comes down the track straight towards us at speed. Before Tate can complete the manoeuvre, it slows and then stops in the middle of the road. The sun is reflected on the windshield of the tinted window, so I can't make out who's in the front.

'What does he think he's doing?' says Tate, taking his foot off the gas, so that our car is now at a right angle to the other car. 'Where's he gonna go? How I'm supposed to get past him?' He moves to open his door.

'No,' I snap and lean over him to grab his arm to stop him.

'What?' He rolls his eyes and flops back into his seat. 'Please don't tell me you think this guy's a threat. He's just some redneck waving his dick around.'

The headlights on the other car flick to full beam,

dazzling us, and suddenly the car is moving, at speed, straight towards us.

'Shit, he's going to h—'

Our car rocks as the driver rams us, hitting the back passenger door on my side. The rear of the car takes most of the impact, and mercifully none of the windows break, although the airbags deploy. For a moment, it's a touch of déjà vu, except this time the other car keeps moving, pushing us inexorably towards the water.

'Fuck,' shouts Tate. 'Are you okay?'

I nod, my body still vibrating from the force of the hit. Then before we can gather our wits, our car is forced relentlessly towards the edge of the road. It teeters momentarily and then with a stomach-plummeting fall, flips over the edge, and we land upside down in the water strapped into our seats. The weight of the engine immediately drags the front end of the car down and we stare at each other with horror-struck faces.

It takes me less than five seconds to assess the situation. We're bent double, held in by our belts, gravity turning us into pretzels. Tate's legs are tangled up on the dash and the steering wheel. Blood is rushing to my head.

Tate immediately begins to scrabble with the door handle but it's no good, we're already sinking. If he opens it the car will fill even more quickly. I grab his arm.

'Shit. What do we do?'

'We need to stay calm,' I say, which is far easier said than done, especially when you're upside down and heading to the bottom of the bayou.

I suck a breath as it takes a few seconds for my

training to kick in. Stay calm. I slow my breathing and focus on the out breaths for a few seconds. We have a little time in the pocket of air, although the car is sinking fast and water is trickling in from various directions – there's a full flood running down the windscreen towards the roof below us.

'Breathe, Tate. Calm, slow. We're going to get out of here. Trust me.'

'I don't think I have a choice,' he says with a sterling effort at humour. 'I'm relying on your ninja skills.'

His steady faith gives me a much-needed confidence boost. A training exercise is very different to reality, but I do know what to do.

'Okay,' I call over to him above the sound of rushing water and the groaning of metal. 'We need to carefully undo our seatbelts and get out of our seats to land on our feet to stand up.'

'Let me go first,' says Tate manoeuvring his legs and somehow managing to push his seat right back before he undoes his belt. With his superior upper-body strength, he rights himself with impressive ease and then helps me as I follow suit and undo my belt. He eases me down and leaves his hands on my waist as we stand knees bent in the cramped space.

There's a jolt as the car comes to land on the bottom of the bayou, rocking slightly with the impact and we almost lose our footing, both of us making a grab for the steering wheel.

The water is rising rapidly and it's already above our knees.

I try to open a window, but the electrics have already failed.

'Now what?' he asks. I'm impressed that he's staying calm, though I can see from the rise and fall of his chest that he's focusing on deep inhales and exhales.

'We're going to get out.' I kneel down in the cold water, which is rising second-by-second, to tug at the head rest, removing it from the top of the seat. I hand it to Tate, the metal struts facing him.

'Let's get that muscle to work. You need to smash the window.'

He gives me a grim smile and takes the headrest. 'Just like that.'

With what is clearly all his might, he launches it at the window, which is below his knees and beneath the rising water level. I think the glass cracks on first impact, but I can't be sure. It's difficult to see through the murky water.

'Keep going,' I urge.

With Tate's second swing of the headrest, a gush of water bursts through. Tate keeps hammering at the window and I can see pieces of glass floating on the surface of the water in the car which is now rising even more rapidly. Now, time *is* against us.

'Go,' I yell above the torrent flooding in. 'I'll be right behind you. This is important. Swim as far left as you can towards the swamp cypresses before you surface.'

He gives me an agonised look, takes a deep breath, bends down and thrusts himself through the window, his broad shoulders just making it through. Taking a deep breath, the water up to my neck now, I duck beneath the surface onto my knees, holding my nose and keeping my mouth closed and forcing my eyes open. Through the muddy water, I can see the window beneath me, and I half swim, half push myself towards it grabbing hold of the steering wheel to haul myself forward against the water gushing in through the window. I grab the edges of the window, my hands catching on bits of remaining glass, and heave myself through, fighting against the current forcing its way inside. Wriggling free, I push myself off the side of the car and swim away from the vehicle. With the weighty drag of my clothes, it's hard work, and with the fear of running out of breath, I have to fight the urge to swim upwards.

At last, I deem it safe to surface, which I do with a gasp and immediately search around for Tate. My nose is full of the smell of brackish water, and I wipe unidentified bits of leaf, slime and weed from around my mouth.

'Over here,' he calls in a low voice. Treading water, I spin round towards his voice. He's holding on to a log and I swim towards him, realising that we're hidden in the shadows and shallows of the trees. The bright lights of the white car are shining out over the water trained on the spot where the car went in. Bubbles rising from the stricken car below mark the point of entry and subsequent landing spot, a good couple of metres from where we are. Here, among the trees, we're out of view. Unless the driver decides to sweep his headlights this way.

Over to the left something surfaces in the water startling us both, but not as much as the crack of gunfire that immediately follows. A bird takes flight with an angry squawk.

'Fuck,' says Tate in low quiet voice. 'They're shooting at us.'

'What they *think* is us,' I say in a low flat tone, reaching over to touch him.

The car sits there and the quiet is oppressive, although I'm gradually aware of the sounds of the night. The low grunt of a bullfrog. The rustle of things in the trees and the occasional gentle splash of water.

Tate once asked me what I was afraid of. I'm pretty sure at this moment in time it's alligators. I swallow back my fear.

'Bastard is waiting to make sure he finishes us off,' says Tate, his voice rough-edged with fury.

'Looks like it,' I say grimly, my hand working its way beneath my trouser cuff to free the knife I keep holstered there. I'm not sure how effective it's going to be against an alligator but the thought of being able to defend myself is making me feel a lot better.

'Good call to suggest swimming this way,' says Tate through chattering teeth, the cause of which could be cold or shock or a combination of both.

'Yeah, hopefully whoever it is, is going to figure we've drowned.'

We wait surrounded by the sounds of the night, the seconds dragging. The cold is permeating my skin now, and I'm gritting my teeth as hard as I can to stop them chattering, too.

After what feels like forever, the lights on the car brighten and I hear the engine fire up. The beam of the highlights swing away and then around as the car turns and drives off.

'Thank fuck,' says Tate, his teeth chattering even more furiously.

'We need to get out of here.'

'Yes, please.'

I point to the opposite shore and we swim there in silence. Thankfully, my feet hit the bottom of the bayou quite quickly, even though we're still a little way out. From there we have to splash our way through the shallows, tripping and falling over hidden roots and debris lurking in the thick mud. I pray there are no slumbering alligators in the vicinity that we're about to disturb. Finally, we clamber out of the water, our clothes covered in muddy sludge. The smell is rank and insects buzz around us as I drag my hair back from my face.

I pat down my pocket and withdraw my phone. Dead of course. Not that I expected otherwise.

It's dark now and difficult to see our footing as we tread carefully.

'I think there was a house over that way,' I say, pointing to where I'd seen a roof what seemed hours ago.

'There are no lights.'

I stumble and he grabs my hand, hauling me to my feet. 'Watch your footing if you can, don't want to tread on a sleeping alligator.'

'Thanks, Tate. The one thing I wasn't worrying about.'

He gives my hand a squeeze. 'They're more scared of us.

With all the noise we're making, they'll have skedaddled long ago.'

'Promise,' I say in a small needy voice, of which I'm immediately ashamed. I don't do distressed maiden – ever.

He swings an arm around my shoulder. 'Cross my heart and hope to die.'

'I'm going to hold you to that,' I say, finding a bit of my backbone.

'Says she, holding a knife. Where the fuck did that come from?'

'Ankle sheath.'

'Of course it did. You going to use it to build us a shelter for the night.'

'Not if I can help it.' I hope we'll find some sign of habitation, even if it's a bird hide or a fisherman's cabin. I'm desperate to get my wet, very smelly clothes off and I'm wondering what's lodged down my bra. The fabric feels very gritty.

Every now and then there's a burst of noise, a rush of wings as we disturb nesting birds or a sudden rustle through the undergrowth.

I trip over a tree root and go flying through a shrub and – glory be! – realise I've stumbled onto a track.

'Tate!' I say with a little burst of adrenaline-fuelled excitement. 'It's a path.'

'Great.'

'Paths lead to places. People.'

'Which way?'

I look up, there's no light pollution at all and the sky is full of stars.

Tate follows my gaze. 'Looking for the Pole Star or something?' he asks. 'Are you going to navigate us back to civilisation?'

'Not today. We need to make a fifty-fifty decision. We could toss a coin.'

He lets out a mirthless laugh. 'I'm too cold to be digging through my wallet, which is probably full of leeches and other stuff. Let's keep moving.'

'This way, then,' I suggest and point to the right. 'A path must come from somewhere and go somewhere, so by rights there should be something at either end.'

We fall into step, our feet trudging in unison, flicking through the long grass and squelching in the sodden ground. After walking for no more than twenty minutes, a shadow looms up out of the trees. A cabin.

'Hallelujah,' says Tate, our steps quickening as we approach the quiet building. In the dark it's difficult to assess what sort of state it's in. It could be a holiday home, a hide or a smugglers shack.

When we get nearer we peer into the shadows to see a shiplap-clad cabin perched on wooden stilts. A set of steps lead up to the wraparound veranda. We mount the stairs in silence.

'If anyone's home, we're gonna scare the shit out of them,' says Tate.

'No, we're going to play the famous ball player card like never before,' I say. 'About time it paid off.'

'You say the sweetest things.'

'I know.'

The house is in darkness, although would it even have

electricity out here in the middle of the swamp? Tate knocks on the door. 'Hello, anyone home?'

There's no reply.

'Let's take a look around,' he says and starts to walk along the veranda. The cold is starting to bite.

I run my hand around the door frame and around the doorstep in case someone's left a handy key. Unfortunately, no such luck.

I tap at a pane of glass with my knife before exerting more force and smashing it in.

'Lily!' Tate hisses from a few yards away. 'What are you doing?'

'Breaking in.'

'But—'

'Tate. We're cold and wet, and I'm not saying we might die of hypothermia, but we need to get warm and dry ASAP, especially if you're going to play the game of your life in just over a week. Think how proud the owner of this place will be, saving The Don's life.'

'Good point,' says Tate. 'You're really catching onto this fame thing.'

During this conversation, I've slipped my hand through the broken glass and turned the latch to let us in.

'Hello. Anyone home,' I call. 'Can you help us?' I don't want anyone coming out brandishing a shotgun. 'We had an accident in the bayou,' I call.

Nothing. I think it's fair to assume the place is empty.

Tate flips a switch and light floods into the large front room. It's neat and uncluttered and there's no sign of current occupation. Our eyes meet and we give each other a horrified stare.

'Shit,' says Tate. 'I'm guessing I look as bad as you.'

'Right back at you.' I say between chattering teeth. 'Let's find a bathroom.'

'Copy that.'

Off to the left there's a small kitchen, which given our remote location is pretty modern. At the back of the living room there's one large bedroom and an en suite bathroom. We barely glance at the bedroom, although I'd have to be blind not to notice the big king size bed with plump pillows and a crisp white quilt.

I let out a little sigh at the sight of the big shower, the high-end toiletries and the pile of white fluffy towels. This place is definitely a rental or an Airbnb.

Tate turns on the water straight away and holds a hand under the spray. 'Glory be, it's warm. Sorry, Lily. Fuck modesty. I need to get warmed up. Both of us do.'

I am not about to disagree.

He begins to strip off his clothes, shucking his soaked and filthy jeans down his legs. A piece of slimy greenweed is wrapped around one calf, and tiny specks of dirt freckle his skin. He's right. Neither of us are in any state to worry. I follow suit because I can't bear to be in my clothes a moment longer. My skin itches and my scalp prickles at the thought of the small insects and beasties we've waded through.

The overhead shower is plenty big enough for both of us and I step in behind Tate. Instant bliss. Hot water streams down over my head, warm rivulets chasing their way down my body. I'm trying not to stare at Tate's muscular back and that insanely hot ass. Instead, I focus on looking down at the water in the white shower tray, which is swirling with mud, twigs and other tiny bits of leaf mulch.

'Oh God, this is heaven,' I groan, closing my eyes and revelling in the temperature of the water and the feeling of my body warming up. Now I can admit to myself just how wet and miserable I was. And how close we came to not making it. Fuck it. We could have died. I am done fighting this. I press my body into Tate's. My legs start to shake. Post-adrenaline shock. I know the science, but my body doesn't seem to be getting the message.

Me and Tate. Together. My eyes are closed, squeezed shut against the image of what could have happened if we hadn't got out of the car.

'Lily?' Tate puts a hand on my shoulder. I'm shaking.

I open my eyes and his deep blue eyes are focused on me.

My heart turns over, a long slow tumble. And I feel the fall. Emotion rushes at me from every side. Love as bright and furious as a starburst explodes inside me. Tate could have died. I lay a hand on his broad chest. I never stopped loving him. I'd buried it deep and then piled life on top so I didn't have to examine it too hard.

He wraps his arms around me and pulls me close to his warm, wet, naked body. My body melts into the landscape of his, like it's supposed to be part of him. We stand together absorbing the feel of each other, chest, thighs, arms, belly and I sigh against his skin, water coursing across my face. Home. I lift my face and kiss the underside of his chin, my lips dragging on the slight roughness of his bristles. I taste him lightly with my tongue, tightening my hold on him because I'm scared to let go but it's okay because I feel the flex of his arms banded around me. He's not letting go.

He leans behind himself and switches off the shower before ducking his head and his mouth captures mine in a slow kiss that deepens the second my tongue touches his. For a few seconds we're taking our time, balancing out the fear and easing our way towards each other. But then there's too much space between us and our mouths press harder together. Suddenly, it's too much and I can't get enough of Tate, the span of him, the width of him, I can't get close enough. I thrust my hands into his hair and hold his head, his hands are hugging my ass to him. I want to climb inside him and as he clings to me with the desperation of hanging onto life, I know he feels the same.

Every nerve ending is alight, my skin tingles and inside I'm hot to the core.

My hands move to his hips, my thumbs skating inwards across the smooth skin down towards his groin. I'm in too much of a hurry, driven by the aching need that's been dormant for far too long. I slip my hand to cup his hard, smooth cock. Silken and strong.

His guttural groan makes my clit sing.

'Fuck, Lily.'

I stroke him a couple of times, revelling in the burn of heat between my legs, before he slaps his hand over mine. 'Slow down,' he murmurs, easing back and pressing a kiss on my throat. When he cups my breasts, his large hands dwarf them, his thumbs rolling over the nipples. I've always been way too sensitive there and the quick friction almost sends me tumbling. His grin is wolfish because he knows.

'Some things never change,' he says, his eyes intense as he takes my hands and holds them above my head, clasping them in one hand, while the other comes around my waist to support me. He stares down at me, his expression full of intent. I catch my lip between my teeth. My body knows this song. I'm quivering with anticipation. He ducks his head to take one nipple in his mouth. There's no gentleness here and I don't want it. I need the strong pulls of his mouth against my tender flesh, and as he sucks and teases, tormenting me, I gasp, unable to distinguish between the pleasure and pain. The sharp tugs are echoed between my legs. The more I call out, the harder he sucks.

My knees are weak. I cry his name out.

When I can take no more, I finally say, 'Stop. Please. Stop.'

He lifts his head and gives my nipple a quick kiss, cupping the other breast with his free hand and rolling his thumb over the neglected nipple giving me a satisfied smile. 'I haven't finished yet.'

I swallow, my nipple throbbing, radiating desire throughout my body.

He stares down at me, lifts an eyebrow and waits. He knows I can't say no. I close my eyes and suck in a sharp breath when he takes my other nipple into his mouth. He takes his time, leisurely licking, sucking, swirling his tongue. It's torment. I want it hard and fast, and he knows it. He's breaking me down and I love it.

Eventually I have to give in. 'Please, Tate.'

'Please Tate, what?'

I hold back the words. Not wanting to capitulate, wanting him to work for it.

His mouth lets go of my nipple with the pop of a cork, the loss of his warm, wet tongue makes me whimper.

'Tell me what you want, Lily.'

'Suck me. Hard.'

I'm relieved I don't have to beg.

'You have such responsive tits,' he murmurs and ducks his head again. I squirm against him trying to free my hands, although its half-hearted. Much as I want to touch him, the pleasure he's giving me makes me submit. I close my eyes, lost in sensation, only conscious of my laboured breaths and his hot mouth pulling pleasure from my tender flesh.

The tension in my core spirals, but it's still not enough.

'Tate,' I cry. My voice is stretched thin and high and I'm hanging on, but only just. I try and pull free from the hold he has on my hands. I'm greedy for more, want to touch him, stroke him. Hurry him along.

He moves to my lips with an open, hot-mouthed kiss but doesn't release me. I groan into his mouth, my breasts burning and tingling like they're on fire, fiery bursts of pleasure licking at me.

Tate's dick is butted up against my stomach, granite hard. I push against him trying to take charge.

'Nuh-huh,' he teases, pulling back. 'Only good girls get what they want.'

He pushes me back against the tiles and changes his hold on my arms, forcing them higher above my head.

'Are you going to be a good girl?'

I glare at him, and he smiles when I try to shake his grip.

He grins. 'Oh Lily, you're going to be so good.' His voice is gravelly, and damn it, my heart expands. He's in control, just the way I like it. And, God help me, I've always liked it. Being under him, giving him what he wants. It gives me an extra thrill, even though in all areas of my life I'm assertive and in charge. With us, it's always been like this. Him dominating me, overpowering me with his masculinity. My guilty secret.

I still don't say anything because I don't like to make it too easy but I'm pretty sure my breathless moans are all the answer he needs.

He slides his free hand between my thighs, pushing me so that I have to take a step to part them. Without more ado, I feel the pad of one of his fingers at my entrance.

'So wet,' he whispers into my ear and slides his finger in with slow, insistent pressure.

A garbled moan escapes me as I tip my head onto his chest. I think I'm losing my mind. Lightning heat is burning through my core, the pressure building. I rock onto his finger.

'No, no,' he whispers and withdraws. I protest. He raises his hand to lift my chin and stares into my eyes. 'I want to watch you come.'

My eyes plead with him. This is too intimate. Too much. But I'm desperate to feel him. For him to make the emptiness go away.

This time he slides two fingers in, stretching me, with a firm slow pump. My legs are shaking. The need rising and rising. I hold his gaze with desperation because I can feel it coming. Feel that I'm going to be vulnerable to him. Something I swore I'd never be again. This is capitulation but ... the orgasm bursts. Sparks of sensation burst through my body like a meteorite shower, hot bright and incandescent. I let go as I'm swamped by the flood of feeling, my eyes never leaving his face.

He lowers my arms and wraps his around my waist pulling me to him, his lips nuzzling at my neck. I cling on like a shipwrecked sailor to a rock. Limp and spent. My heart is still pounding and I'm totally spaced out. I close my eyes and let my breathing settle. I have no words and I'm grateful he has none either. How do you talk after that? Although I'm conscious that he's still fully erect. I smile to myself. Tate's iron control. He's always taken care of me first.

I'm a little too hazy to function yet, even though there's the niggling thought that I haven't taken care of him. I stiffen slightly and start to pull away, my hands moving downwards.

As if he reads my mind, he kisses my neck, holds me closer as if he's never going to let me go and murmurs in my ear. 'There's all the time in the world.'

I close my eyes again and let myself enjoy the embrace.

Chapter Twenty

TATE

M y dick is still throbbing and jerking, wanting release, I'm close, but when I finally take her, after all these years, I'm going to do it in a bed and take my damn time.

But the sight of Lily, her head thrown back, her lips swollen and her eyes glazed with passion, is a near spiritual experience and it's challenging my resolve. I've never seen anything so hot in my life. I take my dick in my hand and watch her eyes widen. I feel a sense of relief. I watch her watching me as I pump real slow. She's fucking beautiful, especially now as she's coming down. Soft, helpless and mine.

Oh God, yes, she's mine. I can't do it anymore. Pretend she doesn't mean anything to me. I want Lily Heath underneath me, over me, in front of me – every which way I can, and it frightens the fuck out of me. Something squeezes my heart like an iron fist and everything I've been trying to fight backs off. I stroke harder, my eyes never leaving her face, her parted lips, the hunger and curiosity in her eyes. She bites her lip and I can see the battle going on in her: she wants to watch but she also wants to help. But it's a turn on, her watching me.

'Next time,' I grunt. I can feel the tingle at the bottom of my spine, my balls heavy. My muscles clench and then … the release, the rush, that whoosh of getting there. I ejaculate with a fierce flood and close my eyes, sweat beading my forehead as my cum drips onto the floor.

Lily touches me, placing a hand on my chest, almost anchoring me as I stand there, legs apart, breathing hard.

'Fuck.' I blink at her coming back to reality. Her eyes are still wide and a little startled. There's still that innocence in there and my heart does a funny little flip. I ease out a breath and feel my heart rate start to settle.

I turn the water back on and squeeze the shampoo dispenser on the wall, pumping a handful into my palm and dumping it on my head. Then I go back for more and lather it into Lily's hair, even though I want to soap her breasts and start all over. But I don't want our first time to be a quickie in the shower. I'm going to do this properly because it might be the only chance I ever get. Lily ran once, she'll likely run again.

Lily lifts her hands to her head and starts to massage the soap in, her tits rising with the movement. She lets out a small 'Mmm,' as the hot water runs down her body.

'That good,' I ask.

'So good. I've never felt so filthy in my life.' Our eyes catch and I grin at her unintended double entendre as my eyes drop to her naked breasts.

'They look fairly clean to me,' I tease.

She huffs out an exasperated sigh, but she doesn't mean it. Lily's nipples are still tight, rosy buds and I know it won't take much to start her up again, but I'm planning to take it slow from here on in.

That doesn't mean we can't have a bit of fun getting there.

'But it's good to be thorough,' I add, soaping her tits, my hands gliding over the pert mounds. 'Perfect tits,' I say, and her eyes go wide again. I love teasing her like this, especially when I hear her sharp intake of breath. But I go easy on her and slide my hands down to her waist and around to rest on her butt. My thumbs massaging her skin in small circles.

She leans over and takes a handful of soap herself and presses her hands against my chest, massaging my pecs, and she grins up at me.

'Nice body. You've put some work in.'

I stand still, my feet planted and focus on breathing slow as her small hands explore my body, rubbing and stroking their way along, assessing each and every contour of my shoulders, my neck, my chest. Her skin is pale against mine, her slender fingers searching and seeking, light and firm. Then she checks out each of my abs working her way down with a thoroughness I'm loving, teasing and testing me. She pays particular attention to my hips and the creases below, running her palms down them. I'm captivated by the feel of her touch and the concentration on her face, and that slight smile dancing at the corners of her mouth as if she's making interesting discoveries.

'We're gonna run out of hot water,' I say, and we agree to finish up.

There's a pile of white towels and I can't help myself, I do the gentlemanly thing and snag one to wrap it around her before I take one for myself.

'Thanks,' she says, her nose wrinkling at the sight of our discarded clothes on the floor which are giving off a distinct swamp smell.

I don't want to break the spell, but I think we're both coming back to reality.

'Now what?' I ask.

'I need coffee,' she says. 'And we're kind of stuck until we have clothes.'

'Not a problem here.' I tuck the towel around my waist.

She looks at my chest. 'Show off,' she says with a laugh and tucks her own towel around her. It leaves her long legs on display.

'I've got no complaints.'

'We are going to have to leave here eventually,' she says and scoops up her wet clothes and heads out of the bathroom. I pick mine up, amused that she's made it clear she's not about to do my laundry, and follow her through to the kitchen and to the laundry room out back.

With the quick efficiency I've gotten used to, Lily gets the washing machine working and then moves back into the kitchen, going through the cupboards and freezer.

In minutes, she's got the coffee machine on, too. The hot shower and sexy interlude might have warmed us up, but I'm still feeling cold on the inside. She hands me a mug of black coffee, and by mutual accord we go through to the living room. When she sits in the armchair, I sense she's distancing herself to regroup, get her head back in the game, because there's no doubt we're up the creek without a paddle.

I watch her take a sip of her coffee.

'Now what?' I ask.

She gives me a surprisingly radiant smile. 'We stay put and relax.'

'I can get with that programme, but what's happened to my bodyguard.' I'd have expected her to be plotting and planning how we get back to civilisation as soon as possible.

She lifts her shoulders and gives a negligent shrug. 'We're warm, safe and dry. No one knows we're here. And the bad guy thinks you're dead. This is the safest you've been for a while. And at this moment in time, no one's going to worry.' She catches her lip between her teeth. 'It's going to take a day or two before anyone figures you're missing, and when they do Winston will do anything he can to keep that quiet.'

'The shit will hit the fan then. He'll go crazy.'

'I'm not planning for us to be missing that long.'

'What are you planning?'

'We stay here. Tomorrow, I'll leave you here and try and find a way of communicating with Winston to let him know you're still alive. We can use this to our advantage.'

'I need to get back and train.'

'Tate. Someone tried to kill you. You need to lay low for a while. This is the perfect cover, them already thinking you're dead.'

'Yeah, but if the team find out, it will kill morale.'

She gives me a long, level look. 'I'm even more convinced that someone on your team is responsible.'

I didn't want to hear this when she first said it, and I don't want to hear it now.

'No way.'

'Tate. Someone followed us here from New York. Someone must have followed us to the car rental.'

Okay. I can't deny her logic, but there's no way any of my teammates would do something like this. They're my brothers. I mean, we don't always get on, there's plenty of rivalry and trash talk, but we're a team and on course for the biggest fucking victory of our lives. Not one of them would jeopardise that. We've all lived and breathed football since we were kids. This is the ultimate prize.

I shake my head and she gives me a look full of sympathy.

'I refuse to believe it,' I say, scowling at her. 'It's not true.'

'Okay,' she says with calm dispassion, which even though my stomach is churning, I have to admire. 'Who else might have a grudge against you?' She frowns. 'Unless it isn't you they hold the grudge against…'

'What do you mean?'

Her frown deepens. 'Until today.' She steeples her hands together, pressing her index fingers to her lips. 'I didn't think…' Her pause is lengthy as she studies my face. 'I didn't think they were serious.'

'Now you tell me. So, this whole bodyguard business was a means of getting up close and personal?' I'm trying to lighten the mood because I'm nauseous. My leg starts to jig and a wash of sweat floods over my body. Sitting here drinking coffee in this pleasant room seems a miracle when I remember the car sinking and having to swim out of the smashed window. Taking that last breath, ducking beneath the water and forcing my way out, leaving Lily and oxygen behind, was *the* hardest thing I've ever done in my life.

Lily immediately gets up and comes to sit beside me. She kisses my cheek. 'If that hadn't happened, I might not have had the best orgasm of my life.'

I'm tough. Strong. A man. But right at this moment, I feel weak, scared and clueless. All I know is that Lily is my anchor right now. I need her more than I've ever needed anything. The touch of her hand on my thigh is all that is stopping me heading for the toilet and throwing up.

'Second best,' I tell her, trying to regain control.

'Second best?' she raises an eyebrow playing along. I know she can see that I'm out of kilter.

'Yes. The best is yet to come.' She bursts out laughing.

It breaks the ice and all the tension.

'I think we both need some food.' She pauses a moment before adding, with a quick smirk. 'There's plenty of pizza.'

Chapter Twenty-One

LILY

We sit in the living room, eating pizza that I found in the freezer, and watching an old episode of *SWAT* on Netflix. It would be ridiculously domestic except for the distinct sexual buzz in the air. We're sitting side by side on the couch, in our towels, not quite touching but certainly not avoiding each other. He's gloriously bare-chested, and it's difficult for me not to sneak glances at his broad, smooth pecs and those tight square abs. I can smell the shower gel we both used earlier, woodsy, with a hint of pine. I hide a shiver of desire, the hairs on my arms bristle with awareness at his nearness. Between my legs there's a growing dampness, and even though he's not looking at me, every part of me is on slow-burn in anticipation.

Through the windows the trees are an amorphous dark shadow, silhouetted beneath the slightly paler sky. Not a single light breaks the wide horizon. We're completely alone in the middle of the swamp. We've lit a couple of lamps, which give the room a warm glow and cast a golden light over Tate's face. I turn to look at his profile, a bare kiss away, at the stubbled, square jaw, the tiny creases at the corners of his eyes and the slightly forward thrust of his chin. I hold my breath trying not to give into the urge to trace his jawline with my lips, to smooth his cheekbones with my fingers. Being this close to him. This is an expectant lull before the storm.

I've experienced plenty of close shaves before, but this, this time it's different. Inside I'm shaky. Unbalanced. For the first time since I walked away from Tate eight years ago, I don't know what step to take. I can no longer rely on the ground beneath my feet, it could fall away at any moment. I need to hold on to him. I don't know what it means but I'm going to take everything I can while it's on offer. I can worry about having my heart broken again, another time. For now, I'm holding on to this, and whatever it brings.

'This was good pizza.' Tate licks his lips and pushes away his empty plate, grinning at me. 'I'm always going to have fond memories of pizza.' His smile is quick and dirty, ramping up the low-level buzz of excitement radiating through me.

'I think you've said that before.' I try to sound normal, but my voice is breathy. I want him, all of him, for however long we've got.

'Just reminding you in case you'd forgotten.'

For some reason, despite our intimacy earlier, I blush, and his grin ratchets up to a whole new level, a gleam of lust in his eyes. I swallow and he sees it. The telltale sign of my nervous arousal.

Without a word, Tate rolls off the couch to his knees and

advances towards me. He stops in front of me and looks me dead in the eyes before he parts my knees and slides his hands up the back of my legs to pull me forward. My towel unfurls and my legs open, exposing me, and his eyes gleam with satisfaction.

'And there she is,' he whispers. 'Fuck, you're beautiful, Lily. That is one gorgeous pussy.' He dips a finger into me. 'So wet.' Then he takes his finger and puts it into his mouth.

I clamp my mouth together, trying to hold back the involuntary gasp, shy and turned on at the same time. Tate has the power to excite and terrify me at the same time. It's like being on the high diving board about to jump, knowing that it's scary but that you'll love it at the same time.

I close my eyes and hold my breath waiting for his mouth to touch me.

'No, no, no,' he says and pinches one of my nipples.

I inhale sharply.

'Watch. Enjoy. You know you want to.'

I nod, because I do. He always teased me about my English reserve, but I've never been able to do anything like this with any other man. Only Tate.

His dips his head between my legs and I gaze down at his dark silky hair as his mouth latches onto me, hot and wet, his tongue swirling over my sensitive nerve endings, the sensation so intense I almost hyperventilate. I drown in sensation as he licks and sucks. It's a while before I realise the high-pitched keen is mine. I'm losing control, and I try to wriggle free. It's too much, but not enough. I'm climbing higher but I need more. Tate's hands hold my hips, keeping me firmly in place. I'm panting, desperate to get there, but he's in control, holding my orgasm at bay with the constant teasing: advance and retreat, lick and suck.

'Fuck, Tate.' I clutch at his head. 'Please. I need—' It feels like my clit is on fire, it's so swollen. I need friction, hard thrusts.

He lifts his head. He rubs my clit with one finger as he studies me for a second.

'What do you need, Lily?'

'You. I need you.'

He rises to his feet and pulls me up, scooping me up into his arms and striding to the bedroom. His profile is stern and serious. God, what am I doing? This is it, after all these years we're passing the point of no return, but I couldn't stop now even if I wanted to.

He puts me down and then releases his towel, standing in front of me, his huge erection proudly at attention. I swallow. Christ, I want him.

'I want you,' I say looking him straight in the eye.

'Don't look at me like that. I might not last,' he grumbles.

I take his hand and lead him towards the bed, then I turn him round and push him down. He takes me with him and I'm lying on top of him, feeling his warm skin against my body. I inhale sharply at the feel of him beneath me, my nerve endings dancing with delight and wild abandon. He rolls us over so that he's above me, taking his weight on his elbows.

'Are we really doing this?' I ask softly, scarcely able to think straight. I'm consumed with aching need, but at the same time it almost feels too special to spoil. I want to hold onto the magical anticipation a little while longer.

He looks down at me. 'I want to say the right thing – only if you want to – but the honest truth, Lily, is that I think I want this more than I've ever wanted anything in my life.' He places the softest, gentlest kiss on the corner of my lips. 'But if you've changed your mind …'

I put my arms around his back and hug him to me. 'No.'

'You know I don't have any protection on me,' there's a wistful expression on his face.

'It's a good job I'm on the pill.'

'I'm clean.'

'I know you are, after all the time we spent in the shower.'

He smiles and leans forward, pushes my hair from my face and kisses me deep and I want to inhale him, draw him into me.

The mood changes, serious and intent now, as the kiss consumes us. It's my entire focus, his mouth roving across my lips, and I'm aware of his body, hot and heavy over mine. Our breaths turn to pants, our bodies pushing and pulling towards each other, and I can feel the strong tug of desire pulling me down into another place where there's only him.

I lift my hips, desperate and needy. At the touch of him, I push forward, wanting all of him, and then in one slow but sure push, he thrusts inside. He's heavy, stretching me, filling me. It's heaven and I want more. He groans.

'Lily…' He holds for a second and I can feel tiny pulses inside me. Then he surges forward again. 'You…' He withdraws and then glides back in hard. 'Feel…' He slides back. 'So…'

He thrusts harder again. 'Fucking…' He pulls back and this time slams home. 'Good…'

I lift my hips, push for push. His forceful pace is slow and steady, but my body welcomes each lunge, the friction a delicious burn of heat and fire. He sets a pace, reaching into me, over and over again. Pleasure mounts with every movement. I cry out his name, barely able to hold on, but he's relentless, driving into me, and I'm breathing hard trying to keep up with the punishing pace, rising to meet each push. My skin is covered with a sheen of sweat. My orgasm is hovering, elusive and out of reach. Frustration makes me moan.

He adds a finger rubbing over my clit and I cry out his name at the sensory overload.

'That's it, Lily.'

His jaw is tense, the muscles in his neck corded with tension. His powerful arms bulging with the strain of his weight.

'Please, Tate, please.' I'm not even sure what I'm begging for.

'Fuuuuck. I'm coming. I'm coming,' he shouts, and with one last thrust I feel him come inside me just as the wave of intense pleasure hits, washing over me. I collapse back into the pillows clinging to Tate's sweat-soaked back and he lowers his body onto me. I sigh, welcoming his weight. There's something satisfying about being anchored beneath him and I hold onto him, savouring the tremors and aftershocks in my core and the feeling of him inside me.

After a while, Tate rolls onto his side, taking me with him. We lie studying each other in the lamp light.

'Well, that was worth waiting for,' he says, stroking a finger down my cheek.

'It was,' I say. My heart rate may never return to normal. I feel like I could float off the bed.

'It's never been like that with anyone else,' he says, a rasp to his voice.

I'm surprised that he's being so open with me, and it forces me to be honest with him. 'Nor me. I … I'm not normally that intimate with anyone.'

He touches my face. 'It's a turn-on, you know.'

'What is?'

'You being shy.'

'I'm not shy, I'm just not … not used to…' The truth is I've avoided real intimacy. Never allowing anyone to get too close. Sex is always businesslike and perfunctory. Almost transactional. I never stay over or let anyone else do that with me. I've always told myself that it's the nature of the job, it's important to stay independent, but the truth is, I've never felt I could be like that with anyone else but Tate. He always had my back. All that time ago, I always knew I could rely on him. He looked after me in a way that no one had ever done. I'd trusted him to look after me.

It would appear I still trust him. With my body, at least.

Chapter Twenty-Two

TATE

I wake up to sunshine spilling through the windows and dancing across the planes of Lily's body. She's sprawled next to me, one leg touching mine, her arms under her pillow. I study her smooth, pale skin and a large freckle to the right of the cute dimple in her lower back.

I'm used to waking up after indifferent sleep in impersonal hotel rooms, but today my body feels well-used and well-slept. The bed is comfortable, cocooning my heavy, lethargic limbs but despite this, inside I'm alive and buzzy and today is bright and brilliant. I turn, and there she is, asleep next to me, her blonde hair spread out on the pillow like every dream you can imagine. She's like a mirage. She's really here, and last night we had mind-exploding sex, not once, not twice but three times. On the third occasion, all inhibition blown out of the water, she rode me like a cowgirl, grinding down on me so hard I almost saw stars, although I'm not sure I'll ever forget her perfect tits bouncing above me, or her head thrown back, face contorted with ecstasy as she shuddered through the orgasm I felt rip through her.

Sex with Lily was so much more than I could ever have imagined. Was it because we waited so long? Or was it the near-brush with death that sparked a basic need to redefine our existence. Celebrate life in its rawest terms?

She stirs and rolls over, one arm thrown above her head, and the sheet falls aside leaving her back and shoulders exposed. Her smooth muscle tone beneath the soft skin is clearly evident, reminding me who she is now.

'Stop watching me,' she mumbles. 'I'm sleeping.'

'How can you know I'm watching you, if you're sleeping.'

'I have eyes in the back of my head. Go make coffee, if you need something to do.'

'Someone's grouchy.'

'Seriously? You've forgotten I'm not a morning person.'

'No. I remember, but I'm trying to figure – in your line of work, do you tell the bad guys not to bother you before 9am?'

She rolls over and puts an arm across her eyes. 'Very funny. When I'm working, it's different. I could still pin you to the ground in an instant, if I wanted to.'

'I'll go make that coffee,' I say and drop a kiss on her sulky mouth.

'And for the love of God, put some clothes on,' she adds, as I stand up. 'How am I supposed to resist that ass?'

The contrast between who she appears to be – ninja bodyguard-princess – and the reality of the slightly shy but passionate lover, makes me smile. But it also reminds me that we are stuck in the middle of nowhere and that tomorrow the rest of the team is flying in. Practice starts then, and I *have* to be there.

I'd gotten caught up in the sex. Forgotten about what's important. What I've been working towards my whole life. This is not some grand reunion. Eight years ago, I let Lily Heath get under my skin and I fell apart when she left. That isn't going to happen again. Yesterday we almost lost our lives. It was good sex, hell, fucking great sex and I'm up for us enjoying ourselves as long as we're here, but I can't afford for this to derail my future. She almost did it once, she doesn't get to do it again.

But even as I study her smooth back and the indentations of her spine, which are begging me to kiss each and every one, right down to the swell of her cute ass, I think about what her skin will feel like under my tongue. My dick stirs and I promise myself, one last time. I lean over and kiss the very top of her spine. She wriggles and looks over her shoulder at me with a sleepy smile. 'What happened to coffee?'

For a moment I'm transfixed by the sight of her and the uncomfortable thump of my heart. I turn and go make some coffee, wriggling my hips to give her an eyeful.

When I return ten minutes later, Lily's lying on her front dozing, and I put the coffee next to her and study her sleep-tousled hair and her relaxed face.

Her eyes open. 'Morning,' she says with dopey smile, and right there I'm gone. I kiss her mouth and press her back down, moving to sit astride her, keeping my weight on my knees as I slip my hands under her to fill my hands with her breasts. She squirms, her ass rising up to kiss my balls. I squeeze her nipples as I start to work my way down her back, nuzzling and kissing her skin. She wriggles but I clamp my knees on her hips, and with my mouth I press her into the bed. There's silence apart from the rustle of sheets. I can feel her heartbeat rising as I lick and kiss my way down. When I reach the hollow of her spine, I shift back and put my hands on the top of her ass, kissing the very top of the crease there, and she moans. I start to slide a finger all the way down between her ass cheeks and she moans, her hips tilting up slightly to give me better access. I pause at the tight pucker and hear her sharp inhalation, but her hips rise a fraction. I toy with the tiny circle pushing one finger against the tense muscle. She lets out a soft murmur, which I take as encouragement, and I push a little harder, making her moan. I trace down with my other hand, finding her wet and oh-so ready.

Without any preamble, I thrust two fingers inside Lily and pump her without any finesse. I know I'm punishing her for me not being able to resist her, but she takes it, murmuring, 'Yes, yes, yes,' between pants.

I love how fucking tight she is, how responsive, and how she takes everything I give her. I push a little deeper with one finger, continuing to pump her. My dick is hard, so fucking hard. I lift her hips and drive into her hot, wet pussy, balls-deep. As I close my eyes and feel her around me … fuck … I think I've died and gone to heaven. This woman. She clamps tight around me.

'Lily. Oh, fuck.' The garbled words are involuntary, I'm lost to the sensation of her sweet pussy pulling me in as I drive into her, over and over, and she meets me, thrust for thrust. My orgasm comes so hard and fast, there's no warning. The intense pleasure almost paralyses me, and I collapse on top of her, my dick throbbing and pulsing. I gather her up to me, spooning her to me, my hands cupping her breasts. 'Fuck, Lily. Fuck.'

She's hanging onto me, stroking my arm, and I'm not sure if either of us know what is up or down at the moment. My chest stops heaving at the same time as the guilt creeps in. Fuck, I used her, really used her for my pleasure.

I turn her to face me, prepared for recrimination and ready to apologise the shit out of things. 'Christ, Lily. I'm s—'

She lays a finger on my lips. 'Don't.' Her eyes are serene and there's a soft smile on her face. I'm confused.

'I should have slowed down. At least waited until you woke up properly.'

'Did you hear me complaining?'

'Fuck, no,' I say remembering her breathy, incoherent cries, which even now make my balls tighten.

Her eyes brighten and the smile turns a touch smug. 'I like that I can do that to you.'

'You do, do you?'

She nods, soft and sated, blooming with feminine power. 'It's a good feeling that you can bring someone to their knees.'

I decide to bring her down a peg. 'For that pussy I'm happy to go on my knees any time for you. Pizza or no pizza.'

She bursts out laughing. 'You just have to have the last word.'

'Always,' I agree, and kiss her on the lips. She responds eagerly and all my intentions about getting up and out vanish.

'I don't like it,' I say, sipping black coffee as I stand in the kitchen listening to the sound of our clothes in the dryer.

'Of course you don't,' says Lily with a long-suffering sigh. She wants us to stay here for another night, which, despite my dick jumping and down, saying 'fabulous idea' I'm not sure about, at all. I need to get back to the structure of training and routine. They've shaped my life this far, I need that.

'Look, Tate, while you're in this house, you're safe.' Her voice softens and it does something to me inside. She cares about me.

'There's a someone out there who wants to kill you. You're safest while you're – I'm sorry to say it'—she uses her fingers to punctuate the word—'dead.'

Sudden fear tightens my muscles. I don't need reminding of our close call yesterday. It brings back last night's dream, where I was trying to give her mouth-to-mouth in a car full of water before she turned into a rotting corpse and floated away.

'Tate.' She turns round to face me, her hip propped against the kitchen counter. With the sun shining through the window, lighting up her hair, she's so beautiful, but her face is filled with worry. Her expression makes something shift in my chest. I'm not sure many people have actually worried about me for a long time. They might worry about the outcomes of things I do. How I play. Whether I score. But they don't care about how I feel inside.

'Something has changed,' she says and her words are urgent, emotion spilling from them. 'The previous attempts were loud, attention-grabbing...' She shakes her head. 'They were amateur, like they weren't trying too hard... It's been bothering me for a while. None of them were that serious.'

'You are kidding, right? I mean, being ditched in the bayou felt pretty fucking serious to me.' I'm trying to lighten the horror of it, even though it doesn't feel real. I'm just a ball player, this is outside my remit.

Lily straightens up and comes to stand beside me, laying a hand on my arm. She sighs. 'I have to say this because I need to be honest with you, and you wouldn't thank me for trying to protect you from the truth. With the previous attempts, the peanut-tampering, the firebomb, they left the outcome to luck, to chance, whatever. But yesterday,' her voice lowers and I can hear the vehemence in her tone, 'yesterday was different. They meant business. They hung around to finish the job off properly. That was much more ruthless.'

'Before, I was doing a job, I was making sure you were safe. Going through the motions but...' She takes my face in her hands and holds it, her bourbon-brown eyes piercing mine.

'Now I'm scared for you. Someone wants you dead.'

It's the gesture as much as the words, that catch me at my core. It's humbling, that she cares so much. I feel the slow tumble of my heart as I fall headlong back in love with her.

'Lily, it's okay,' I tell her, even though I know it isn't. Someone wants to kill me, and I have no idea who could hate me that much. 'We can stay put for the time being, but I need to train.'

'I can help you with that,' she says and a wicked twinkle lights up her eyes, banishing the previous sombre tone.

Chapter Twenty-Three

LILY

The warm water laps around my shoulders and I look up into the night. There seem to be more stars than sky. I take a sip of my red wine and sigh. I can't remember the last time I felt this relaxed. It might have something to do with all the exercise I've done today, supporting Tate. God, the man is superhuman. I had a hard job keeping my hands off his hot, sweaty body as he worked out in his boxer shorts.

'Come here,' says Tate now, from the other side of the hot tub. 'You're too far away.'

I smile because they're words he's used before, beside a campfire on a beach when we were in college. I move over and before I can sit beside him, he catches my hips and positions me between his legs. His arms come around my waist and I lean back against his chest as he kisses the top of my head.

'This is nice,' he murmurs.

'Mmm,' I say, relishing his warm skin against my back

and the feeling of being cocooned in his embrace. It's quiet and comfortable. Safe. It's home, and my heart turns over in my chest, grief, sadness intermingled with contentment. I mourn what we lost, summoning the dull ache that has always been there and examining it. It dawns on me, too many years too late, that I ran away because I expected him to bail on me at some point. I'd been so conditioned by my upbringing, that at the first sign of history repeating itself, I fell into line, into the narrative my dad had taught me. Why the hell hadn't I confronted Tate after I heard him talking to his dad? Why aren't I demanding an explanation now? Is it because I know I was as much to blame as he was?

Enjoy it while you can, I tell myself, not wanting to delve too deeply into the past. There's no turning the clock back or seeing into the future, but I can savour every second of the now. I can draw every bit of pleasure from it, because this time these feelings might have to last me a lifetime.

Tate's hands very gently slide up to cup my breasts. I relax against him, my head on his shoulder and enjoy the sensation of the water lapping at my skin and his barely-there touch. It's hypnotising, this closeness and ease. He kisses my neck and he sighs and I feel his warm breath against my ear. I'm loose and sated from our earlier pre-dinner encounter, fast and furious on the sofa with not one or two, but three orgasms. Tate is nothing if not diligent.

His hands splay across my stomach holding me against him, anchoring me to him.

We sit in easy silence, my limbs loose and lethargic.

'Lily?' The single word quivers with question.

'Mmm.'

'Why did you leave when you did?'

It's like he fired an arrow and the point pierces. I close my eyes, trying to keep the truth out. I want to tell him, but how can I without revealing the damage he did to my heart and the fallout afterwards.

'Lily?' he prompts.

'I had to. My Dad had a heart attack.'

'I know that. But you didn't have to cut me off like that. I wanted to be there for you, but I never heard from you again. You didn't answer my calls, texts and then you blocked me.' I can hear the hurt in his voice. 'It was like being cut off at the knees. And not knowing why. It killed me.'

His words settle on me, the sadness in them permeating and wrapping around like a blanket of sorrow, and I ache for him, because there's pain in every one of them.

Suddenly I'm sick of the bullshit. The hurt that has never really gone away. I want to fight back. To challenge him, even though I'm completely mixed up inside.

'Tate. Don't do this. Don't lie to me. You might have been upset I'd gone, but I know you were planning to dump me anyway.' My own pain makes me sound a little hard and resentful. 'I walked away before you got the chance and I guess that hurt your ego.'

He lifts me over his leg so that we're side by side and he can see my face.

'What? I was never going to dump you. You walked away because you never really cared that much.'

'I didn't care? What the hell, Tate. I heard you.'

'Heard me what? Phoning you over and over, when you never once picked up or called me back. That's cold.'

'It was self-preservation,' I snap, hurt by the accusation. It had been so hard to ignore those calls, most of which came while my phone was switched off because I was in the hospital in ICU with my dad. I hadn't dared reply to any of them because I would have begged him to come. I needed him so much at that time, it hurt to breathe as I sat by the hospital bed listening to the beeps of the monitors, Dad's breaths on the ventilator, wishing that Tate was there to hold me. Afterwards, I promised myself I'd never be that weak, needy girl ever again, because Dad was right. Caring about someone makes you weaker. Makes you vulnerable. I changed my phone number, deleted all my social media and became invisible. I finished my degree and, as soon as Dad was better, I trained as hard as I could to find a place in life where I could stand alone. Self-reliance became my mantra.

'Then why did you leave?'

'Because I found out that … I honestly believed that you loved me, but then I heard you say to your dad that you were just filling time with me before the draft. And don't deny it. I heard you.'

He stares at me, shock in his eyes, and then he puts his head in his hands and huffs out a mirthless laugh. 'I don't fucking believe it.'

He looks up at me. 'I told my dad what he wanted to hear. To get him off my back. If you heard, why the fuck didn't you ask me about it? The Lily Heath I knew would have burst in and given me shit. Why didn't you?'

'I'd just heard my dad had had a heart attack. I needed

to go back to England. As quickly as possible. I didn't have the energy to fight.' Even as I say the words, I know I'm lying.

'Did you really not know that I loved you?'

I'm shocked to see the pain tightening his face. Guilt twists me up. I hadn't answered those calls because I was trying to prove to myself that I could go on without him. That I could cure the pain by cutting myself off, like my dad did when I was a kid. It was much easier not to speak to him.

I was a coward.

'Why?'

'Why what?'

Why did you tell him what he wanted to hear?'

'Because I was a fucking coward. I knew that he'd give me grief if I told him that I was planning to ask you to marry me. I wanted to show it could work, that once I was drafted he'd see that it could work. That we were a team.'

'Marry me?'

'Yes, of course.'

I'm really knocked for six by this admission. It's like a punch to the gut and all I can do is stare at him as my stomach churns. I think I might be sick. I got it so wrong.

'Shit,' I murmur and start to rise to my feet. It's like I'm having an out-of-body experience. I need to escape, I can't face all this emotion. And then I realise that's exactly what I did then, and what I've done ever since. I ran away because I was scared he didn't want me and that I wasn't as self-reliant and independent as I'd been brought up to be. The realisation makes me sick to my stomach. All these years

I've been lying to myself. Living a lie, priding myself on my self-sufficiency. I needed Tate that day, needed him so much it had scared me. So, I'd run as far away as I could. And now I'm still as much of a coward as ever. What if he hurts me again? I can't let him in again, and that's what I'll do if I tell him that I ran because I was scared.

I owe him an apology, but it's too late. Far too late. So where does that leave us now?

I let go of the breath I've been holding. I'm not going to run this time.

'So where does that leave us now?' I ask, not sure I want the answer. Everything is a little raw inside. Maybe too much time has passed. We're not teenagers, anymore. We're both older and wiser. The sexual chemistry might be as potent, but we aren't the same people we were.

Tate looks at me, a touch of defiance in his eyes. 'All I know is that nearly dying gives you a new perspective on life. I don't hate you anymore.'

'Good to know.' I sound flippant, but I'm hiding the fact that I hated him for what he'd made me feel. For making me feel back then that I wasn't enough for him. If I'm honest, hate and bitterness carried me through a lot of years.

'I'm not sure I ever did. When I saw you at that dinner, a few weeks ago it all went out the window, and I was so pissed with myself. I've rehearsed for years how it would go if I ever ran into you, and there you were the same beautiful girl that fell at my feet the night we met, all indignant and furious and...' He trails off.

'What were you going to say?' I'm intrigued.

He laughs. 'I wasn't going to say anything, I was going to pretend I had no idea who you were. Make out that I barely remembered you, let you know that you'd had no impact on my life, that you definitely hadn't once smashed my heart to pieces.

'We really fucked up something good, didn't we?' Tate says. 'Where does it leave us now?'

'I … I don't know,' I reply. 'This –' I wave a hand between us '– this could just be some post-traumatic reaction. An innate need to prove we're still alive.'

'It could. Or it could be feelings that have been in hibernation and are finally allowed to surface.'

Tate stands up, takes my hand and leads me out of the hot tub across the deck, through the French windows and into the bedroom.

'Why don't we take each day as it comes until we figure it out,' he suggests as he takes my mouth in one of those delicious, long, drawn-out kisses.

Chapter Twenty-Four

TATE

'Are you sure you're going to be okay, on your own?' I ask for the second time, even though it's only a three-mile walk. I don't want to let her go. We found a map in one of the drawers that showed us we're not that far off the beaten track. The highway is only a mile to the south of us and the town, in the opposite direction. Suggesting I go with her is a non-starter, we both know that I'm instantly recognisable, Superbowl fever is running high. There's much less chance of her being noticed when she walks into the small town to pick up supplies and, most importantly, a new phone. Good job credit cards are waterproof.

Lily takes my face in her hands and kisses me on the lips. Immediately, I think of her mouth around my dick less than an hour ago, and I deepen the kiss because I can't help myself.

When we part, her face looking delightfully flushed, is earnest.

'Tate, I've been taking care of myself, since I was a child.'

'Yeah, doesn't mean you should always have to, though,' I grumble.

'Don't forget, I'm a trained killer.' She winks, and I love that she's trying to lighten the mood because she doesn't want me to worry. 'Quite capable of snapping a man's neck with my bare hands.'

I raise an eyebrow and play along. 'And have you?' Although I'm sure she's capable of it, it's hard to reconcile that with the sweet, sexy woman of earlier who was on her knees in front of me.

She gives me a flirty smile and in a low, throaty voice says, 'Not telling, I like keeping you guessing. Keeping you on your toes.' She kisses me again, full on the mouth, and I laugh – probably as she intended. She's walking into Belleton to let Winston know that we're safe but keep our precise location on the downlow. It hurts like fuck that she's still adamant someone on the inside, on the team, is involved. But after our near miss, I'm inclined to follow her advice, even though I'm convinced she's wrong.

'I should be a couple of hours, but I'll be back with some more breakfast options and protein-friendly meals.' Pop-Tarts and pizza aren't exactly nutritious and we're both craving a decent cup of coffee, the limited supply in the cabin is long gone.

'You'd better get Winston to speak to my dad,' I say. 'If he hasn't heard from me, he's likely to raise the alarm, and if the media gets wind all hell could break loose, which won't do the team any good. This close to the game, they need to focus.'

'As soon as I get back with a new phone you can contact

him yourself,' she says, then opens the external door. 'Will you be okay?'

'After you've nearly sexed me to death?' I tease.

That rosy blush tints her cheeks, but her eyes sparkle with amusement. 'You're so not funny.'

'Oh, but I am.'

'Don't answer the door to anyone.'

I raise an eyebrow. 'Who do you think is going to come calling?'

'No one, I hope. It's called sensible precautions. Don't do anything stupid.'

'Stupid? Like what?' I have every intention of doing a very physical workout. The big game is coming up faster than I'd like, and I need to make sure I'm in top condition. I've already missed a day's weight training and conditioning, and all that sex, great as it was, sadly doesn't count.

'I don't know with you,' she says.

'You had no problem with anything I was doing last night.'

Her mouth twists in amusement. 'That was last night.'

'Or this morning…' I can't help pressing her.

She gives me a reproving grin. 'You never give up the advantage, do you?'

'Nope. It's one of my strengths, on and off the field.'

'I'm going,' she says, shaking her head, but she's smiling, too. 'I'll be back as quickly as I can.'

'Don't stay out too late, honey.' Again, I have to have the last word.

I stand on the veranda and watch Lily walk through the trees until she's swallowed by the shadows and disappears from view. Leaning on the balustrade, I listen to the sound of the bayou around me, the birdsong bouncing over the nearby water and the wind whispering through the trees. The encroaching sounds reinforce the silence of the cabin and amplifies the sense of isolation. Being alone has never bothered me, I've always filled the space with training, watching football clips, listening or viewing sport, but I don't like the quiet. I like noise, background sound.

With my AirPods at bottom of the bayou, no doubt well and truly waterlogged, I put the TV on a music channel and turn it up full blast so that I can hear it outside on the veranda to do a HIT workout.

Conscious that this has to count, I sweat my way through squats, burpees, lunges, twists, and push-ups – and hold a plank for five minutes.

The workout focuses my mind. My muscles are primed, my body is conditioned and ready to go. I am in the best shape of my life. I've worked for this. It's going to be okay.

Even so, frustration starts to creep in. I feel like I'm in one of those dark fairy tales, where temptation is dangled and the protagonists have to resist.

These last few days are so important.

I should be out on the gridiron.

I need to be throwing and catching the ball, dodging and manoeuvring with my teammates. Practising drills and working on our plays.

I do another round of lunges.

Shit, I hope Lily speaks to Winston first. Coach will lose his shit if I'm not at practice. I don't even know when it is.

Even though my muscles are fatigued, I push myself to do more reps of squats.

And what about my teammates thinking that I get a pass on training? That will create resentment. Destroy trust. A knot ties itself hard in my left shoulder. This week I should be with the team masseur; she's got strong, skilful hands and keeps my muscles in tiptop shape. She's been instrumental in preventing injuries.

I shake my head. This is not like me. It's additional nerves with the game coming up. My mind is spiralling like crazy.

I take a long shower and my thoughts turn elsewhere. The cold tiles at my back, Lily's hot body pressed up against my front while water cascaded down us both. I smile to myself, that was another workout. I wander out in a towel and consider helping myself to another couple of Pop Tarts. I could murder a protein shake, too. My diet has gone to hell this last forty-eight hours. I flex a bicep. Muscle loss can occur after twenty-four hours if you don't eat any protein.

At least I can stay hydrated. I console myself with a pint of water, loaded with ice and go into the lounge to turn off the thudding base that's still pounding out of the TV speaker. At the last minute, I flip the channel because I feel a bit dislocated from real life being stuck out here and find a local news network. There's a piece about an alligator getting into a supermarket and spending the weekend there before being chased out, which amuses me and then the studio presented announces we're going live to New Orleans' city centre.

The scene cuts to a local news anchor outside a very familiar scene, I perch on the edge of the seat. It's the hotel Lily and I are staying in – if we manage to get back there. As I watch, a luxury coach with dark tinted windows pulls into the turning circle in front of the building.

'And the Superbowl excitement notches up another level with the arrival of the Austin Armadillos, who flew into New Orleans earlier this morning.'

What? I sit bolt upright. That's a day early.

'This afternoon, they'll be taking part in their first pre-game practice at a top-secret location in the city.' The anchor grins at the camera and then steps closer, lowering his voice as he speaks into the mic. 'My money is on the Strawberry Fields Stadium. Stay tuned to WWL-TV to keep abreast of all the football news you need to know.'

I snap the TV off as the ad break comes on.

'Shit,' I say out loud. The team weren't due until tomorrow. Practice this afternoon! I have to be there. I can't miss it. No way. This is my life. I check my watch. It's just after 11am. If practice is at three, like it usually is, I can be there. If I make it to the highway I could hitch a lift.

I look towards the door that Lily walked out of a scant hour and a half ago.

Shit.

I can't walk out on her … not now.

But I have to. I have no choice.

This is bigger than both of us.

This is the Superbowl, the thing that kept me sane after she left, what I've been striving towards nearly all my life.

This isn't just about me. It's the team. My responsibility as Captain. My dad has spent his life supporting me, putting me ahead of his marriage because Mom didn't understand how passionate he is about my success.

I check the time again, the second hand ticks by, relentless and insistent. With every tick, my decision firms. I have to get back to the city. I try to tell myself, Lily will understand, though I know in my heart of hearts that she'll be furious with me. But this is more important than what I want, or what she wants. This is outside of us. My dad taught me that football is bigger than everything else. I've come so far and people are depending on me, fans are relying on me. This is not about me and what I want, it's about delivering on my promise. I *have* to be at practice this afternoon.

I gather up my stained sneakers, which still smell of swamp water, and pull on my crumpled T-shirt.

Checking the map, I work out that if I walk due south, I'll hit the highway, from where I can thumb a lift. There are some bonuses to being a famous athlete and a hot-news contender for the Superbowl. I'm confident I'll get picked up pretty quickly.

I pause. Lily. I ought to leave a note for her. I rummage around in a couple of drawers and find a pen and pad of paper.

I write the first words.

Lily. I'm sorry

My pen sticks to the sheet. What do I write next. *'I'm sorry, but…'*

That's a cop out. It means I'm not sorry at all. And I am sorry. Really, really, really, really sorry. How do I tell her, I *have* to go to practice. For so many reasons, I *have* to.

I screw up the sheet of paper. What I really want to say is that I love her, but at the same time I'm walking out on her, choosing football over her. Again.

The fact is, I don't have a choice. The Armadillos may only ever get one shot at the Superbowl. I owe it to my dad, my team, the fans, everyone.

This isn't about me and what I want.

Chapter Twenty-Five

LILY

The grocery bag I'm clutching to my chest is weighed down with two steaks, some potatoes and greens, as well as a quart of milk. I'm never going to win medals for being a domestic goddess, but the idea of taking care of him is... I'm not sure how to describe it, but it makes me happy, and I think he deserves it. It's kind of sad that no one does that for him. It strikes me that we've both had fucked-up childhoods, lacking in any emotional support or being cared for, although we've both turned out okay.

I can see the cabin ahead through the trees, and I pick up my pace, my feet sinking into the cypress needles on the path. I'm already imagining Tate, half-naked. I bet he's been training the whole time I've been out. The man is a machine, so dedicated. But he needs other things in his life. Like love, sex and fun. These last forty-eight hours have been amazing. Our connection is stronger than ever. I'd forgotten the depth of feeling he'd stirred in me. I should be cautious about telling him how I feel, but a part of me can't help thinking that it would mean something. That it would make him happy.

I mount the steps of the cabin and I'm about to open the door but something stops me. The hairs on the back of my neck prickle, telling me something isn't right. Damn, did I get it wrong? I'd weighed up the risk of leaving him on his own, factoring everything in. Standard procedure. I'd evaluated the data, which told me the risk was low to non-existent. Has someone found him? Has someone been here?

My heart squeezes so painfully I have to stop a minute to take stock, and not burst in. Emotion is out-talking, which isn't going to help Tate if he's in trouble. I have to force myself not to give into the desperate need to call out his name.

Caring about someone can get you killed.

This is exactly what my dad was talking about. I haul in a deep breath, trying to quash the potential images of Tate's broken body that are clouding the front of my mind. It's stupid, I never think like this on an assignment. But then, I'm not normally in love with my client.

Come on, Lily. You can do this.

My arms are shaking as I carefully lower the grocery bag onto the wooden decking of the veranda. Taking a composing breath, I duck under the kitchen window, listening hard. I'm not sure what has spooked me, but my gut instinct always serves me well, so I creep around to the back of the house, my ears primed for the slightest noise. Nothing. When I reach the bedroom window, I go down onto my knees and risk peeping through the glass. My gaze slides over the rumpled bed and my usual clear-minded focus is disturbed by the mental image of Tate's tanned skin against my pale flesh, his muscled limbs tangled in the sheets. I close my eyes briefly then force myself to scan the room for signs of anything amiss.

Reassured that it's safe to do so, I slide open the glass door of the bedroom, easing my way in without making a sound. My heart is pounding. Shouldn't have left him on his own. Shouldn't have left him on his own. I take off my shoes and, keeping low, I slide my feet across the wooden floor towards the bathroom. It's empty, although the last vestiges of steam around the bathroom mirror and the slight damp air tell me that Tate was alive and well very recently.

It's too quiet. Where is he? Knots tighten in my stomach as I edge out of the bedroom into the lounge. The only sign of life is the half-empty glass of water on the living room table.

I inch over to the kitchen. It's clear, as is the laundry room. Relaxing slightly, I straighten up. No bloodied body and no sign of a struggle. Nothing to suggest that anyone else has been here. I should feel reassured but I'm not, the sense of foreboding is stronger than ever.

Even though I know he's not here I can't help calling, 'Tate?' Just in case he's in hiding or something. There's no answer. I swallow and try to consider the possible rational options. Since when have I found it so hard being sensible?

He could have gone out for a run. Something spooked him and he's outside somewhere in hiding.

I step out of the front door of the house and call his name again. The only response I get is a couple of pigeons taking flight and skimming the tree branches in their haste.

Where the hell is he?

Come on, Lily, you can't walk around in circles all afternoon, I tell myself. There has to be a logical explanation. He could walk back through the door at any moment. He's probably gone for a run.

I go back into the house and, determined to keep myself occupied, I unpack the groceries, stashing the steaks and the bottle of wine, which he may or may not share with me, into the fridge.

With that done, I wander back into the lounge and pick up the glass of water, which is when I spot the pen and paper on the sofa. My pulse speeds up in response to the alarm bells ringing in my head. It's almost a relief to see that there's nothing written on the pad but then I begin to wonder why he would have taken them out from wherever they lived. The sense of foreboding is suddenly heavier and punchier. I take the notebook over to the window and tilt it so the surface is bathed in light. I can see the indentations left by the sheet above and Tate's strong handwriting.

Lily. I'm sorry

I grip the pad and the words settle into my brain like they've been branded with a red-hot poker. For a moment I'm stuck, as if my feet have taken root, and then it all starts to add up. I sink onto the sofa, my knees stupidly wobbly. He can't have…

I'm cold. I'm hot.

He has.

Tate has gone. He's left.

I'm so fucking stupid. He's gone. Of course he's gone. He's got a football game to play.

How could I have even believed for one fucking second that he would stay?

How long after I left did he hightail it out of here? Did he watch until I was out of sight?

Did he walk in the opposite direction so that there was no chance of us bumping into each other?

Hot tears threaten to spill and I brush them away, angry at myself for being such an idiot. For falling for Tate all over again. For letting history repeat itself. Football is always going to come first. Caring for someone is a fool's game. I let my guard down and made a huge mistake.

Chapter Twenty-Six

LILY

Two hours later I'm in the back of a taxi, heading back to New Orleans, my jaw is clenched and I'm watching the scenery pass with total disinterest. I refuse to think about Tate or what I'm going to say to him. I've taken refuge in focusing on the job. I've spoken to Winston and Tierney, filling them in on what has happened. Both are suitably shocked, and Tierney's team is on standby waiting for Tate to turn up at the hotel – which we've all agreed is the most likely scenario. I've filed a police report and signed a statement with the local sheriff's department, who are en route to the bayou to bring the car up. All I need to do when I get back is to resign from the assignment for my serious error of judgement in leaving Tate on his own.

I have no alternative, I fucked-up big time, even though Pennington assured me that I did a proper risk assessment. He's wrong. I should have known that Tate would run first chance he got. I let myself be blindsided by sexual chemistry … again. Leaving Tate on his own had gone against all my training. I messed up.

All that matters to Tate is football. And, like my dad taught me, relying on someone else for your happiness is a fool's game.

Caring about someone can get you killed.

I thought the pain had lessened over the years, but it's come roaring back and I can still hear Tate's voice in my head. *'Surely, I'm allowed to have a little fun between now and then. It's not like it's serious or anything.'*

Is that what these last few days have been – a little fun before the big game?

Football was always going to be the winner.

I lift my chin and look out of the window, grateful that the driver is not predisposed to be chatty. When my phone rings two minutes out from the hotel, I snatch it up.

'It's Tierney. Tate's just walked into the foyer.'

'Is he okay?' I ask.

'Sure, cocky bastard looks fine, although no thanks to you. You screwed up there.'

I breathe easily for the first time in hours. He's safe. I don't even care how fucking smug Tierney sounds that I messed up on my watch.

I walk into the foyer and pause in the doorway. Tate is surrounded by a bevy of people including Winston, Shane, Tierney and a beaming elderly couple.

A flood of adrenaline races through my system. Relief wars with fury. He's alive. I drink in the sight of him. Tall, powerful, strong and gentle, so gentle when he wants to be, and also relentless when he wants to be. I have to block out the image of him parting my knees and tugging my hips closer. My body betrays me, though, and I feel heat between my legs.

Furious, as much at myself as him, I stare at him, at the crinkly-eyed smile he bestows on the elderly couple, and I remember the way he smiled down at me in the shower.

I curse his easy manner as he chats away to everyone like he's some returning hero and hasn't just ripped my heart out. As I move closer, it's quickly apparent that the elderly couple gave Tate his second ride back to the city. Apparently, he hitched a couple of lifts which would explain how I managed to catch up with him so quickly.

Over the heads of everyone, Tate spots me. For a moment, there's a guilty expression on his face, as if he's been well and truly caught with his hand in the cookie jar. But it's soon replaced with a bland smile as he gives me a cool nod.

I'm not prepared for the punch of pain that fills my chest. I'm embarrassed to find that tears are stinging my eyes. I concentrate on the sensation of my nails digging into my palms as I clench my fists hard. Fuck you, Tate. In that moment, I realise that he isn't sorry at all. He ran because he could. Because I didn't matter to him. I'm the fool here.

I glare at him and watch as his lips purse and he turns away. Inside, I feel that awful falling-just-before-sleep sensation.

'Meeting, my suite,' says Winston, his sympathetic gaze sweeping from me to Tate. 'Ten minutes.' His tone almost floors me. I don't want anyone to be nice to me.

Backing away from Tate and the cluster or people

around him, I know I need some respite. I don't want to ride up in the lift with everyone. I need some space. With Tate's back to me now, I slip into a conveniently placed alcove behind a little tree. Numbness has settled in, it's the only way I'm going to be able to function. I've blown it. Falling in love with Tate, all over again.

I pull on all my reserves, my training, my ability to compartmentalise. I don't need Tate Donaghue. I have a job to do. From here on in, it's strictly professional. I'm not even going to speak to him about the last forty-eight hours. What happened in the cabin, stays in the cabin. I'm going to be so glacially cool and indifferent to him, he might just find his balls have frozen off.

I straighten and peer through the tree as the entourage bears Tate towards the lift.

I catch sight of Winston's wife, Pammie, entering the hotel foyer with several large designer shopping bags, an abundance of ribbon handles hanging over her wrists. She stops dead, right beside the tree, although no one around her seems to notice. Intrigued, I watch as her eyes zoom in on Tate and widen. She stares at him, her mouth open until the lift doors open and he disappears from view with the others.

Pammie puts down her bags and I see the shock on her face, before she puts one hand over her mouth, as if she's holding back an exclamation of some sort.

She stays like that for several, long, seconds before she takes her hand away, and I hear her murmur, 'Oh my god, he's *alive*. He's alive.'

I'm trying to decipher her tone – is she relieved or

amazed? – when she bursts into tears and hurries away to my left towards the ladies' restrooms.

I'm about to step out from behind the tree and follow her when I notice the grim-faced Scandinavian guy – name of Sven, according to Tate – stalk after her. It's the first time I've been able to take a proper look at him and then it clicks. I know him. I've not met him, but the face is one I recognise from a data bank. I dig the cheap phone I picked up earlier out of my pocket and take a quick picture of him through the foliage. He's still moving, so the shot I take is not the best quality, but it might be enough. Then he disappears through to the bar.

I move down towards the restrooms, planning to catch up with Pammie. I need to talk to her. But as I start down the corridor, Tierney steps out of the men's restroom. Damn, I thought he'd gone upstairs with the others.

'Miss Heath. You're headed in the wrong direction.'

'I'm going to the ladies.'

He blocks my path, rounding me up like a sheep dog, and while I could easily take him out, at the moment it's probably not politic. He's never liked me.

'For some reason, despite your very obvious fuck-up, Winston wants you present to discuss strategy and we're short on time. The team is headed out to practice in half an hour. You can use the restroom in his suite. But be assured, I've recommended you be fired.'

But over the last few minutes, I've changed my mind. I might be down, but I'm not out. Tate needs me, whether he knows it or not. I'm the best chance he's got because the stakes are much higher than any of us had realised. I will see the job through, even if right now he's stomped all over my heart.

'Why?' I respond to Tierney. 'Because you feel threatened by me?' I toss him a patronising smile and stride ahead of him.

Winston's suite resembles a Cabinet war room. There are various security people gathered around, leaning their butts against everything but chairs. I walk in and take a seat, refusing to take part in the dog-pissing contest around me. I also refuse to engage with Tate, even though I can feel his eyes on me.

Tierney stands behind me like a guard dog, he's so bloody close I can almost feel him breathing down my neck. I suspect he's been waiting for a moment like this, where he can tell Winston that outsourcing protection was a mistake. Much as I'd love to say that I don't care, that I'll happily walk away – I can't. Tierney isn't up to the job. More than ever, Tate needs close protection. My gut instincts are almost climbing the walls. Seeing Sven has triggered all my Spidey senses and then some.

I don't trust anyone else to protect Tate properly. I swallow. If anything happens to him, I wouldn't be able to live with myself, but he doesn't need to know that.

'Lily, perhaps you can give us an update on the current situation.'

I give Winston a level look, refusing to be cowed by the tense situation in the room.

'Sure,' I say, in a matter-of-fact, clipped tone. Laying the facts out. 'The county sheriff reported back in the last half hour. They've located the car and are bringing it up. Unfortunately, they've not been able to locate any bullets for ballistic analysis. Divers are returning for a second search later this afternoon. It's an attempted-murder investigation and they are liaising with the police department in New York.'

Tate's mouth tightens as I talk, but I refuse to look his way.

'We need to discuss security going forward,' says Tierney. 'Clearly Miss Heath is not up to the job. Our security team can manage protection now that the team is all here in one place. Practice, the schedule, media appearances will be under tight security and we're liaising with the stadium, event organisers and the media.'

Tate sits there and I notice that his eyebrow flickers at the 'not up to the job'.

'Sorry, John, I disagree,' Winston interjects. 'Without Miss Heath's astute action, and the fact that she got him out of that car and stopped him being shot, Tate would almost certainly have died. If he was stupid enough to scoot off the minute her back was turned, then he's the fool.' Winston turns to Tate.

'Tate, you might be my number-one ball player, but you, my friend, are a horse's ass.'

I allow myself a very tiny twitch of the lips. I really like Winston.

He turns to me, and I see the corporate spine that earned him the fortune to buy a football club.

'Lily, I want you to stay on the job. John, you will manage the security when Tate is on the field, that's your area of expertise. But Lily stays on close protection. There's a shindig tomorrow night. Lily, you'll be with him and at every other public event. And while I appreciate your dedication to the team, Tate, I will not appreciate it if you get yourself killed doing so. Today's stunt will not be repeated. You will stay close to Lily. You will do as she tells you. Is that understood?'

Again, my lips twitch but this time I glance at Tate.

'An apology is due to Lily for you hightailing it out of there. She has a job to do. You might not like it, but her job is keeping you safe. How in hell's name can she be expected to do that if you take off by yourself whenever you feel like it?'

Tate looks a little chagrined. To my amazement, he looks me in the eye and holds my gaze.

'I'm sorry, Lily,' he says. 'Really, I am.'

I regard him coolly. Maybe he's just sorry because Winston called him out. Whatever, I'm determined not to let those sad eyes melt my dumb heart. I can't afford to fall for it, or him. Not again.

I give him a cool nod, then look away. Football can keep Tate Donaghue warm at night for the rest of his life as far as I'm concerned.

Tierney tries to make a token objection, but it's obvious to all that Winston has made his mind up, and the meeting continues as we discuss the schedule and security logistics between now and the final. I deliberately avert my gaze from Tate, though I feel his eyes on me.

Half an hour later, Shane's phone rings.

'The team bus is leaving in five minutes,' he tells us, and everyone stands up to leave, though I really need to talk to Winston about something so I hover.

'Stand down, Lily,' he says. 'John's men can escort Tate down to the bus. They'll be going with the team to practice.'

I nod. Winston is the boss, and I'm glad of the enforced distance between me and Tate. Even though there's so much I want to say … no … yell at him, I'm going to keep it inside. He will never know the terror I felt when I returned to the cabin to find him gone. We're done. From now on, it is purely professional with a side helping of frost.

Tate walks out of the room with three security guys and Tierney. At the door, he stops and turns around giving me another solemn stare. It's obvious he's still trying to say sorry but we both know he would do the same thing all over again if he had the choice.

Chapter Twenty-Seven

TATE

I can't believe it. I fucking missed the catch, the third one in a row. I shake my head and run back to position, trying to ignore the crippling fear leaching into my stomach. It's because I've missed practice a couple of times – because of unforeseen events and distractions like fucking allergic reactions and firebombs and fake engagements.

And incredible, hot, amazingly good sex.

'And again,' yells Coach. We run the drill for a fourth time and I'm racing down the field, my legs pumping like pistons. I dodge two players and I'm heading towards the end zone. It's the perfect play, all I have to do is make the catch.

Fuck.

I fumble it again.

'Man, what is wrong with you?' asks Blake when Coach blows the whistle and calls me over.

'Time out, Donaghue.' Coach glares at me. He won't

bawl me out, it's not his style, but I will get the 'I'm-disappointed' silent treatment for a while. Not that I blame him. I've been shit all afternoon. My teammates are giving me unsubtle frowns, and I can tell my missteps are affecting them. I hunch over my knees avoiding eye contact with anyone. I'm so pissed at myself.

One of Tierney's goons is sitting in the seats, clearly bored out of his mind. Apparently, he's more of a baseball man, a pertinent reminder that perhaps there is more to life than ball. Which then makes me think of Lily. I've really fucked up there. I shouldn't have left without talking to her. I should have made her understand why I had to leave. Walking out made it seem as if I couldn't give a shit what she thought. I'm a selfish bastard. I was only thinking of what I wanted, and she deserves better. A lot better. How do I apologise, when I know I'd still make the same decision and leave her? There's no room in my life for her. I need to suck it up and get my head back in the game.

Blake flops down beside me, his helmet dangling from his hand, and his shoulder pads brush against mine.

'What's going on, Donaghue?'

I shrug.

'And where the hell have you been?' He clutches his chest. 'You ghosting me?'

I laugh at his melodramatic tone.

'Lost my phone.' And because Blake is my best friend I add, 'In a bayou.'

Suddenly, it's a relief to be able to talk to someone about the whole ordeal of going into the water in the car. I've been blocking it from my mind. Winston doesn't want anyone to know but I need to talk about it.

'What the hell were you doing in a bayou?'

I wince and look around to check no one is listening.

'Lily and me, we had a mishap.'

I tell him what happened.

'Fuck, Tate. That's not a mishap, it's a nightmare. You coulda died.'

'Thanks, Sherlock, that didn't cross my mind.'

He reaches across and pats my thigh. 'Sorry, man. That's serious shit. How are you feeling?'

I shrug again.

'Good job you had Lily there,' he says, and something loosens inside me.

'Yeah, it was,' I say, before adding in a heartfelt voice, 'fuck, Blake, she knew exactly what to do.' I look at him. 'She saved my life, twice over, because when we got out of the car, she had us swim into the trees. Whoever it was started shooting at the car when a big air bubble broke the surface.'

'Fucking hell, Tate.' He stares at me with horror on his face. 'You're kidding... No, you're not, are you? That's insane.'

'It'd have been a hell of a lot more terrifying without Lily.' I pause and emotion bubbles up. It's more than gratitude, it's something much bigger and deeper. 'She's amazing.'

Blake gives me a shrewd look but doesn't say anything. He keeps watching me, like he knows I'm here for the full confessional.

'I think I've fucked up.'

He nods. I stall for a minute and I'm grateful when he prompts, 'What did you do?'

I give him the PG-rated version of events and Blake listens without a single comment.

It's only when I tell him that I left without leaving a note, that he speaks.

'You asshole. But I can tell you exactly why you did that.' He's pleased with himself, but I'm not going to let him beat me to the punch because I've finally pieced it together for myself. Even though it's all a bit hopeless, I feel a burst of elation as I finally admit the truth.

'Because I'm in love with her.'

'That right there. And you ran scared.'

'I ran because of this,' I wave my hand around. 'I can't afford the distraction. You know what I was like when you first knew me.'

Blake stares at me as if I'm talking gibberish.

'Yeah. Heartbroken.'

'Exactly. I very nearly threw my football career away, letting myself get distracted, took my eye off the ball, lost my focus.' I repeat the phrases that are my mantra, hearing my dad's voice as he said them.

'Man.' Blake shakes his head and crosses his legs, leaning back, a puzzled frown on his face. 'What are you talking about?'

'I can't afford to let it happen again.'

'Bullshit!' He punches me in the arm. 'You need to get your head out of your dumb ass. Did your game suffer when you were with Lily in college? Were you or were you not scouted at the college championship game?'

I frown at him. 'No. Yes, but—'

'But nothing. When you were with Lily, you were on your game. I didn't know you then, but I knew you after, and you took the split hard. Everybody knew you were in love with her.'

'I was, but Dad—'

'Your dad is … is a solid guy, but no disrespect, he's got the emotional intelligence of a dead rat.'

Now it's my turn to stare at Blake. 'What?'

'Tate. He's … obsessed. With football. Why do you think Coach banned him from watching practice games?'

'Because he got a bit overwrought,' I start to explain. 'He wants to be involved.'

'Yeah … *he* wants to be involved.'

I frown.

'It's all about him. I get it, he's proud of you. My mum and dad are proud of me, but if it all fell apart tomorrow, they'd still be proud of me. All they want is for me to be happy.'

We're both silent while I digest the words. 'Dad's … Dad. He's…'

Sound blurs out for a minute, the action on the field receding into the background. All I can hear is Dad:

'Fuck's sake, Tate, what was that pass in the third quarter?'

'Good game, but I think you coulda taken that all the way.'

'Losing is for losers. You don't want to be a loser.'

I try to think of the times he's been happy about a result

without having some criticism, some negativity to counter it. There's always been a sting in the tail.

'Great win today. Think you can repeat that play? Let's hope it's not a fluke?'

'I told you if you got your lazy ass to train harder, you'd win this game.'

'If it weren't for me, son, you wouldn't have any of this.'

Lily tried to point it out but I didn't listen. She's right, my relationship with my father is conditional. His approval is based on my performance. My achievements are always thanks to him. Not my own hard work or my talent.

'Does Lily make you happy?' asks Blake very quietly.

I think it's the seriousness of his intonation that gets to me. It's such a direct, devastating question, stripping back everything.

There's only one answer. I think of the thousands of ways she makes me smile, the way she can turn me inside out, how I feel as alive with her as I do when I make a great play.

I feel stupidly wobbly, but I owe him the answer. I need to say the words out loud to reinforce them, prove that they're real in the outside world.

'Yes, she does.'

'So, what are you going to do about it?'

I sink my head into my hands again, ruffling my helmet-flattened hair.

'I don't think an apology is going to cut it.'

Blake shakes his head. 'Fool me once, fool me twice. You've struck out there.'

'You're not helping.'

Blake laughs, the sod. 'It's kind of cute seeing you felled for a change,' he says, then sobers for a second. 'Although I'm not sure how you're going to explain it to Coach.'

Out on the pitch, Coach is beckoning us over.

We run out onto the field to join our teammates and join in the catching drills. For some reason my legs feel lighter, and when the ball comes flying towards me, sweet as a peach, I snatch it out of the air, grinning at Blake and make the twenty-yard run to touchdown.

'Thank fuck, you've finally got your head in the game,' he says, when Coach blows the whistle an hour later to signal the end of practice. 'I was worried for a while that you'd lost it.'

'Oh no. I know exactly what I'm doing,' I say because as soon as I get back to the hotel I'm going to talk to Lily. Tell her I messed up. Tell her I love her.

We leave the college ball-stadium where we've been playing and head out to the bus. Suddenly the three security guys grab someone who's approaching.

'Fuck's sake,' yells a familiar, angry voice. 'I'm Frank Donaghue. The Don's father.'

'It's okay, guys.' I nod at them.

They release Dad and he brushes down his shirt. 'What the… And where the hell have you been? I've been calling you and texting you. No one at the hotel knew where you were.'

'Sorry, Dad. I lost my phone. There was an incident.'

'Get a new one and fast. How did practice go today? You feeling confident? You need to keep your focus for the next few days. I know you gotta to do a lot of the monkey-suit crap, but make sure you eat properly and don't stay out late.' He claps me on the back. 'Hell, son, it's like you're twenty-one again and I'm having to make sure you're not sneaking beers behind my back. What you doin' for the rest of the evening?'

I roll my shoulders. 'Getting a massage. And I've got an official dinner thing tonight with the sponsors. Attendance is non-negotiable.' I wince, because I'm going to have to spend it with Lily and, despite my fighting talk earlier, what are the chances she's going to accept my apology. Her expression in that meeting with Winston could have frozen hell several times over.

The thought settles like a heavy lump in my stomach.

'Gotta keep those sponsors happy, they're your paycheck.'

'How's your hotel?' I ask, wanting to change the subject, but I immediately realise it's a lame attempt to please him.

'Fine. Would have been better if it was where you and the rest of the team are staying.'

'I can change the reservation,' I offer.

'No,' he gives me a smirk. 'I haven't drunk the minibar dry yet.'

'You do realise it's cheaper to drink in the hotel bar,' I tell him.

'Son, you'd begrudge your dad a drink?'

'No, not at all,' I tell him and I don't. I earn enough for him to drink every mini bar dry in the whole of the United

States if he wanted. I always pay for his flights and accommodation wherever we're playing. It's the least I can do after all he's done for me, although Blake's comments, which echo Lily's, are lodged firmly in my brain.

'Why don't you go back with the team and then I'll come over and we can talk game-plan? You can tell me what Coach is thinking.'

'Sure.'

But for the first time ever, I wonder what else Dad has in his life during the season and in between my games. I wonder if he's happy.

Chapter Twenty-Eight

LILY

Three pictures spill out of the envelope into Winston's hand.

'That's why Pammie and I split up,' he says bitterly.

As soon as Tate had left the room with Tierney's team escort, I'd cornered Winston. There was something I had to ask him.

'Can you tell me what went on with you and Pammie?'

During the meeting, my subconscious had been ticking furiously, and I had a ton of questions. When he tells me that out of the blue she demanded a divorce after receiving incriminating photographs, things start clicking into place.

I take the pictures over to the window and examine the images in the light. They're fairly conclusive. Winston, hand in hand with a gorgeous brunette. Winston kissing said brunette. Winston leading the brunette into a hotel foyer towards the lift.

'And they're fake,' I state, because though they look real,

they're too obvious, too convenient. They're the best fakes I've ever seen.

He nods, his face grim. 'She refused to believe me. I even had them checked out by an expert to prove it. But he said that if they were fake, he couldn't tell.' He shakes his head. 'What I don't understand is how she could possibly believe that I would be unfaithful. I've never so much as looked at another woman.' His jaw tightens. 'I loved her.' I can tell he's keeping a tight rein on his emotions as he grinds out, 'But the next minute, she's moved in with her freaking tennis coach. I should have known, the way he's been sniffing around.'

'How long has he been her tennis coach?'

'A couple of weeks. Now they're shacked up together.'

'When did she bring the photos to you – before or after the Conference Championships?' I ask. They're the equivalent of the semi-finals of the Superbowl.

'The day after.'

'Do you mind if I show these pictures to one of our experts?'

'Sure, although what difference is it going to make now?' The Winston I'm used to seeing reasserts himself. 'The damage is done. All I care about now is the team, and them playing the game of their lives. Win or lose, we made it to the Superbowl final. No one can ever take that away from us.'

I think of Tate, and even though I'm still furious with him, my heart aches for him. Will winning ever be enough?

Back in the hotel suite, the plan I have in my head is almost derailed at the sight of a pair of his sneakers abandoned by the coffee table. It brings back memories of him, in jeans and with bare feet, at the cabin. I'm unable to stop the images of him flooding into my head, and for a moment I give in. God was it only this morning. My body tingles.

I force myself to concentrate on the task in hand. I speak to Pennington and arrange delivery of the photos to a local FBI contact, and I also send over the picture of Sven, taken with the cheap phone. I make arrangements to get new phones for both me and Tate, too. I'm not being kind or helpful to him, it's a basic safety precaution – or at least that's what I'm telling myself.

Then I try to track Pammie down. I need to talk to her. She's involved in all of this, all the way up to her pretty neck, but now I'm sure there's more going on than a plot to stop Tate playing in the game. We've lost sight of that with the murder attempts. No one this afternoon even suggested that he be pulled from the team. It was never considered. And it never would have been.

Which leads me back to the original threats and the half-hearted initial attempts and the fact that the last one at the bayou was so different. None of it makes sense.

After a fruitless few hours trying to find Pammie, who has apparently checked out of the hotel, I send a report over to Pennington with my thoughts. The FBI contact has sent through the detail of one tiny mistake that shows that one of the pictures is a fake. It's a shadow in the wrong place. I wonder why Winston's expert didn't spot it, but it's possibly not enough to convince Pammie of the deception – even if I could find her.

She and Sven seemed to have vanished without a trace. The hotel CCTV has no record of them leaving, although their room is empty. If they've booked into another hotel or an Airbnb, they've used an alias. With thousands of people descending on the city for the game, it's impossible to check every new reservation or check-in. But their disappearance confirms my theory that they are involved somehow.

I message Pennington and ask his digital geeks to try harder with the picture of Sven. I've trawled Pammie's social media, and it's painfully obvious that Sven has been doing his best to stay out of sight. In the few photos of him online, he's turning away from the camera or his cap is pulled low down over his face. There's no doubt he's a pro, and that is ringing all sorts of alarm bells. The Superbowl is possibly the biggest televised event in the States. Last year's viewing figures topped over 123 million. It's a live event. My gut instinct is on super-high alert. If you wanted to make a statement, making it during the world's biggest football game would be the time to do it.

What if that was the target all along? What if the threats against Tate were a diversion? But why then get serious in the last attempt?

None of this adds up, although I'm convinced Tate's in as much danger as ever.

I'm still studying my laptop screen when I hear the click of the suite door opening and Tate appears in the doorway.

We stare at each other, both frozen in position. He fills the doorway with the breadth of his shoulders outlined in the sharp suit. The dress shirt is moulded to his chest, and all I can think of is the tanned skin beneath the pristine, white cotton. Every bit of moisture evaporates from my mouth, so I'm not sure I could speak if I tried.

My fingers could map every last millimetre of that gorgeous body. The feel of his skin is branded on my fingertips. My hand curls, fighting the longing to touch him again.

Tate breaks first and closes the door behind him.

'I'm sorry, Lily. I shouldn't have run out on you like that.'

'No, you shouldn't,' I acknowledge, and return to my laptop. My stupid pulse is leaping about like a live electric cable in a rain puddle.

'I made a mistake.'

'Yes, you did,' I say, without so much as glancing up. Inside, I'm fighting a battle, but the head is trouncing the heart.

'And you're not giving me an inch here, are you?'

'No. You're my client and that's it.'

'You don't mean that.' His smile is teasing, and it makes my resolve waver.

'I do mean that.' I can't afford to fall under his spell again. I'm here to do a job. His life is on the line. 'We had sex, it was long overdue. We got it out of our system. We can move on.'

'Fuck, Lily. That's cold.'

I can see I've made a direct hit with my callous words.

'It's the truth,' I insist.

'No, it isn't, and you know it.'

His words hit home but I don't so much as flinch.

'It is now.' I deliver the line like I mean it, even though inside I'm dying with regret. It has to be this way.

He pinches his lips. 'I take it you're coming to the dinner tonight.'

'I am. Like I said you're the client, you're the job. We're leaving at seven. There's a car picking us up from the foyer.'

I stand up and grab my laptop. 'I'll see you then.'

'Lily, wait.'

I shake my head. 'No, Tate. We're done.'

I walk out of the room into my bedroom, closing the door behind me and wondering how I'm going to get through the next few days when I'm so stupidly in love with him.

But if I'm going to keep Tate safe, I *have* to keep my distance.

Chapter Twenty-Nine

TATE

I check the knot in my tie one last time and smooth down the sleeves of my thousand-dollar suit jacket. I'm going into battle. I'm not giving up on Lily. Not this time. I messed up but I'm going to fix it, even if I'm not sure how.

I gave up on her when she went back to England. I know that now. I should have chased her down and brought her back, even if I had to kidnap her. I could have waited for her dad to be well again. I chickened out because I believed I needed football more than anything else in my life. My dad might have wanted the best for me, but his brand of tough love isn't enough to sustain me anymore. It's going to be difficult, but I'm going to have to talk to him. Put some boundaries in place. I love the game, but I love Lily, too. Not that I've demonstrated that very well.

Things are going to be different from now on. This is one game I have to win, because without Lily, winning anything else is meaningless.

I open the door and almost swallow my tongue. I've

seen Lily naked, casual, sex-tousled, every gorgeous which way, but tonight she looks … hot, hot, hot, and so fucking distant.

'Whoa,' I say, and then at her icy stare, add, 'You look nice.'

'Thanks,' she says, acknowledging the compliment, although her smile barely breaks a sweat.

Is it my imagination, or does she sound a tiny bit put out?

'I mean, you could have made a little bit more of an effort,' I add, aiming for funny to hide my admiration.

My eyes stray down her slim figure and the sequinned tunic, which skims her body, clinging to her hips and bottom and stopping mid-thigh above a pair of cowboy ankle boots. Her blonde hair is a mass of curls that snake around her collarbone. She's done something with her eye makeup, too, that makes her big brown eyes appear soft and smoky. I think my heart actually misses a beat. Damn it.

'Holy fuck!' I say when she turns around. 'The back of your dress is missing.'

She glances over her shoulder with a cool smile that twists me up inside.

'Good job I'm not making much effort, isn't it.'

Fair enough.

'Shall we go?' I put a hand beneath her elbow and guide her out of the room and along the hall to the elevator. When we step inside, she stands in front of me so that I get the full effect of her dress and her perfect, creamy skin.

I take a sharp breath in and clench my hands to my sides to stop them from grabbing her shoulders and turning her to face me so that I can kiss away that pleased little smile I can see in the mirror. Kiss my way down the dents of her back, slip my hands around her waist under the silky fabric and cup her breasts.

'Are you wearing a bra?' I ask.

In the mirror, Lily raises one haughty eyebrow without turning my way. 'What do you think?'

'Hell, with you in that dress, rational thought isn't possible. Every man in the room is going to be wondering the same question.' And I don't like the thought of that at all.

'You'll have to stick close then,' she says.

'Isn't that your job?' I ask and immediately regret it.

'So it is.' Her tone might be mild, but the look she gives me could take a layer of skin off me. 'As long as you don't run out on me.'

Ouch. She's taking no prisoners. Not that I'd expect her to. I get a kick out of the contrast between her kick-ass attitude and that initial shy reserve in the bedroom before she loses her inhibitions. Those little gasps she makes when she can't help herself.

She's such a gorgeous contradiction.

My brain is filled with the memory of her sweet pussy, the breathy moans that she can't hold back and the fierce flush that rises up her breasts, throat and cheeks when she comes.

I grin at her.

'What?' she asks suspiciously.

'Nothing,' I say, with as much innocence as I can muster, deciding that I'm going to do my absolute best to keep her off-balance until she finally caves in and recognises that resistance is futile.

'You're really not going to forgive me, are you?' I ask her conversationally.

'Not in this lifetime, no,' she replies as the lift glides to the ground floor. 'You're strictly business.' With that she lifts her chin, regal as ever, and when the doors of the lift open, she steps forward without even glancing back at me, making it clear she is having the last word.

Like I'm going to let that happen.

We step out into the media spotlight, quite literally. It's not just the sports journalists, but the celebrity writers and of course a bank of photographers.

I catch up with her long-legged strides. Man, she's sexy in the short dress and those cute little cowboy boots. I slip my hand into hers and, taking advantage of our audience, I lift her knuckles to my lips.

'Behave,' she murmurs and squeezes my fingers with a grip that might terrify a lesser man.

'Of course, darling,' I say, in a voice loud enough to carry to the bank of photographers lined up on our right.

'Do you really want to keep playing this game, darling?' she murmurs in my ear. 'Because I'll win.'

'Win?' I ask.

She shoots me a smouldering look, which has the paparazzi springing to attention.

'Yes.' Her answering smile is dangerous.

I grin back at her. 'We'll see about that.'

With my hand lodged in the small of her back touching her bare skin, I guide her across the foyer to the sponsors' backdrop where we're expected to pose for a few pictures and where I'll have to do a few press interviews before we're released for dinner. Football really has come to town, and the whole place is decked out with balloons and bunting, like Christmas on steroids. Outside, there's a line of media vans and behind them a security cordon holding off a sea of fans. I'm used to the attention at games, but this is a whole new level.

A harried publicity girl comes straight over. 'Mr Donaghue, can we get some pictures.' She urges me and Lily towards the backdrop as photographers and journalists jostle for position, shouting their demands and questions.

'Can you face this way?'

'How are you feeling about the game?'

'Over here.'

We stand together posing for pictures, my arm loose around her shoulders, one hand touching her glorious hair, rubbing the silky texture between two fingers.

'Cut it out,' she whispers through gritted teeth, her smile a touch forced.

'I'd say make me,' I murmur back, giving her a wicked smile, 'but then you might bring me to my knees.' I pause and then add, 'And we both know how much you like me on my knees.'

'Tate!' she says with an involuntary gasp. I love the blush infusing her cheeks.

'Yes, darling.' My voice is sultry and the colour flushing her face heightens. It's all very satisfying, although my dick is starting to join in the fun.

'How long have you known Miss Heath?' yells a female

journalist with a very welcome interruption. 'It's a very sudden engagement. Is it for real?' There's a challenge to the question before she follows up with subtlety. 'Some people are saying it's a publicity stunt.'

'People can say what they like,' I tell her, stiffening a little.

'Are you being paid, Miss Heath?' the journalist presses, her beady eyes watching us both.

Lily simply gives her a disdainful smile and doesn't deign to answer.

'You haven't known each other very long,' she persists, 'to get engaged?'

Lily looks up at me and gives me a beatific smile, that's the only way I can describe it. Then she winks at me, her face angled so that only I can see it, before she turns to the journalist.

'I guess it depends whether you think eight years is long enough,' she says. 'We met in college. We were at Radley together.'

I'm amazed that Lily has shared this, but I realise it's typical of her generosity. She's protecting me, taking care of me again.

'You should check out the college yearbook,' she adds. 'There's the cutest picture of Tate.'

'Not as cute as you,' I respond. 'You had those…' I waggle my fingers in the air on either side of my head remembering how I used to untie them and pull her hair loose.

'Braids,' she supplies.

'Yeah.' I grin. 'Do you think you'd wear them again for me?' This time I wink at her in full view of the press.

There's a burst of laughter from photographers and journalists, while the latter frantically scribble notes or start scrolling on their phones. I've got a feeling our yearbook photos will be all over tomorrow's press.

With photos done, journalists given brief interviews and radio and TV crews provided with a few soundbites, we escape the media scrum and are escorted out to the waiting car by Tierney's men. Once we are safely behind the tinted windows, Lily leans back into her seat and sighs.

'How many days until the game?'

'Only three. Think you'll survive?' I tease.

'Of course,' she says and then leans down to ease off her boots.

'If it's any consolation, they're as sexy as fuck,' I tell her.

She tries to school her face, but the disapproving expression misses its mark.

'Or rather, they make you look sexy as fuck,' I add. If I'm going down in flames, I might as well add some accelerant.

She shoots me a snow-queen stare of utter disdain and stretches one of her feet, rotating it at the ankle.

'Give it here.' I grab her leg and swing it onto the seat so that her foot is resting on my lap. 'I'll give you a foot rub.'

She tries to wrestle her leg free. 'I don't need a foot rub,' she says.

'No one needs a foot rub, but they're very nice.' I grin at her and dig my thumbs in the delicate high arch of her foot.

'Ah. Oh, Mmm.'

I stroke my thumbs hard along the length of her foot and then back again.

'Mmm,' she moans again.

'That good?' I ask, watching her. Her eyes are closed, and I can see she's trying hard not to let the pleasure show on her face.

I knead a little harder on her sensitive instep. 'Stop,' she whispers and sucks in a strangled breath. 'No, don't stop.' She flops back in the seat and writhes a little before letting out another, 'Mmm.'

'What is it you want me to do?' I ask. 'Stop or don't stop. I'm confused.' Even though she's still got her eyes closed as if she's hiding from me, I smile at her. Her face is contorted with a combination of pain and ecstasy.

'Just massage my foot, you big dumbass,' she mutters before adding begrudgingly, 'it's very good.'

I oblige and I'm caught staring at her when she opens her eyes.

'What are you doing?'

'Nothing, apart from massaging your very pretty feet.'

She looks suspiciously at me. 'Why are you staring at me?'

'I like seeing the pleasure on your face,' I say softly.

Her lips press primly together but she doesn't say anything, instead she closes her eyes again as if to shut me out and separate herself from the touch of my hands.

For a minute or two, I rotate my thumbs over the

underside of her foot, listening to her quick intakes of breath. She's not unmoved and neither is she pulling away. I skim my hand along her calf, lifting it up a little and kneading the taut muscle. The hem of her dress rides up her thighs and I can see the silk panties she's wearing at the top of her smooth, creamy thighs.

Her eyes fly open, and seeing the direction of my gaze, she immediately tries to close her legs.

'Don't,' I say. 'I'm enjoying the view.'

She stills, her eyes holding mine.

The air in the car has become thick and tense and I'm conscious of my own careful breathing.

I can see her throat dip as she swallows.

'We shouldn't be doing this,' she says.

'Doing what?' I ask, my fingers creeping a little higher and stroking the delicate skin on the underside of her knee.

'This,' she whispers, but hasn't snatched her leg away.

I push the hem of her dress a little higher. 'But what if you like it?' I murmur, holding her gaze. At the sight of her, relaxed, with that familiar uncertainty in her expression, my dick hardens. Fuck she's the sexiest thing I've ever seen.

'What if I don't?' she replies, her eyes a little glazed.

I smile very slowly. 'Oh, I think you do.' I move my gaze back to her panties and the evidence of her arousal spreading across the pale blue silk. 'You look wet to me.'

There's a light frown on her face and that shyness that is such a turn-on. I know no one else does this to her, makes her overcome her inhibitions.

'Are you wet for me, Lily?'

She nods. Her eyes pleading with me. I love that she can't lie to me.

'And what do you want me to do about it?'

Her mouth opens and I cock my head waiting for an answer. She stares at me, hope and desperation bright in her eyes.

'I'm waiting.' I love that I can turn the tables. That here, I'm in charge. Kick-ass Lily softening under my hands into sexy, submissive Lily. It's such a turn-on.

'Please, Tate, don't do this,' she says. 'It's so hard to fight it.'

It's the pleading in her eyes that undoes me.

I gently move my hand and guide her leg back so that her knees are primly locked together.

'Perhaps I should have told you before I started seducing you.'

'Told me what?'

'That I'm in love with you.'

Lily's lips part, and I swear I see something glisten in her eyes.

'We're two minutes away, sir.' The moment is shattered by the discombobulated voice coming over the intercom.

Lily eases out a long breath and looks me squarely in the eye, her face wiped of all emotion.

'This can't happen again, Tate. I'm your protection detail. Nothing more. I've got a job to do. I have to keep you safe.'

She takes a tube of lipstick out of her purse and calmly reapplies it, while my heart crumples like a discarded tissue.

Chapter Thirty

LILY

I fold my dress, put it into the suitcase, then close the lid. All packed. I look down at the ring on my finger and toy with the idea of slipping it off now. It would be easier to leave it in the hotel suite.

With one finger I caress the big fat diamond, moving it so it sparkles.

It's light refraction, I tell myself sternly, but I hold it up again. I don't want to take it off. It's final. This job is at an end or rather it will be in a few hours' time.

I might as well leave the ring on until the game is over. I don't want any eagle-eyed journalists spotting its absence and the news overshadowing Tate's big day. At least that's what I'm telling myself.

The last three days have been pure hell. Tate has been subdued and withdrawn. I know I hurt him, and he has no idea how that open declaration of love affected me. It was everything I wanted to hear, but I have to protect him. The closer it gets to the Superbowl, the more my gut twitches.

Pesky instinct is working overtime, seeing shadows everywhere. There's been no further attempt on Tate's life, but there's also no sign of Pammie or Sven. I'm constantly checking over my shoulder for them, and despite Pennington, back at HQ in London, running face recognition software for the last forty-eight hours, there's been no ping on Sven's identity.

In the lounge of the suite, I find Tate dressed in his smart suit.

He focuses on the case in my hand.

'Going somewhere?' he asks. There's a stillness about him that I remember from before when he had an important game. He was very good at staying calm and collected, on and off the field.

'Home, after the game. You're not going to need me anymore. My contract finishes with the final whistle. Winston's idea of a joke, I think.' My words come out in a hurried rush, hiding my worry.

I've been overruled. Even though I'm convinced that Pammie and Sven are out there plotting something, Tierney is adamant that the threat was always about stopping Tate from playing. He's stepped-up security in the final build-up to the match, and everywhere Tate has been he's been accompanied by me and at least three of Tierney's team.

'And then what?' he asks. 'Another assignment?'

'Probably,' I say, although I've lost my appetite for it. The thought of staying in one place and spending time with one person has a certain appeal. I must be growing old.

'I know you're mad at me for running out on you – but I

think you're running, too. You've never stayed anywhere or settled. What are you running from, Lily?'

'What's this, amateur-psychology hour?' I drawl, and I'm grateful for the beep of his phone signalling a text.

He checks the text and his mouth tightens into a straight line. 'The bus is here.'

I escort him downstairs in the lift. The foyer is crowded with people: other players, team officials and various other hangers on. I scan the faces urgently, on the lookout for anyone who seems out of place or sets off my internal radar. I stand in front of Tate.

'Put your arm around me,' I tell him. 'And stay close.'

This is one of the last opportunities a killer could get close. My system is flooded with adrenaline, my eyes darting in every direction ready to identify any potential threat. I'm achingly conscious of the heat of Tate's body next to mine and the weight of his arm around my shoulder. I'd do anything to soften my body into his, but I can't relax for a second. Members of Tierney's team at our front, back and sides as they push their way through the crowds. I'm tense and I walk with Tate to the front of the bus.

'Try and stay out of trouble,' I tell him, as he waits to board the bus with the rest of the team.

'I think I'll be okay,' he says, shooting a sidelong look at the three police patrol cars flanking the front and back of the bus.

'Let's hope so,' I say, giving him a big smile for the benefit of the cameras who are trained on us.

'Worried about me?' he asks, leaning in, as we're having an intense conversation.

'No,' I say.

'Going to miss me?'

'Like a hole in the head. Although I'll still be around, I'm working through until the end of the game. I'll be with Winston. I'll probably see you in the locker room before the game.'

'Security is tight on game day. No one is getting through.'

'I'd like to make sure for myself. It's kept me and my principals alive this long. And it's standard protocol.'

'And you always do everything by the book?' Tate's eyebrows lift in question.

I ignore him and turn to Blake, who's come to stand beside us, grinning. 'I love it when you give him shit. Must be love. People never give him shit.'

'Plenty of people give me shit,' protests Tate.

'No one that counts,' says Blake, with a laugh, and he claps Tate on the shoulder. 'Come on, man, let's get going. See you later, Lily.' He climbs aboard the bus.

'Well, this is it,' Tate says, his jaw tight.

I nod, not quite trusting myself to speak. This is harder than I thought it would be. But then goodbyes always are if you get too involved. I've done the very thing that I was always told I shouldn't do. Care.

He lifts a hand and caresses my face. 'Take care of yourself, Lily.'

I cover his fingers with mine.

'And good luck with the game.' I pause and give him a brilliant smile, which is probably extra glittery because of the tears shining in my eyes. 'You'd better win.'

'I'll do my best, but I know you'll forgive me if I don't.' He gives me a sad smile. I think of his dad, continually pushing him.

'Always. Play the best you can and enjoy every minute. It's only a game.' I give him a last, brave wink and step back as he turns and climbs onboard.

When the doors finally close with a hydraulic hiss, I heave a sigh of relief that I've managed to hold it together.

I'm met at the stadium entrance assigned for the Armadillo team officials by a young woman. She's wearing a headset, has a walkie talkie in one hand, a mobile phone in the other and the biggest radio-mic pack on her hip that I've ever seen, along with an accreditation label around her neck, the size of a paperback book.

'Hi, I'm Vicki. I'll take you over to Winston and the family enclosure. 'She hands me a pass bearing my own photo. 'Keep this on at all times. And can I have your signature to say you've received it.' I sign, date and time her clipboard and hand it back to her. 'Follow me,' she says.

The place is heaving as we head out onto the field. Crash barriers divide the space, with huddles of people talking and gesticulating at various points. Huge billboards and banners have been installed in every free space possible and there's an entire media village built over one end of the stadium. Huge, thick electrical cables traverse the floor and hundreds of people with headsets and clipboards are scurrying about. There's so much activity I have to dodge in and out of the people yelling out curt commands or corralling others into position, including the fresh-faced boys of the college football team who are standing in for the real heroes, as they head out onto the pitch to mark positions for the camera crews in readiness for the game.

Ed Sheeran is doing his sound check. It's all a bit mind-blowing, and you could be forgiven for thinking it's chaos, but everyone seems to know what they're doing and they all have a job and a task. The atmosphere is electric with industry and intent. It's a huge operation.

Above me, a fifteen-foot hoarding featuring the Armadillo's symbol – a tough-looking scaly creature outlined in bright blue – is being hammered into place from the platform of one of six cherry pickers around the venue. The huge TV screens around the stadium are showing a run-through of the players and, suddenly, there's Tate looking straight into the camera, his hair's tousled and his eyes feel like they can see right into me.

I stop dead, my heart clenching in fear and pain. This place is huge. Once he's out on the field, anyone in the stands from any angle could take aim at Tate. What if he is Sven's target? I feel sick with fear, fuelled by the vivid image of Tate being felled on the field with a single shot. Blood bleeding into his white football shirt. It paralyses me and my legs almost buckle under me. I'm scared for him. Truly scared. The lesson my dad drummed into me, comes home to roost.

'Miss Heath?' The woman I was following has turned around. I'm several feet behind her. 'Are you all right?'

I can't answer her. I look at the tunnel where the players

will emerge in a short while. Where is Tate right now? Down in the bowels of the stadium with his teammates? How is he feeling? Regret pinches hard and I really wish I'd told him the truth when he'd asked, 'Going to miss me?'

I am going to miss him for the rest of my life and my heart sinks, a lumpen lead of misery.

The woman is tapping her foot slightly. I rally, because she must have a million and one things to do today.

'Let's go,' I say, sounding way more in control than I am. Inside, adrenaline has turbo-charged my system. My pulse is speeding, my breaths are shallow and I'm as jittery as a pre-schooler high on sugar.

She takes me right up to Winston and Tierney, and stands beside them as if she's awaiting further instruction.

'Lily, good to see you,' says Winston, with a friendly beam, which belies the strain around his eyes. Tierney, wearing sunglasses, flashes me a cool, resigned smile. He's not happy about me still being here, but he's got over his initial offence at my request to do a recce of the stadium myself.

'Hello, gentleman,' I say, realising that despite Tierney's subdued greeting, it's obvious he's as gassed as Winston is. There's an air of excited disbelief about them. Don't they see the potential danger, all around us? I try to pull myself together. It's not like me to catastrophise like this. Normally, I assess and respond to risk based on the available facts. Not go off on some mad flight of fantasy and all the possible 'what ifs'.

'This is quite some undertaking, isn't it?' I say.

They both nod solemnly and then I add with a smile,

because I'm trying really hard to act normally and they're obviously so buzzed, 'You guys must be thrilled to be here.'

I think of Tate's calmness earlier. I know him well enough to know that it's deliberate camouflage. He's always loved the thrill of the game. He loves football. I just wish it could love him back, the way he should be loved.

Dread and pain swirls in my stomach. I wish I could see Tate. I have so much to tell him, and now… What if it could be too late? Why was I so bloody stubborn? Caring has made me vulnerable, brought down my defences, but the opposite side of the coin is that it makes me happy. Life with Tate was filled with joy before we broke up, and spending that brief precious time at the cabin was a glimpse of what life could be again.

I've messed up. I wonder if there's any chance of getting down to the locker room before the game, or am I being selfish? He needs to focus.

I realise Winston is grinning at me and lifts his sunglasses so that I can see the billion-dollar smile crinkling his eyes. 'To be honest, Lily. I'm so gassed I might pee my pants, but I'm trying to be cool. Do I look cool?'

'Boss,' drawls Tierney, also raising his shades, definite warmth in his eyes for once. 'Anyone who asks do I look cool, is not cool. Besides, you got your jacket on inside out.'

Vicki and I exchange a female-to-female pitying smile, although I get the impression she's pretty excited to be here, too.

Winston glances down and then play-punches Tierney, before taking off his jacket and turning it the right way round.

'It's awesome. Just being here.'

'Are you nervous?' I ask.

'Not now. I'm so damned happy to be here. This moment in time, I don't care who wins – I'm soaking up the atmosphere. Isn't it something? But come this afternoon, I'll be as jumpy as a box of frogs, and I'll want to win so bad I'd steal my grandma's teeth.'

I can't stop thinking about Tate. He must be revved. The pressure over the last couple of months has been enormous, not to mention the anticipation and staying the course to get here. He's had a season of seventeen gruelling games with only one week off in week ten. And I know he's given it his all.

'So.' Winston gestures to one of the seats. 'This is the friends-and-family section for the Armadillos during the game. I've allocated you a seat here. I can't have you on the sidelines.'

'That's fine.' It doesn't really matter where I am – I won't be enough to stop Tate getting hurt. There are going to be 73,000 people in the stands, plus all the people that work here and the support teams. Tension rides every last one of my muscles.

'There'll be security teams sweeping the back areas and corridors the whole time,' says Tierney, as if he's read my mind – or maybe he can tell I'm uncharacteristically still. 'We've actually increased the security numbers.'

'Good to know.' Even though it's a needle-in-a-haystack scenario and I don't even know if there's a needle in there, I intend to take good look around, which is why I insisted on an access-all-areas pass.

'You still think there's a threat?' asks John and I realise that the question is rhetorical. He's no fool.

'Yeah,' I say, letting my anxiety show.

'You're worried,' says Winston, sitting down, and I sit next to him. 'But we're nearly home and dry.'

Tierney, still standing, exchanges a glance with me and I realise that he's not taking anything for granted. Like me, he's still cautious.

'That last attempt is bothering me.' I glance at Tierney who nods. 'And so is Pammie's disappearance.'

'We've got as much in place as humanly possible,' he says. 'The stadium is covered. No one is getting in here that shouldn't. All the contractors, TV crews – every last person has accreditation. It's ticketholders only and they'll all go through security to get in.'

I give him a bland smile and he misses the sympathy in it. He's ex-police. He expects the system and processes to work. I'm less confident. I've worked on too many assignments where people don't give a stuff about such things and are driven to achieve their goals by any means, including utter madness.

'Oh, you don't have to worry about Pammie,' volunteers Vicki, joining in the conversation. 'She's here. I saw her a little while ago with her –' she darts an anxious look at Winston '– boyfriend, when they picked up their accreditation. They had Teddy with them,' she says brightly, as if trying to soften the news. We all turn and stare at her. 'That's one cute little dog,' she adds nervously.

Chapter Thirty-One

LILY

'Did I do something wrong? asks Vicki.

My mind is elsewhere, and I study Vicki's photo pass again.

'Do you have copies of everyone's accreditation photographs?' I suddenly ask.

'Yes,' she says hesitantly.

'How quickly can you get me one of Pammie's boyfriend?'

'Er ... well.' My sudden question has put her on the spot and then she shoots me a brilliant smile. 'I've got it right here.' She pats her phone which is also hanging on a lanyard around her neck. 'Everyone emails them to me, and I arrange for them to printed off with the barcodes, which determine what access they have.'

'I need it now,' I snap and hold my hand out as she finds the picture on her phone. It's still not a great shot, but having another one adds to the data points needed for facial recognition. I hold her phone, still attached to her neck, and take a picture on my phone, then send it to Pennington.

'What sort of access do they both have?' I ask, releasing her phone. She rubs at her neck where the lanyard has loosened.

'Everywhere. I mean … all areas. Because…' Her words falter and she looks at Winston again. 'Pammie still owns half the … the team.'

Shit, the sense of foreboding that has been dogging me all week gathers apace.

I ring Pennington.

'Middle of the night, Lily,' he mutters.

'Photo incoming. Of Sven. I need identification ASAP.'

He snaps into action. 'On it. I'll call you back as soon as I get a hit.'

I turn back to Vicki who's wide-eyed and very pale. 'Have I done something wrong?' she asks a second time.

'Not at all,' I reassure her. 'But when was the last time you saw Pammie?'

'When they arrived.'

'Did you see which way they went?'

She shook her head. 'Sorry.' She waves her hand at the chaos around us. 'I was busy.'

I snatch her clipboard. 'Here,' I say running my finger down the names on the printed sheet until I find the entry I'm seeking. 'They got here a little over an hour ago.'

'What the hell is going on?' asks Winston.

'I don't know,' I say honestly. 'But we have to speak to Pammie. Find out what she knows. She's involved. I'm sure of it. She's—'

My phone rings. I answer, knowing it's Pennington.

'It's not conclusive yet, but there's a possible match. Anders Gustafsson. Brother of Lars Gustafsson.'

'Shit,' I say. Lars Gustafsson was part of a terrorist plot in Paris that I helped to foil last year.

'If it is him, and it's an *if*, you've got a situation. It's alleged that Anders could have been the bomb-builder in Paris.'

'Bomb-builder,' I echo, immediately thinking of Pammie's outsize purses.

Winston and Tierney swing round, alarm etched on their faces.

'*Alleged*. No proof,' clarifies Pennington.

'Have you got enough to persuade the authorities to evacuate?'

'Let me get onto my contacts at Homeland Security and the Critical Incident Response Group.'

It all makes perfect sense to me, though. Pammie was the perfect target, owner of half the football team with complete access on Superbowl day. All it took was a few dodgy photos and the shoulder of a sympathetic, handsome Swede – and hey, presto, bomb-maker Anders Gustafsson has the opportunity to make some kind of statement to over 123 million people.

The threats to Tate had been a diversion to keep everyone off balance. It was highly possible Sven recognised me, though, which would explain the change of MO and the serious attempt on Tate's life that wasn't aimed at Tate at all.

'Is that the best you can do?' I say. 'It's the bloody

Superbowl, Pennington. In a few hours this place is going to be filled with over seventy-thousand people.'

'I'll get on to the authorities, like I said. But in the meantime, see if you can persuade the powers-that-be to get the place evacuated. Use your charm, Heath.'

I hang up.

Seems my charm has run out of steam.

'You have to be fucking kidding,' says Tierney when I explain it all to him and Winston.

'Even you say yourself, there's no evidence,' says Winston. 'I've been married for twenty-five years to Pammie. There is no way she's involved in this. She's the sweetest, kindest woman. Oh, fuck!' He puts his head in his hands. 'And I still love her. It kills me that she believes I'd cheat on her. She would never in a million years do anything to hurt anyone. I promise you. And as for her boyfriend wanting to blow up the stadium. Have you any idea how crazy that sounds?'

'It might sound crazy,' I tell him. 'But people like Sven don't follow normal rules. What if he's got a gun? A bomb? Maybe he doesn't care about the means, maybe he just wants to cause disruption on the biggest scale he can.'

'So you want us to shut down the Superbowl, the biggest sporting event on the planet'—Tierney's voice rings with undisguised scepticism—'based on the fact that this Sven guy might be a bomb-builder or a sniper? You don't even know which. I'm telling you it's skinny. And have you any idea how much money we're talking about? Millions.'

Winston shakes his head. 'Sorry, Lily, you work for me. Pammie wouldn't be mixed up with anything like this. Seriously, you think she'd threaten Tate?' He actually laughs. 'You've forgotten that this is a plain old protection detail. You're not on His Majesty's Secret Service anymore. I think you're seeing conspiracies and plots where there are none.'

'But what if I'm right?' I can't believe they're not taking this seriously.

But a seed of doubt is there all the same. Like, maybe my judgement is seriously skewed by my feelings for Tate. I've not been acting rationally since I set foot on the field.

'Honey.' It's the first time I've wanted to take Winston's legs out from under him. 'If you're wrong, the TV advertising people would sue the ass off us, not to mention the NFL, the fans – I can see the class actions lining up.' He shakes his head. 'And while I'm not happy about Pammie shackin' up with her tennis coach, I know her. You got the wrong people.' He sighs. 'Stand down, Lily.'

'Winston, you can't take the risk, you need to evacuate the stadium,' I persist, studying the stands above us which are starting to fill up. I'm realising that Winston and Tierney have probably led comparatively sheltered lives, whereas my dad brought me up to expect the worst. I haven't got time to explore why that may not be a good thing. Right now, I want to eliminate as much risk as possible when it comes to Tate.

'I can't do it, Lily.' Winston studies me. 'Find Pammie.

Talk to her. And if she does have anything to do with those threats to Tate, well, I'll eat my own shoes.' He lifts his highly polished leather brogues. 'There's less than an hour until kick-off.'

'Okay.' I shove my phone into one of my boots, because I don't have any pockets in the mini skirt and shirt that I donned as my blend-into-the-crowd outfit, and I don't want it knocked out of my hand. Unfortunately, Tierney refused to let me bring a firearm into the stadium and the tight security getting in would have busted me if I'd defied him. I always pick battles I'm going to win. I start moving before either of them has a chance to say another word.

My all-areas pass works like a charm and no one gives me a second look when I ask them if they can direct me to the security offices.

Once I'm there it doesn't take me long to find a room filled with TV screens and a young man monitoring them.

'Hi,' I say. 'Sorry to bother you, but I need some help,' and smile sweetly at him.

His eyes sharpen with interest.

'Sure, what can I do for you?'

'I know you're busy but I'm searching for someone. We think she might have obtained her accreditation by fraud.'

The security guy in the CCTV room perks up even more. I guess scanning a dozen TV screens all day isn't terribly exciting.

'I know the time she arrived at Gate B, and she has a little dog with her, so she's not difficult to follow.'

'On it,' he says, turning and starting to type quickly on the keyboard in front of him.

'That her?' he says. He points at an image on the screen of Pammie and Sven, with Teddy trotting along beside them.

'That's her. Great. Are you able to track her?'

'Sure,' he says, as if I'm asking him for cents when I could be asking for dollars. With my heart thumping, I watch the screen as it cuts from camera to camera.

Pammie is oblivious to the surveillance as the pair of them make their way up to the executive offices on the top floor and enter a door, after which they vanish from view.

'Do you mind if we keep watching, check she's stayed put?' I ask.

'No problem.'

My patience pays off. Five minutes later, Sven leaves the office alone.

'Can you track him?'

'Of course.' My new friend is delighted to be able to show off his prowess, but thirty seconds later, when Sven slips through a non-descript grey door, he sighs. 'Ah, looks like this is where it ends. He's gone into a maintenance area, and there's no coverage down there. No need for it.'

At least I know where Pammie is. 'Where's that office?'

He tells me the sector number and gives me directions.

Hopefully, Pammie can tell me what the hell is going on, but I'm pretty sure that Sven's been using her as a mule to ferry something illicit into the building. A bomb, most likely, as its individual components might not be picked up by security.

I phone Pennington as I race up the escalators. 'No dice on evacuation yet, this end. Winston won't risk it. But I've watched some CCTV footage. Sven is in the maintenance area. Section 4 on the top level of the stadium. Let Tierney know. I'm going to find Pammie.'

It takes me ten minutes to locate her, and the black eye is the first thing I notice when I open the interior office door. Teddy is cowering behind her, his little face peeping out. Pammie peers up at me out of the swollen lid and lifts her head very slowly. She's chained to the heating pipes, her legs fastened together with cable ties.

'He's got a bomb,' she says. 'He's going to blow up the stadium. When the national anthem's playing. You've got to go and tell someone. People will die.' I can hear the desperation in her voice, but I'm also impressed that she doesn't even suggest I free her.

Her words confirm my worst fears, and a cold run of fear ices its way down my back. As I step towards her, the dog whimpers and starts to shake.

'No,' Pammie croaks, her eyes suddenly fearful.

'It's okay,' I say, gently, because I can see the finger marks around her neck as tears run down her face.

But too late, I realise she's trying to warn me. Out of my peripheral vision, I see the shadow behind me, and even as I'm ducking to the right, a strike of pain reverberates through my skull as something hits the back of my head.

As I crumple to the floor, my last thought is that I never told Tate I loved him.

Chapter Thirty-Two

TATE

The locker room is tense, even though the guys are wisecracking and joshing each other. I sit on my own on one of the benches, Lily's words revolving around in my head. 'Play the best you can and enjoy every minute. It's only a game.' She really meant it.

'You okay?' asks Blake, flopping down beside me. He's trying to pretend that he's cool but none of us are. This is the game of our lives.

'Sure.'

'You're an idiot, you know that.' Blake folds his arms and gives me a superior cocky look.

'And this is based on…?'

'Why the hell haven't you told her you love her?' Blake stares at me. The guy really is the closest thing I have to a brother, and while it's tempting to tell him to fuck off, what's the point.

'Because…'

'Because she sure as hell loves you. I've got eyes, you moron. You're just going to let Lily walk out of your life?'

I look down, close my eyes for a second. 'I tried… I told her I loved her.'

'You did?'

I nod. 'But I guess I said it at the wrong time, because it didn't make any difference.'

'Words,' said Blake. 'Sometimes you've got to back up the "I love you" words with actions.'

I frown. 'You mean—'

'I mean. You've got to *prove* you love Lily, not just say it.'

'It's too late. She's leaving after the match,' I say.

'You know, there's this amazing technology these days that means these giant metal birds – airplanes, I think they're called – can take off and fly in the sky … all the way over the Atlantic. All you need to do is buy a ticket.' Blake scratches at his chin in an annoyingly infantile way. 'I mean, with your money, you could probably charter your own.'

'You're hilarious, you know that.'

'It's a talent.' His face turns serious, then, and he grabs my arm. 'Tate, make a decision now. Then you can stop thinking about it during the game. You're either going to go after her or leave it, but it's your choice. Take control for yourself.'

I clap him on the back because right there, he's right. It's all so simple. It's like the sun coming out after a day of rain. I grin at him.

'I'm going after her. She's not running out on me,' I say, with more certainty than I've ever felt. I've been accusing Lily of running away, but I've been running away, too, in the opposite direction. I need to give chase, show her I'm serious. Like I should have done the first time.

'Great,' says Blake. 'Now, get your head in the fucking zone. We've got a football game to win.'

And it *is* great. Decision made, I already feel calmer and I'm ready to get out on the pitch and 'enjoy every minute'.

Time is ticking and there's only half an hour before we have to be on the field for the national anthem. Winston, Shane and Tierney come into the locker room with Coach and his team for one last pep talk. I scan the group for Lily, even though there's no way I'm going to get the chance to talk to her.

Winston, Tierney and Coach separate and huddle together in the office next door. I watch them through the doorway, curious about the furtive air about them. They're talking in anxious whispers, their hands gesticulating frequently and there's lots of head shaking.

'Where's Lily – Miss Heath?' I ask Shane, who is standing nearby.

Shane, who is normally imperturbable, scowls. 'She's gone to find Winston's wife.'

I smile. Of course, she is. Lily is nothing if not tenacious. She's been looking for Pammie all week, although she didn't say why. I admire her for her thoroughness and determination. She is loyal, fierce and strong. She's amazing.

'Yeah, Pammie and her douchebag boyfriend are here in

the stadium,' adds Shane, glancing anxiously over at Winston, Tierney and Coach. Winston is on his phone and so is Tierney.

'So what's the problem with Pammie?' I ask, following his gaze.

Shane's mouth flattens and he hesitates. 'Lily thinks Sven is planning something here. Her boss has been onto Homeland security and the CIRG are holding a meeting right now, trying to decide whether or not to evacuate the stadium or not.'

'Evacuate the stadium. You're kidding.'

'I wish I was. There's a possibility that Sven is an alias and could be a known bomb-maker. But no one can come up with any evidence to prove it. At the moment, it's pure supposition. There's a lot resting on the game, so there's a lot of people fighting hard for their corner and equally people fighting hard for public safety. It's one hell of a hot potato. I'm glad I'm not having to make the call.'

I stare at him. Too stunned to say a word.

'As an added complication, the CCTV system has gone down, so no one knows where Pammie and Sven are.'

'Or Lily?' My limbs seem to freeze. Losing the CCTV sounds like too much of a coincidence to me. Surely that was a red flag. Lily certainly would have thought so.

'She was headed up to the management suite about ten minutes ago because that's where Pammie and Sven were last seen.'

I look at the door out of the locker room and stand abruptly. 'I gotta go.'

'Go where?'

'The john,' I say, pleased with my quick thinking. 'Nerves getting the better of me.'

'All of us,' said Shane, with a sympathetic smile. 'I'd better go over and find out what the latest is. And Tate, keep this between us, I only told you because you asked about Lily. I should have been more discreet. Don't give it another thought. In another half hour you'll be out there on the field singing your guts out to "The Star-Spangled Banner".' He nudges me in the arm.

I nod but my mind is shooting off on another tangent altogether. I *have* to find Lily. She was so sure that Pammie held the key to things, and I trust Lily's instincts. She saved my life, not just by getting us out of that car, but also by telling me to swim away from where it went in. If I hadn't, whoever was out there would have picked me off. Fuck, I love the woman. The thought of anything happening to her…

I leave the locker room in the direction of the restrooms and find Blake in there. Shit.

'Where you going?' he asks.

'I've got to find Lily.'

'Now? The game starts in less than half an hour. Coach will kill you.'

'I *have* to find Lily, Blake. I think she's in danger.'

'And the game?' Blake's face is a mixture of apprehension and admiration.

'Fuck the game.' I yank open the back door and start jogging down the hallway. No one is going to stop me. I'm going to find Lily.

I attract quite a few startled stares as I barrel past the

security people and the marshals. Fans stare at me, open-mouthed, quite a few try to high-five me.

I'm heading towards the main escalator when the fire alarm starts shrieking and a voice comes over the Tannoy.

Please evacuate the building via the nearest exit.

The escalator. Staff start pointing to the exits and gather at the bottom of the escalator which has now slowed and stopped. People turn around and start walking back down.

'Out of my way,' I say as I push past them. I get to the top and a security guard bars my way. 'You have to leave the building, sir.'

I shake my head and barge past him, sprinting to the staircase, fighting my way through the tide of people, all of them telling me I'm going the wrong way, then staring after me. I can hear the questions as I fly by.

'That's Tate Donaghue.'

'What's he doing?'

'Where's he going?'

The crowd thins with each level of the stadium. I'm grateful for the signs directing me to the Management Suite and when I reach the final floor, equally grateful for the hard yards I've put in in the gym and out on the field, it's deserted.

I try to think what Lily would do. This is her field of expertise. She'd be methodical and leave nothing to chance. Nor would she advertise her presence, I remember her stealthy approach in my apartment corridor before the firebomb, and my heart does that miss-a-beat thing. I remember so many things about Lily, so many things I love.

And I might not get to tell her. The fire alarm is still deafening, the shrill scream piercing my skull.

I work my way along the corridor, peering through the windows of the offices, all of which are in darkness, though there's enough ambient light to see if there's anyone inside. I reach the fifth one down and I can't see anyone, but suddenly there's an excited yip and I see Teddy jumping on the desk, barking furiously at me.

I push open the door and the dog bounds forward, jumping around my ankles with feverish excitement before taking off through the open door. It's only then that I spot the woman lying on the floor, chained to a pipe on the wall.

'Lily!' Fuck she's bleeding, there's blood all over one side of her face.

I bend, taking her hand and feeling her pulse. Weak, but still there. Her eyes open and she groans slightly, then attempts to sit up.

'Tate…' She focuses on me. 'What are you doing here? They're … evacuating the building. You shouldn't be here…'

'What the fuck do you think I'm doing?' I say, gripping hold of her hand, because I'm worried that my capable, gorgeous girl is going to lose it if I don't act decisively and as if I have the first clue I know what the hell I'm doing.

I examine the chain holding her to the pipe.

'What happened?'

She swallows. 'Sven? God, I was so stupid. Pammie was here chained up, and then … he came up behind me. He hit me over the head, and while I was out, he chained me up and now she's gone. I don't know where he took her, she's banged up pretty good.'

I nod, deciding not to tell her that she's looking pretty banged up, too. The blood has matted a patch of hair on the top of her head. Instead, I wordlessly tug at the chain that's looped around a pipe and padlocked to both of her hands. I can see that her wrists are raw and bloody where she's tried to pull the pipe away from its fixings and I wince.

Lily's mouth tightens. 'Sven's set the time to blow during "The Star-Spangled Banner". Tate, you've still got time to get out. Please. There's nothing you can do here.'

'Fuck that,' I tell her. 'You think I'm going to leave you.'

Her eyes are pinned on me, wide with terror. 'We're right at the epicentre of the bomb... It's through there.' She indicates the office next door.

I put my hands on the pipe and yank as hard as I can, but it's going nowhere. But neither am I. I pick up one of the chairs and slide the metal legs behind the pipe to use as a lever, but it's no good. Then I examine either end of the pipe where it goes through the walls.

Lily is silently watching me, her lip caught between her teeth, and I can see the tears shining in her eyes.

'Please go, Tate.'

'Lily, like I'm going to do that. I love you and I'm not going anywhere.'

'If you loved me, you would,' she says, and I stop and stare at her.

'Emotional blackmail is not going to work,' I say, trying for humour because I know she's scared. 'I'm not leaving you. I ran out on you twice before. This time I'm sticking.'

'This time, you'll die. I don't want you to die. I want you to go out and win the Superbowl.'

'Lily, football is football, but you… If I don't have you in my life, none of it is worth anything.' As I'm saying all this, I'm still working at the pipe, but I know it's futile. The chain is heavy-duty, with large links. I look around to see if there's anything heavy to smash the padlock, but I can't see anything.

'Any suggestions?' I ask.

'Yes.' There's entreaty in her eyes. 'Leave.'

'Never happening. So, Plan B. You know how to defuse a bomb?'

Lily frowns, though I can see her brain springing into professional mode, like the all-action heroine she is. 'Yes, in principle,' she says. 'But I need to see it. And I need some tools. A screwdriver, a pair of snips, although scissors would do. It depends on the complexity of the bomb.'

'What if I described it.'

'Tate, I'm not sure—'

'I don't see there's any other choice. If only I'd brought my phone. Fuck.'

'I have mine.' She nods down at her feet.

'What?'

'In one of my boots.' She wiggles her foot. 'Don't ask.'

I pull the boot off and the phone drops to the floor with a thud. I hold it up to her face to open it up. And because I can't help myself, I lean in to kiss her. A swift, heartfelt kiss full of promises for the future. We are going to have a future. I refuse to believe that we're not going to get our happy ending.

I run to the room next door and it's not difficult to find – the bomb is sitting under the desk, the countdown lights winking like they do in every action thriller you ever see.

'Take pictures of everything you can see,' Lily calls.

I take several photos, including some close-ups, and run back to her.

Like every bloody disaster-film cliché, the clock is counting down and we've got nine minutes.

I hold the phone up and she studies the images, her brow furrowed in concentration.

'Nine minutes,' she says. 'Bags of time.'

'God, I love you.'

She chokes out a very small laugh. 'You can do a lot in nine minutes.'

'Well, when we get out of here. You can show me,' I tell her. 'In the meantime, talk me through it.'

'Can you focus on the section to the right of the time? The wires there.' She frowns as I do so. 'Now scroll down.'

Studying the picture, she tilts her head to try and get a better view. 'I need you to zoom in on those wires, and if you can, without touching it, take a shot of the side view of where the wires go into that box, as close as you can get.'

'Coming up,' I say and run back towards the bomb. 'Is it a big one?' I ask, horrified by the plastic-wrapped grey bundles surrounding the timer, which I've already photographed.

'Mmm,' she replies. 'Do you want the good news or the bad news?'

'Bad first.'

'It's a very big bomb.'

'And the good.'

'If it goes off neither of us will know a thing about it.'

'We'd better make these last eight minutes count, then.'

There's a silence as I take the picture she asked for.

When I return, her face is soft and her eyes a little luminous. I don't need the words I can see it in her face as she studies me as if she's trying to memorise my features. 'Now's probably a good time to tell you that I love you. I never got over you. No one has ever measured up since.' She lifts her bound hands, but the chain pulls them tight. 'I want to touch you. Your face.'

I swallow. I can't bear this but I'm not giving up. Not yet. 'We're not dying today.'

But at what point do I make the call to spend our last minutes together. At five minutes. At four. At three. At two. One?

And I realise it makes no difference, there's never going to be enough time for us.

I hold the phone screen up for her and she leans forward studying the new picture, chewing at her lip.

'Okay. There's some scissors on the desk. You see the black wire there. That's the one you need to cut.' She frowns. 'It's a very simple circuit. Either Sven didn't expect it to be found or … there's a very clever booby trap in there that I can't see.'

'So, once I cut that, that's it.'

Taking a big breath before she speaks, she says, 'That's it, either the clock stops or…'

I put the phone down and lean in to kiss her.

'Or I need to make the next seven minutes count.'

She lets out a painful half laugh. 'You going down to the wire, then?'

'Fuck, that's terrible.'

'I know. Gallows humour.' She smiles sadly up at me. 'We really made a mess of things, didn't we?'

'Well, I'm going to spend the rest of my lifetime, making it up to you.'

We both laugh this time. She pulls at the chains again and I lower my face so she can run her fingers along my cheekbones, across my eyelids and then to my lips.

'You're a beautiful man. Inside and out.'

I kiss her fingers, I can't speak.

A tear slips down her face. 'We wasted so much time. And all for nothing.'

I swipe my finger along the trail of her tear, my heart hurting because I want more than this. I lie down next to her and take her in my arms. We stare into each other's eyes, and I kiss her, barely grazing her lips because she's so precious to me. I trace her face with my hands trying to absorb a lifetime of love in the few minutes we may have.

The moment is too big, it's as if we're teetering on the edge of our own personal black hole. My heart expands as I look at her beautiful face.

'I love you,' I tell her one last time. 'So much.'

She nods and I can see in her eyes the words she wants to speak, but she's too choked up to get them out.

I check the time on her phone. Four minutes left. It's a lifetime. With one final kiss, I force myself to my knees and stand up.

I take the scissors out of the pen pot on the desk and the Stanley knife also lying in the desk tidy.

She gives me a tremulous smile. 'I love you right back. For the rest of my life.'

I swallow and give her one last look and cross the few feet through to the office next door. My hands are sweating, and I pray I can keep them steady enough to cut through the wire and that there is no booby trap.

I lift the scissors with trembling hands and manoeuvre them into position, sliding the wire along the blades as far as I can. I glance back through the doorway. I can't see Lily's face, just her legs. I close my eyes and pray like never before, then I squeeze the handles of the scissors to close the blades.

Chapter Thirty-Three

LILY

Deafening silence might be a cliché, but it's born of truth. The absolute quiet weighs heavy in the room. The querulous fire alarm has stopped, and I'm aware of the solid thud of my heart in my ears, each pump of blood an ominous countdown.

My job has always been dangerous, there was always a chance things would end badly. Dragging someone else into it is wrong, but I could no sooner walk away from Tate than, it appears, he could from me.

I wait. My eyes closed, focusing on how much I love Tate. If that's my last thought on earth, it couldn't be better. I'm trying to be brave and hold back the tears. I hate feeling this helpless and not being with Tate, even though he's only in the other room.

The silence drags on, and I open my eyes to see Tate standing in the doorway still clutching the scissors in his hand. My heart sinks, he hasn't had the courage to cut the wire and I can't blame him. He's shown so much courage already, just by being here. That do-or-die moment is terrifying. It's unfair of me to even ask it of him. Sometimes it's better to leave it to fate.

Then he gives me a crooked grin. 'Who knew disabling a bomb was so easy?' he says.

I almost pass out with the sudden relief.

'The clock has stopped.'

I'm beyond words. We both are.

He comes to sit beside me, scooping me onto his lap. I ignore the bite of the chain at my wrist. The pain is more than worth it. I lean into him, aware of his solid body. My home.

After a while, each second spent savouring his very being, my head pressed against his chest, listening to the comforting beat of his heart, my body limp with relief and gratitude, my brain starts to process.

'Tate?'

'Mmm,' he says from above me, his chin resting on my head.

Something has been puzzling me. 'The alarm had only been ringing for a little while before you got here.'

'And?'

How did he know where to find me? That's one of a dozen questions I have.

'You must have set off before it went off.'

'Mmm.'

I jerk my head out from under his chin and tilt my head up at him.

'Did you know they were going to evacuate the stadium?'

'No. Apparently there was some discussion taking place, but everyone was keen for the game to go ahead.'

'And you left the locker room?'

'Lily, I had no idea where you were. Of course I left the locker room.'

I stare at him. 'What about the game?'

'What about the game?'

'It's the freaking Superbowl, Tate.'

He grins at me. 'I know.'

For some reason, we both find this funny and there are still tears rolling down both our faces, our mutual pent-up hysteria spilling out, when a couple of suited men, who are clearly some sort of federal agents, appear at the door with their weapons drawn.

'Put your hands up.'

Tate does as he's told. I have more difficulty, but I hold my chained hands in full view. It would be the ultimate irony if anyone got trigger-happy now.

'There's a bomb next door,' says Tate casually. Both men freeze.

'A disabled bomb,' I qualify.

One of the men crosses to the doorway of the other office.

'She's right. Fuck that's one hell of a bomb. We still need to get you folks out of here.'

One of them is on his phone already and I hear the wonderful words, 'We're going to need a bolt cutter.'

Tate doesn't leave my side, even when the firemen appear with the heavy-duty equipment to free me.

'Do you know anything about the little dog out there? He's sitting whining outside a cupboard, but it's locked?' asks one of the agents as a fireman snaps the metal links in half.

Tate and I exchange a quick look. 'Pammie?' he says and I see fear on his face.

'Pammie Radstock?' asks the agent.

Tate and I both nod and I explain that she was here earlier and that I'd taken her place.

The agent leaves the room and a minute later we can clearly hear the sound of breaking wood.

Thankfully, when they break the door down, she's alive and indignant. I think I really like Pammie. I hope she and Winston can sort themselves out.

In minutes, the room is full of agents and uniforms, policemen and firemen.

I rub my wrists as I'm finally free and Tate loops an arm around me, clamping me to him.

The debrief is brief. Apparently, there's quite an appetite for a football game and it's of national importance that it goes ahead as soon as humanly possible. The usual crime-scene protocol is being abandoned, not that Tate or I care.

We're being escorted down the escalators. 'Excuse me, officer,' Tate says with a charming smile. 'Are we free to go?'

'Sure. As soon as you're downstairs and back in the locker room, we're good to go and reopen the stadium.'

Tate links his fingers with mine. 'We can see ourselves down from here. You don't need to stay.'

The policeman frowns with uncertainty.

'I've got a few things to tell my girl before I go play ball, if you don't mind,' says Tate, with an all-men-together sort of conspiratorial tone.

'Oh. Yes. Of course, Mr Donaghue.' The policeman gives us both a salute and hurries off. Below us, the doors open and people begin filtering back into the building.

Tate pulls me through the nearest door. We're in one of the executive boxes.

He takes my face in his hands. 'Someone once told me they could do a lot in nine minutes.'

'Did they now?' I ask and kiss him. 'Lucky for us we've got a lifetime.'

Epilogue

LILY

'It's Donaghue taking it all the way to the touchdown!' yells the announcer. I'm screaming as he hurtles into the end zone with minutes to spare before half time is called.

The Armadillos are two points ahead of the Sarasota Snakes, and I might need a defibrillator before the end of the game. Can my heart take much more of the excitement? It's already had a year's worth of adrenaline overload in the last couple of crazy hours.

The whole stadium is a blur of colour and noise, and my pulse has been pumping at double time since the first strains of 'America the Beautiful' drift up from the stage in the middle of the field. Like everyone in the family-and-friends enclosure, tears run down my face as the gospel choir belts out the chorus. I might not have quite the same attachment to the US national anthem, but I was deeply moved and felt the tremor in my heart at the fierce pride of the crowd and quite possibly at the sight of Tate on the field singing along. Once 'Lift Every Voice and Sing' finished, I was a mess.

Thankfully, the military bands and the flypast, exciting as they were, pressed pause on my emotional overload. At least until the moment Tate and the team ran out into position, in their blue and white kit, to the storming bass of DJ Katz. My heart pretty much stopped with pride.

'Doesn't he look fine,' yells Pammie beside me, who, despite her ordeal has fared well, although that might have more to do with her tearful reunion with Winston and the proprietorial arm he has around her shoulder, as if he's never letting go.

'Hands off my boyfriend, you've got your own man,' I tease her, although I have to agree, Tate looks mighty fine.

We're now in the final seconds of the second quarter, and Pammie and I keep anxiously checking the clock, waiting for the referee to blow the whistle. Being in the lead at halftime is a huge psychological advantage, or so I've convinced myself.

As the players leave the field, there's a rush of activity as a stage and music kit appear, almost as if by magic. Here in the enclosure, drinks and food are being served, and I find myself with a large plastic cup of beer and a mustard-smothered hot dog. The smell of onions is so tantalising, I manage to scarf it down despite the nerves twisting my stomach like a double helix.

'It's soooo exciting,' Pammie says, with the biggest, broadest smile on her face. 'And I'm so glad Tate's found you again. He needs someone on his side. His dad is not an easy man. Ambitious for himself as much as for his kid, if you know what I mean.'

I nod. I've got a pretty good idea.

'I was so happy when I heard about your engagement,' Pammie goes on. 'It always worried me a little that he might never have anyone love him properly, but I can see you do.'

'I do,' I tell her earnestly. 'I really do.'

'And he loves you. I can tell from the way he looks at you. Like he'd go into battle a dozen times over to keep you safe. It's kind of hot, if inappropriate for me to say.' She grins.

Suddenly the crowd quietens, and a solitary guitar is amplified throughout the stadium as the figure of Ed Sheeran and his pedal loop take the stage.

There are another couple of songs before, with the same slick efficiency, the stage is dismantled. The brief interlude has been a bit of relief on my poor stress-laden body, but now every cell is back on tenterhooks. The teams run onto the field.

'Here we go,' says Pammie.

And suddenly, just like that, my nerves melt away. Whatever the outcome of this game, it doesn't matter. For the first time in forever, a sense of peace – fulfilment, even – descends on me. I don't need my career to define me anymore. I've always been striving for a nameless, nebulous something, taking assignment after assignment to find a purpose. I've no idea what the future holds, but I know with Tate sharing it with me, we can do anything we want.

My smug contentment is quickly kicked to the curb –

my nerves crashing back with annoying enthusiasm – seven minutes into the third quarter, when the Sarasota Snakes take the lead by one point.

They're still in the lead at the end of the quarter.

During the break, I find myself pacing, unable to drink a sip of my outsize beer.

When the whistle blows for the final quarter, I'm sitting on the very edge of my seat, my thighs tense with the effort of keeping still as I watch every movement on the field with laser focus. I can hear Tate calling out a play, and I grip my knees with my hands as the ball flies through the air. It's hard keeping track of where it is, with bodies flying this way and that. There's a fumble and the Armadillos lose the ball. I groan, and Pammie beside me drops her head in her hands.

Right at the front of the enclosure I can hear Tate's dad screaming abuse at the player. He's avoiding looking at me, and if he knew what Tate had done earlier, abandoning his team and the game, he might never speak to me again. But he's going to have to learn to live with me... Not literally but figuratively, because I'm not going anywhere, and Tate's already acknowledged that his dad needs some help and that their relationship is going to be different going forward.

I cover my eyes with my hands. 'I'm not sure I can bear to watch.'

'It's only a game,' says Pammie, before adding, 'you have to watch and tell me what's happening.' When I turn to her, I see she's peeping through her fingers as well.

The game is hotting up and tempers are starting to fray.

There's a flare-up over on the far side of the pitch, but it's quickly doused by the other players, who are obviously worried about a fifteen-yard penalty.

Then suddenly, as I'm really starting to get anxious, Blake intercepts a pass from the offence, and in a perfectly choreographed play, the ball passes from player to player before being captured by Tate. He tucks the ball under his arm and dodges around a player, head down, forcing his way through to reach the end zone. I'm on my feet, clapping and screaming.

There's a roar from the crowd when he slows on the line and slaps the ball down with arrogant panache before pointing one finger and dancing to an invisible beat, his arm scanning around the stadium until it reaches our enclosure. He blows a kiss.

They're four points ahead with less than a minute to go. I swear everyone in the stadium holds their breath as another one of the team steps up to take the conversion.

We all hear the thud as his boot hits the ball and every head cranes to watch as it arcs up in a perfect parabola towards the uprights of the goal. It sails through and the crowd erupts, music blaring, and then it's all over. I'm not sure anyone actually heard the whistle, but when the players remove their helmets it's a signal for the whole place to go completely crazy. I've never experienced anything like it. I'm crying, laughing, screaming, hugging and being hugged by everyone around me. Sheer joy is filling the air around us and my cheeks are wet with tears, my cheeks aching with all the smiling I'm doing. All the while, I'm keeping an eye on the field, waiting for Tate to come closer.

When he starts to walk towards the enclosure, his dark hair plastered to his head with sweat, I focus on his big, strong body and my heart, which has put in quite a performance all afternoon. Tate is smiling at me, all his attention focused my way like a tractor beam. I wiggle my way through the hordes of people, vault over the barrier and run towards him. I launch myself at him and he plucks me from the air, holding me as I wrap my legs around his waist.

'You did it.'

'Fuck yeah.' He kisses me, hot and sweaty and I sigh with pleasure. 'Now, how soon do you think we can get out of here?'

Author's Note

Hello dear readers,

I wanted to let you know that this book was written before the terrible events of New Year's Eve in New Orleans. My thoughts and prayers are with all those that were murdered or harmed that night, as well as with their families.

I have watched plenty of football games over the years but I have to confess the rules remain impenetrable to me, so please forgive any errors I might have made. I also have the temerity to be British and set this book in the US, so please do forgive the lapses where our languages don't always quite coincide.

Lastly, as with a football game, there are as many people behind the scenes as on the field, and it's the same when you publish a book. This is heartfelt thank you to every single member of the team who did their bit to bring this book to publication.

With love,
Cassie x

Read on for an excerpt from *Hot Pursuit*!

In need of the money, Lydia Smith happily signed up to 'flee for her life' on a survivalist reality show but finds herself contemplating running for the hills instead when her partner turns out to be her one-night-stand Tom Dereborn.

The two shared an unforgettable weekend of passion a year ago, but she hasn't heard a word from him since. Now, trapped alone with Tom, with the show's 'hunters' on their tails, suppressed emotions boil over and the past starts repeating itself. Soon it's more than just the money that's at stake – it's also Lydia's heart!

Available now in paperback, eBook and audio!

Excerpt from Hot Pursuit

CHAPTER 1

LYDIA

Flying to Barcelona for the day sounds dead glamorous, except my in-flight bag contains a hi-vis vest, hard hat and steel toe-cap boots. Today's trip hasn't started off well. At stupid o'clock at Heathrow on a Friday morning, I find out my boss Jeff Truman has bailed, some family emergency. A replacement is en route. Which is a bummer. Dependable old Jeff is happily married, with trendy, popular teenagers. They've trained him well – he's never tried to talk me into bed on a business trip or made inappropriate comments. The perfect workmate. Always a plus in my book.

When I land, my phone starts vibrating like a Rabbit on maximum setting, a flurry of texts bursting onto the screen advising me that I'll be joined by a colleague who's just joined the company, so I've not encountered him before. Great. I always love an unknown quantity. Apparently he was on my flight, so our driver can pick us at the same time.

I indulge in a spot of people-watching as the escalator glides down to the main concourse. There are an awful lot of hot Spanish men in their forties with just the right amount of distinguished grey tinting their temples. Is that something in their collective genes?

There's a guy a few steps below. He immediately captures my attention, even from behind. His hair is cropped short at the back, neatly trimmed and leading down into a strong neck, and if you were into that sort of thing, you might fantasise about wrapping your arms around it when you're kissing him. Dark grey suit. Fitted across broad manly shoulders. Long lean legs and the sort of taut arse that makes parts of me sit up and purr. His suit jacket is rucked up by the strap on his laptop case, allowing me to totally objectify the hell out of him. I'm wondering about his haunches, that sexy muscle and tendon bit of thighs and buttocks.

Yeah, I know, a bit weird, but I've had a thing about haunches ever since the time I had the BEST sex of my life. The filthiest, full-on two-night stand that left me starry-eyed and my nerve endings throbbing for a week. Just thinking about it still creates a rosy glow between my legs. I clamp my thighs together. Don't go there, Lydie. Not now, when you're about to meet a new work colleague as well as Señor Lopez, head honcho of the sports retail company that owns the distribution centre that has just burnt down.

I avert my eyes from Sexy Suit man who, to my disappointment, takes a sharp left at the bottom of the escalator, while I turn right, following the exit signs, my eyes scanning the ranks of men bearing whiteboards, handwritten signs on A4 sheets of paper and – fancier – iPads with a variety of international names.

Although I've travelled a lot with my work, it never ceases to be a thrill that someone has come especially to collect me. Someone is here for me.

With the usual burst of happiness, I spot my name.

On. An. iPad.

'Lydia Smith' is spelled out in large white letters out of black. Proper text. For some stupid reason it makes me even happier. Someone had to make an extra bit of effort to do this. Even having to share the billing doesn't dim my delight. Beneath my name it reads 'Tom Dereborn'. This must be the name of New Guy. The surname rings a bell and I feel like there was a girl in my college at university that had that same name. Although I've not met him before, I'm not too worried about him being chucked in at the deep end as I seem to recall he's come from another well-respected loss adjuster.

I approach the driver at exactly the same time as Sexy Suit retraces his steps and comes towards me. Our eyes look at the iPad and then at each other.

Oooooh Fuuuuuck!

Some higher being on another plane is obviously bored today.

I do not sodding well believe it. Seriously?

I know this guy. Intimately. Very, very, very intimately. It's Mr BEST Sex of my Life or at least … I think it is.

There is the faintest flicker of recognition in his steel-blue-grey eyes but then, like a portcullis slamming down, it's gone. He blanks me. Completely. Now there's nothing in his bland impassive face to suggest we had sex numerous times, in numerous positions, in numerous rooms in his apartment. I could almost believe he's never met me before.

A middle-aged man steps forward from behind the driver like a referee stopping me from blurting out, 'You!'

'Señorita Smith. Señor De Reborn. I'm Guido Lopez from Consa-Calida. I thought I'd meet you here and we can go straight to the site for a survey before going into the city to our offices and for some lunch.' He holds out a hand, and as I'm closest, I hold mine out.

So does Tom Dereborn.

The client looks from one to the other of us and out of gentlemanly chivalry takes my hand and shakes it first.

'Mr Lopez,' I say. 'Nice to meet you.'

'You too, Señorita Smith.'

Lopez turns to my colleague. 'Señor De Reborn, nice to meet you.' It must be mild hysteria that makes me want to giggle at his mispronunciation of Dereborn. He repeats the same formalities while the two of us look everywhere but at each other. This cannot be happening.

As Mr Lopez and the driver turn to lead us to the car, I leave Tom De Reborn to make small talk as I try to fathom how the hell this could have happened.

We slide into the back seat from opposite sides as our host gets into the front passenger seat and immediately turns to talk to us. We don't even look at each other but I'm so very conscious of Tom just centimetres from me. My body hums with awareness, every hair on my arms standing to attention, tiny blonde iron filings tuned to Tom Dereborn's magnetic north.

I know this man. I know exactly what he looks like naked. I know how his skin feels. Know what his dick feels like, full inside me. I know what it's like when he whispers shamelessly filthy words in my ear, to make me come, while he's finger-fucking me. For two days and two nights the man knew me inside and out, milked orgasm after orgasm from me. He grunted, groaned and ground. I can still see the tendons in his neck as he's thrusting over me, holding on for dear life, trying to prolong the race to the edge. Hear the long-drawn-out 'fuuuuck' as he comes, pumping and pulsing.

I'm damp, wet and horny. He's ruined me for anyone else and, believe me, I've tried to blot him out. I've tried to erase him. Boy, have I tried, but every sodding subsequent sexual encounter has been a big fat disappointment. So much so – I've given up. No sex, not so much as a sniff, for ages.

I glue my posture upright and forward so I'm not for one minute tempted to look at him, catch his gaze, or even so much as acknowledge him. Thankfully he seems inclined to do exactly the same, although what else can we say in front of the extremely charming Guido Lopez, who seems to have taken a shine to me.

'Señorita Smith,' he shoots an admiring glance at my legs in heels and barely-there sheer tights, 'would you like to stay in the car? After the fire it is … not the place for a beautiful woman.'

I hear a snort come from my left. I don't blame him. I'm here to assess the scale of the loss of the contents of a warehouse which two days ago contained sixty-four thousand square feet of sports equipment. Those football shirts, it would seem, are very flammable. I'm not sure how Señor Lopez expects me to do that from the back of the car.

'Your colleague, Mr De Reborn, will, I'm sure, be able to conduct the survey on his own.'

I give the Spaniard a cool smile. It's not the first time I've been underestimated and relegated to note-taker or back-up partner. Some might say it's because I insist on presenting myself as a smart, feminine woman but why the hell not? This is who I am. It's been hard won and I'm not about to compromise for anyone. I don't have to apologise for being young and attractive or dressing how I want. I'm vain. I want to look good, so I do. But I allow for some practicality – it's common sense if you're working in the field.

When the car pulls up next to the blackened site, buckled and twisted steel uprights testament to the former warehouse, I open my travel bag and pull out a pair of thick hiking socks, my steel toe-capped boots, my hi-vis vest and my yellow hard hat as well as what looks like a brown lab coat.

I try not to feel self-conscious taking off my shoes in the back of the car in front of Tom Dereborn. It feels intimate and far too reminiscent of him unbuckling the straps on my sky-high sandals and running his hands up and along my calves. I gulp and hurriedly pull on my thick, distinctly unsexy, wool socks.

By the time the driver has parked the car, my footwear is on and I've regained a little equilibrium as I step out onto the slightly sticky tarmac, which must have melted in the heat. Acrid smoke taints the air and there's a glow of warmth that has little to do with the local climate. I shrug the overcoat over my suit without saying a word to our host. My colleague mutters, 'Show-off,' under his breath.

Señor Lopez walks us around the site, our feet crunching on broken glass and blackened debris, indicating the warped metal struts – all that's left of the extensive racking that once lined the aisles. His face is twisted with woe and despair as he relays in that spare, hopeless way of the bereft how much has been lost. I have to stamp down on the innate sympathy and the desire to reassure him. It's always sad to see the aftermath of destruction, especially when it's someone's business.

Unfortunately, we're the bad guys sent in to determine the truth of the loss and adjust expectations back to reality. Some clients exaggerate the size of the loss – after all, who does it harm? They've paid their premiums all this time, they deserve the pay-out. But I have a responsibility to shareholders and to other insurance customers to stop out-and-out fraud and keep their premiums affordable. I might sound callous, but I don't mean to. Often we're dealing with shell-shocked, horrified people who've seen a lifetime's work snuffed out in one fell swoop. It is heartbreaking but there is a certain percentage of people who will always try it on. According to Señor Lopez, who has already provided us with extensive figures and details of the amount of stock that was held on this site, the company was holding more stock than it sold in the whole of last year. The figures didn't stack up even back when I was in London.

I know exactly what I need to see and I ask Señor Lopez to show me round the former warehouse. I ask a ton of questions that he quickly starts to get irritated by, but I want a watertight case and for my report to be incontrovertible. I'm known for being thorough.

'For fuck's sake,' mutters my colleague, when I ask Lopez to indicate exactly where the shelves were. When I ask the height of the shelving and how many shelves per unit there were, he tuts under his breath.

I ignore him. I know my job. To be honest it's a relief he's being a complete arse. Stops me remembering all the ways he was so good in bed.

'Señorita Smith. What difference does it make? Everything is gone. You have the figures.' Lopez frowns.

'Yes, Miss Smith,' replies my colleague, undeniable withering sarcasm present in every syllable.

'How wide were the aisles?' I press, pacing across the floor, trying to visualise the scene. Across on the other side of the factory is a skip full of water-soaked sports shirts.

'We couldn't salvage much,' the client says, mournfully trying to steer me away from the skip.

'I'd like to see,' I say and shrug off his restraining hand and march over to the skip. Tom Dereborn follows me, hissing in a low voice, 'For God's sake. Didn't you read the file before you got here? No way in hell did they have ten mill's worth of stock stored here. Any idiot can see that. What are you trying to prove?'

I know exactly that but…

'I'm making sure the job is done properly. I bet you ten quid that there aren't that many shirts in there and the rest have been repatriated by the company to sell on some market stall or car boot sale.'

'So what?'

I whirl on him unaccountably raising my voice. 'So

what?' I put my hands on my hips and glare at him. It feels good to be mad at him, although I'm madder than I usually would be because he's done such a good job of pretending he's never met me before. I want to make him pay for that. Pay for all the other people who've pretended they don't know me because I'm not good enough.

'Yeah,' he says going toe to toe with me, his smart brogues nudging up against my scuffed leather boots.

'I don't bloody believe it.'

'Why are you making a meal of this? The company is obviously inflating the claim.'

'I know that but I'm being thorough.' The word brings back a memory. Tom Dereborn was very thorough, and I flush remembering how assiduous he was… A lick of heat touches my core at the sudden memory – the slow careful slide of his mouth up my thighs and his hot breath teasing my clit.

I suck in a quick breath, to shake loose the thoughts and focus on the specks of white-grey ash dusting the air. 'I want to be able to prove it should they appeal.'

'Our word should be good enough.' His arrogant drawl brings me back to the present.

'We're supposed to be professional. We should be meticulous. Give me a hand.' I regret my choice of words. I've had those hands over every inch of my body.

'What?'

There it is. Just a tiny tell, his left eye twitches ever so slightly.

'I want to get in the skip. Give me a leg up.'

'You are fucking joking.'

'Do I look like I'm joking? Why would you even think that?'

'Because what you want…' The pause is infinitesimal but it's enough. *Tell me what you want.* He murmured it over and over in my ear, followed up with filthy suggestions. '… is for me to do the gentlemanly thing and volunteer to go in there. These are custom-made brogues and a Brioni suit. You going to pay my dry-cleaning bill?'

'I am more than capable of getting into the skip and some of us dressed appropriately. Who the hell wears a suit that needs dry cleaning to go on site?'

'We're representing the company,' he hisses at me. 'And this is a straightforward case. We could be doing this in an office going over the financials. I dressed to look professional.'

'And I didn't?'

He gives my skirt, with its flippy frill, a dismissive look. 'You'll do.'

'And for the record, I don't expect you to get in the skip just because you're a man and I'm a poor weak female. So if you can quit whining for five minutes and give me a leg up, I'd be grateful.'

He holds out his hands and I take great satisfaction in planting a soggy, ash-covered boot in the palm of his hand. 'For fuck's sake,' he grumbles, 'I don't know why you're bothering. We both know the client's a lying sack of shit.' With that he heaves me upwards with more testosterone-fuelled force than necessary and I tumble into the skip, my weight crashing through the pile of soggy empty boxes immediately beneath the surface layer of slithery plastic-packaged shirts. It takes me a while to wade through them and resurface, and when I finally emerge, I spot Señor Lopez scowling behind Tom's back. It's obvious he's heard every word and is less than impressed with either of us.

Somehow, I think lunch is a goner.